CHASING KISMET

*The journey of an Indo-Canadian girl who sets out to discover
her roots, but becomes uprooted instead*

Amrita Lit

ISBN: 1540886131
ISBN 13: 9781540886132

CHAPTER ONE

It's times like these that make me hate the colour of my own skin. Being an Indian girl means being forced to be in situations you'd rather avoid, with people you'd rather not see.

My mother has dragged me to yet another brutally dull banquet hall party. This means we're in the midst of watching my father get completely shit-faced in public, as usual. All while random women approach my mother to inquire about my hand in marriage.

It doesn't matter that they don't know a thing about me. Nor does it matter that I'm only twenty-three years old and extremely mentally unprepared for such a commitment.

All that matters is that from hours of glaring at me from across the room, they have sized up that

I'm tall, slender, have big hazel eyes and sleek dark brown hair. Combine all of that with my light skin-tone and *ding-ding-ding*: I'm these women's dream daughter-in-law. Just slap a muzzle on me and it's a perfect match.

It's too bad that I'd much rather shoot myself in the foot than marry one of their "hood" wannabe sons.

The guests begin to clap and cheer for the *bhangra* dancers performing their hearts out for everyone. I've always found the mini fortune people spend on these parties to be absurd, but to each their own. I have to admit, though; the hall décor is absolutely stunning. The room is filled with crystal candelabras and gold pillars with ivory roses set atop them. The happy couple is perched up on the stage like royalty. No one's even paying attention to them though. Everyone's too consumed with Snapchatting themselves or gorging on the copious free food and drinks. The music in the hall is set to an ear-piercing volume, to compete with the other party happening just on the other side of the extravagantly decorated wall behind me.

Peonies and posies on a wooden frame compose the backdrop to everyone's photo booth pictures. It's unreal how over the top people go with these events. It's just an engagement party. Does half of Surrey really need to be here?

Sometimes I think the only reason my mom even brings me along to these events is to get me matched up with one of these overzealous women's lowlife sons. I'm pretty sure she wants to get me married off as soon as possible, before I get the bright idea of running off with my best friend Roger again.

A few women gather right by our table, and I can hear bits and pieces of their conversation.

"She doesn't even look *apni*," one of them says with as much gusto as a kid in a candy shop.

This is her highest praise: that I don't look Indian. As if it's an achievement to not look like who you really are.

They question my mother about me in excited murmurs, and I pretend to be oblivious to the entire thing. When I was about twelve, I started to notice the looks my mother would receive from people when she would tell them I was her one and only child.

They would say, "Only a daughter? No sons?" Then they'd shake their heads with pity and walk away.

As if it was absolutely unfathomable that an Indian family wouldn't carry on reproducing until they hit the jackpot: a son. All that matters to them is to have a male offspring who can carry on their precious family name. This is obviously because the guys from my community are *such* vital assets to every household.

In this British Columbian town of mine, I grew up around narrow thinking that stems from small minds.

Surrey is a place everyone loves to hate, but no one ever seems to leave. My city has this magnetic vibe that is something you've just *got* to be a part of. It's why we defend the place when out-of-towners diss the "smell of curry in the air." Or make fun of elderly men, a turban in place of a helmet as they ride their bikes, with their beards blowing in the wind. That's what makes this place so great and horrible at the same time. If you live here, you just get it. You know exactly what it means to be born and raised in this infamous city.

"God, this is painfully boring," I say in a whiny voice. I'm more than happy to act like a petulant brat if it interrupts my mom's conversation with these women; they look like they're about to start a bidding war over me right here and now.

She forces a smile at me to make it appear like we're just another normal mother-daughter duo sitting at the party, but the slight twitch in her eyelid tells otherwise.

"The food at these parties isn't even good anymore." I carry on sulking, pushing my fork around in my dried up rice and over-salted butter chicken.

My mom not only ignores my childish complaint, she doesn't even do me the decency of turning to acknowledge my presence.

The promise of good appetizers and butter chicken used to be worth the process of getting ready only to sit in one spot for five or more hours. Unless you count the times I am dragged out to the dance floor by the same aforementioned women to shuffle and clap in a circle. It wouldn't even be so bad if it wasn't for the flock of men at the bar eyeballing me up and down.

My phone battery is pretty much dead, so I can't even text Roop or Serena to pass the time. Instead, I daydream about my last rendezvous with Roger. Oh man, he looked so hot last night, even if we were in back seat of his BMW.

Roger is my friend from pretty much as long as I can remember. We grew up in the same cul-de-sac and spent all of our spare time together. We tried the whole "boyfriend-girlfriend" thing out once the hormone charged teenage years came along. Unfortunately, that idea didn't work out at the time. Truthfully I'm pretty sure I know exactly what went wrong.

We came up with the genius idea of running away together when we were 18. Roger was fed up with the family drama going on at his house, and I would follow Roger just about off the edge of the earth if he asked me to. Our escape plan wasn't exactly well thought out though, so it didn't end very well.

We were caught at a motel by the beach in White Rock by one of his overprotective older cousins. Just about as soon as she saw us, the phone calls home resulted in a whole lot of ear pulling and awkward sex talks courtesy of our parents.

Now we like to keep things pretty private. We don't feel the need to throw a title on our relationship just to know it's real. We know what's between us and that's all that matters. Well, that's how he reassures me when I question him about our future.

Our problem is that he belongs to a different caste than my family. He's a Rajput, and in my mom's world, they're beneath us Jatts. The entire rest of the world is beneath the Jatt caste, according to my parents.

It just so happens that Roger's family has the exact same mentality, except in reverse. I'd really like to have the caste system explained to me, because I thought our religion was all about abolishing that shit.

My mother and I catch each other's eye, and for a second it feels like she can read my thoughts. The women must have taken a hike once she mentioned my father's name. Everyone around here knows who we are; our dirty laundry gets aired quicker than your grandma can hang her *dupatta* outside on a sunny day. People just love to gossip around here, and when it comes to us Sidhus, there's a whole lot to gossip about.

"Sit up straight Tara, and smile for God's sake!" My mom snaps at me. "Do you have to look miserable every waking moment of your life?" She glares at me with a look of utter disgust, as if she loathes my very existence.

"Oh, I'm sorry Mom, is my expression getting in the way of your match-making? I don't get it. What do I do to you that's so horrible that you feel the need to pawn me off to the highest bidder?"

"Quit your nonsense!" she whisper-screams at me in a tone that quickly shuts me up. She narrows her sunken, tired eyes, which is an absolute clear signal the conversation is over.

She tucks her frizzy hair behind her ears and pushes her glasses back up the bridge of her nose. Mom could be such an elegantly beautiful woman if she just put some effort into her appearance. When I tried to get her to wear something other than a ten-year-old plain silk suit to this party, all I got from her was, "I don't even know what the point of going is anyway, your dad's just going to humiliate us before the *shagun* even begins."

I definitely got my looks from my mom. Unfortunately, age, stress, and a loveless marriage have worn her down over the years. Now she looks like an exhausted, desperately sad woman.

She looks especially annoyed with me right now, and I know if I push her any further she'll start up about how much she sacrifices for me.

My dad wasn't always your typical *desi* alcoholic father. He used to have hobbies and interests aside from drowning his sorrows in booze. Over the years, he slowly spiralled into being a man without a job or any ambition. It started with his financial blunders. These range from failed gift shops to buying pawned goods, which some random con artists convinced him were genuine. But the final blow came in the form of family betrayal; his older brother duped him out of his share to his land in India. This was the final straw for my dad. He never bounced back from that one.

I often inquired about why we don't just fight them for it, but each time my parents would brush me off.

"Come on; it's time to go." Mom gestures toward my Dad, who's essentially air-hump dancing his way through a half-empty dance floor.

I grab him by the wrist and try dragging him away. His clothes are stained with *daal*, and he stumbles when I yank him a little too aggressively. Now we've caught the attention of half of the party-goers; they snicker and shake their heads, as if this is the exactly what they expect of our family.

The car ride home goes as anticipated. My mom yells at my dad for being such a useless embarrassment and I try my best to tune them out until we finally reach home.

We live smack dab in the middle of Surrey, in the infamous streets of the Newton neighbourhood.

A place with random instances of petty crime, kids crouched in corners smoking up, and a ton of basement suite renters' cars crowding the road. As soon as we get home, I run up to my room and take a long hot shower to wash away the excruciatingly typical events of today.

I long to just get away from all of this and start my own life filled with fancy shoes, cars, and a kick-ass career. When I was young, I had such high hopes for myself. I was drawn to the fabulous lives of the young, wealthy white girls on *Friends* and *Sex and the City.* I truly believed I was going to find the love of my life, run away with him to New York, and live as a freelance writer or something of that sort.

Perhaps it was all the T.V. shows that ignited my curiosity about sex. Roger was right there with me for all of that. I suppose we became friends with benefits just about as soon as we hit puberty. We traded in jump ropes and games of tag for hours of trying to keep as quiet as possible in his bedroom.

I haven't spoken to anyone but my parents in hours, and suddenly I have a desperate need to hear his voice. He hasn't sent me his usual goodnight text; maybe he's waiting for me to get home first. I call him as soon as I get out of the shower; he answers after the first ring in his sexy, sleep-filled voice.

"Hey, come over?" he asks when he realizes it's me.

This is how it's always been with us. He does me the decency of making it seem like he's asking if I want to be with him or not, but we both know I'll never decline. He has me wrapped around his finger. In about half an hour I'll be wrapped around the rest of him too.

There's just something about him that makes me lose my inhibitions. He's the only person in this world I can completely be myself with. No label could ever mean as much to me as that. Some people call it an "open relationship;" others call me a slut for it. My best friend Roop is actually on my side and thinks that we're meant to be together. Roger is my sanctity and my sanity.

I reach his place (his parents basement) in fifteen minutes. I know my parents always hear the garage open, but they never bother asking where I'm going or where I've been. This is probably because they already know that no matter what they do or say, I'll always find a way to be with him. It's been that way since we were kids.

As soon as I get into his room, he pulls me into his arms. He's wearing his plaid pajama bottoms, with nothing on top. The drawstrings hang loosely around his toned waist. Roger doesn't look like a typical Indian guy. He has a chiselled jawline that makes most girls do a double take whenever he walks by, and his eyes are a striking light grey – which makes him even more alluring to all the brown girls around town.

He runs his tongue over his lips as he grabs me by the waist. I gasp as he pulls me in hard against his chest. He slowly unzips my hoodie and smiles with a sexy half smirk when he sees that all I've got on underneath is a red lace bra. I run my fingers through his hair and kiss him hard before pushing him into the wall behind us. I jump up and wrap my legs around his waist, and he falls back onto his bed. We both laugh as the headboard hits the wall.

"What took you so long?" he whispers into my neck in a way that makes me feel weak in the knees.

I pull his head back by his hair and look into his eyes. They're red and puffy. He's probably high as a kite right now. Even though I despise the ever-popular B.C. bud, his love for it is something I choose to tolerate about him.

Things between us are always this way. We don't talk much, I guess we don't feel the need to. We're better at communicating by making each other whole again in the way we discovered felt right many years ago. I was 16 years old when I lost it to him. He's my one and only - despite what many may believe around here.

I try not to think about whether this is the case for him as well. It doesn't matter in this moment anyway. Right now, as he pulls me closer, he belongs to me, and I to him.

A few hours later I'm awoken by the buzz of my phone. It's a text from Roop.

call me. it's important ☺

I sigh and gently unravel Roger's arm from around me and roll off of the bed as quietly as possibly. It's almost 2:00 AM; my mom will be home from her night shift soon.

"Back to reality," I say aloud to myself.

"Sneaking out on me, eh?" Roger murmurs as I dress in the corner of his room.

"Yes. I don't really want your parents to see me anyways." I say, checking my dishevelled but completely satisfied reflection in the mirror. "Pretty sure I've disturbed them with enough surprise encounters over the years." I smile and grab my keys.

"Walk me out?"

We kiss goodbye despite our morning breath. Just before I leave he flashes me his boyish smile, the one that always makes me feel like the most important girl in the world. It's the dimples–his dimples are a killer.

By the time I reach home, I have about a dozen missed calls from Roop and Serena. I do a three-way call to figure out what the heck is so urgent that these girls need to talk about it in the middle of the night.

"Yeah, what's up?" I say once I have them both on the line.

"Okay, first hear us out before you say no straight away," Roop says in her whiny voice saved for when she wants to get her way.

"Man, I'm tired. I just want to go to sleep, hurry up and tell me what's going on." I say, close to losing my patience. I'd rather be snuggled in bed drifting off to sleep than listen to these idiots.

"Okay. Here it is." Serena cuts in with her valley girl voice. "Us three. May long weekend. Whistler. Let's do it."

"Are you two kidding me?" That's what you wanted to talk about? Fuck off, I'm going to sleep."

I hang up, switch my phone off, and melt into my bed, savouring thoughts of what just happened with the man I hope to marry one day.

CHAPTER TWO

I'm awoken by the sound of my mother in the midst her weekly Sunday morning rants. These episodes are like something straight out of an Indian television drama. They mainly consist of a shrieking woman and the sound of dishes clanging together. Sundays are her only days off, so she saves them exclusively for making my dad's life a living hell. It sounds like today's topic of choice is her asking him to, "At least contribute to keeping the house clean if you're not going help pay any bills."

Even from my bed, I can hear the front door slam. She's probably off to wander around the Indian shopping complex to do some wistful window-shopping.

I take this as my cue that it's safe to leave my room. So I get washed up and head down to our run-down kitchen to make myself breakfast. Though I suppose it's actually lunch, since it's a quarter after 1:00 PM.

I stop in the doorway leading into the den to watch my dad for a second. He looks like a wounded, defeated panda bear, lying there in his beige *kurta-pajama* with his big hairy beer belly hanging out. He looks especially sullen and withdrawn today.

I sit on the arm of the couch adjacent to him to block his view of the T.V. I can't help but wonder what it would take to get him out of his miserable stupor. "Dad, remember those grass hockey tournaments you used to be a part of? I used to love watching you in those. Where did all of those trophies go anyway?"

He looks up at me with a suspicious expression, but he doesn't respond.

I carry on anyway. "So, I'm pretty sure by next semester I'll be transferring to SFU. I'm probably going to live on campus; you're fine with that right?"

He clears his throat but continues staring past me and says, "I don't know. Ask your mom. She's the one in charge around here."

He rolls his eyes, as if to say he's not going to play into this pathetic attempt to get him to open up. Honestly, I can't remember the last time my dad and I had a proper conversation.

He wasn't always like this. I think I got my dreamer personality from him. But for every dreamer, there are ten people waiting to stomp that fire out with a nice big dose of reality.

In my family, the messenger of this is my mom. Then again, without her, this household wouldn't even function. I suppose she's justified in her frustration. She *does* have a fair bit of weight to carry around here.

The problem with my dad is clear: he's clinically depressed. He couldn't handle the inadequacy he felt when he drove us to near bankruptcy. It didn't help that my mom's side of the family had to swoop in and save the day by giving us a loan. We would've lost everything if they hadn't. That kind of blow to the ego is something very few men could handle, let alone a Punjabi man. My dad has too much pride to dust off and start over again. Instead he just drinks himself silly and lies around the house.

I don't know a whole lot about my dad's side of the family, other than the fact they tricked us out of what was rightfully ours. Even before that though, we never really associated with any of them. I learned at a young age to not be too inquisitive about this. The only person I'd ever met from his side was my *bhua* (my dad's sister). I was extremely close with her but she passed away when I was very young.

I don't remember much from that time other than being told that she died of breast cancer. I have a distinct memory of being eleven years old, standing butt-naked in front of my bathroom mirror. The shower was running and steaming the room up, but I stood there crying my eyes out. All while I prayed to a God I wasn't even sure existed that I would never grow boobs.

I had this crippling fear of facing the same illness as my aunt. I've always thought that my fate is intertwined with her. Even though she's gone, I still feel her presence and mentally consult her when I need guidance. She was the one person who was actually in my corner. Naturally, this drove my mother nuts. For a long time whenever she was upset with me she would say, "You're just like her. You two are cut from the same cloth." I never really understood how that was a bad thing though.

On my mom's side of the family the only person who we spoke to was my *mama* (my mom's brother). He battled with schizophrenia for a very long time until finally succumbing to the voices in his head. When he just couldn't take anymore, he jumped off the Pattullo Bridge.

I have no problem admitting I'm bat-shit crazy. But I've learned to hide my crazy and act like a good little Indian girl. I credit this to my bhua. She was only a part of my life for a very short while, but the years that she was there helped shape the person I am today. Although, I'm not too sure exactly who that is. I'm in a kind of limbo state at the moment.

I'm not a kid anymore, but I'm definitely not ready to join the "grown up" world either.

Who cares though? I have a feeling Surrey isn't exactly a reflection of what the real world is like, so there isn't much to look forward to anyway. In my culture, there aren't many fates for a girl to choose from. A woman either grows up to be independent (if she's blessed with forward-thinking parents), but eventually learns her place when her in-laws show her it. Or she never bothers to begin with, and just does as she's told. I'm not sure where I fit in with this. I've come a long way since my teenage years though, that's for sure.

When I was thirteen I attempted suicide. Not in a legit way; but just to let myself know I meant business about really hating myself. Deep down inside, I knew I couldn't actually carry it through though.

I ate a bottle of painkillers and lay on my mom's bed. I had this dramatic expectation for my parents to discover me and rush me to the hospital to have my stomach pumped. Then I realized how stupid I was being and I stuck my fingers down my throat to puke it all up.

Basically, I just became extremely sleepy; I had the most intense nap of my life with some crazy lucid dreams.

Since that didn't go as planned, I turned to cutting. The cutting began as a way to blow off steam whenever I had an argument with my mom. I used the one and only thing my father had ever bought me; a tiny arts and crafts knife he brought home for me when I was six years old. I thought it was rather symbolic to use something I had cherished as a child to hurt myself when I grew up a little.

I used to go into this metamorphic trance when I cut. I wasn't myself - nor was I someone else. I was operating solely on emotion. I was angry, it was a release, so I cut. It was just surface scratches on my inner wrist more than anything. To draw blood would've made me pass out.

Nonetheless, it was a nasty, self-damaging habit. It ceased once Roger discovered this secret and made me promise never to do it again. I didn't need to turn in on myself when I was upset anymore. Instead I turned to him. He put all the pieces of me back together again with just the right words.

The rest of the day seems to float on by as I laze about the house. Roger's watching football with his buddies, and I'm not sure what Roop and Serena are up to today. They're probably brainstorming what excuses to give their parents about Whistler. I suppose that's one benefit of having parents who are too occupied by their own misery to really care about you. This allows me to come and go from my house as I please. My freedom has always been the envy of my peers ever since I can remember. It doesn't feel all that great when you're the one no one cares about though.

I decide to drop by Roop's house to see how her negotiations with her family are going.

Going up to Whistler is not a big deal. It's only like a two and a half hour drive up, and there really isn't much to do there. However, it's well known that on May long weekend, it's a shit-fest up there. Everyone up there is either doing drugs, each other, or both.

Over the years, the crowd who parties there has become progressively younger, but we've never actually gone. Usually, we write it off as being a waste of time and consider ourselves too cool to join in on that sort of debauchery. But the truth is that my friends just can't be let off their leashes long enough to go somewhere for a weekend.

"Where in the world have you been?" Roop says as she grabs me by the arm and pulls me into her house.

"Um, did I miss something? What's going on? Why do you look all flustered? Were you rubbing one out to the *Twilight* movies again?"

"Man, you're so gross! I just need your help convincing my brother. He's being a prick."

"Look, dude. You're twenty-three years old. Don't ask. Just tell."

"Just tell what?" Her older brother says from behind us.

It startles us so we jump, which scares their cat *Mittar*. Roop's brother is always lurking around; it's kind of creepy, but I don't know why it surprises either of us anymore.

"If this is about Whistler, you can just forget about it. I know what goes on up there this time of year. You guys have no business up there," he says, readjusting his Nike hat. I'm pretty sure he hasn't taken it off for at least a decade.

"Harj, you have nothing to worry about. I'm the responsible one. Plus, we're only going for one night. I heard barely anyone's even going this year." I punctuate the lie by playing with my hair and pursing my lips at him.

He looks a little swayed, so I press on, leaning in closer towards him, "Come on, we're old enough to keep ourselves out of trouble," I say in the sweetest voice I can manage without gagging.

I find this whole "asking for permission even when you're an adult thing" ridiculous. Especially from a sibling who's simply projecting his lack of a social life on to us. We shouldn't have to sit at home with our fingers up our asses like him just because he never has *anything* to do with *anyone*.

I can tell he's giving in from the way he keeps shifting his weight back and forth. After a little bit of pestering and a whole lot of arm touching on my part, he finally cracks and says, "Whatever man. Just don't come calling me for help when someone jacks your car or something."

Roop grins at me because she knows I've done it again; I've used his major crush on me to my advantage. Even though he's like almost thirty, it's pretty damn obvious he likes me based on how nervous he gets around me.

We run up to her Barbie-pink room and immediately begin to put outfits together. Out of the three of us, Roop definitely has the best wardrobe.

"Okay, as much as it repulses me that he's probably in his room imagining doing the unthinkable with you right now, I've got to admit we would be royally screwed if you didn't start batting your eyelashes at him like the little skank you are."

I throw a pillow at her and shriek, "I was not! You and I both know it doesn't take much to sway him. He just needed a little persuasion. Do you really think he even cares that much anyway?"

"How about this one?" She ignores my inadvertent jab at her brother as she holds up a black leather dress with cuts on the sides.

I grab it from her and stand on her bed, holding it up to myself. "Oh, how original. Three little brown girls running around scantily clad in black dresses. Not like anyone's ever seen *that* before."

She laughs and chucks a shoe at me. I dodge it and then grab my phone from my bag to check my texts. "Shit, it's already 6:00 PM, I should get home. It's almost time for my dad to take his meds."

This is a completely made up excuse. My dad isn't taking any medicine. Even a multivitamin would probably cause a reaction with all the alcohol in his system. I'm going home because this is my mom's break between shifts, so I don't want my dad to face her wrath alone. What a joy it is to go home to *that* all the time.

When I get home, Dad isn't in his usual spot in zombie mode. There's some commotion from the main floor bathroom; upon getting closer, I realize he's puking his guts up in there.

"Dad, you okay? Let me in." I try opening the door, but it's locked.

After about five minutes of horrifying, inhuman noises, he stumbles out ridiculously drunk. He usually saves this level of inebriation for social gatherings. I wonder what the occasion is today.

"Okay big guy, let's get you to bed." I guide him to his room to begin our regular routine, the one reserved for these lovely father-daughter moments.

I grab a bucket, towel, and a jug of water and place it all within arm's reach on his nightstand. Then, I use all the strength my scrawny butt has to offer to roll him over onto his side.

"Thanks, *putt*." I can't muster up anything close to affectionate in response to this term of endearment.

I sigh and turn to walk away, but he grabs a hold of my hand and stares at me for a moment. He doesn't let go, he just looks at me with this strange expression.

Our family doesn't do emotion. I sit down and place my hand on his rapidly balding head. I look deep into his exhausted, sad eyes, and it all just comes bursting out.

"How long can you carry on like this for Dad? You're not only hurting yourself, you know? You think it's easy seeing you like this every day? How do you think that makes me feel?" I look away when I feel that familiar lump in my throat. I take a deep breath in and try to recompose myself because I know chances like this don't come often.

"My feelings aside, how can you even look at yourself in the mirror anymore? Look at what you've become!"

It's not like me to be so open, but the words come out of my mouth before I even realize what I'm saying. There's a long awkward silence for what seems like an eternity.

"Tara, I stopped being able to face the man in the mirror the day your mother stopped looking at me like I was one." He's slurring his speech, but I can still hear the immense pain in his voice when he says this.

He closes his eyes and turns away, but not fast enough for me to miss the single tear rolling down his cheek. We sit like this for a while, until the steady rise and fall of his chest indicates he's fallen asleep. I get up quietly; perhaps we'll attempt this conversation another time, preferably when he's sober. I stare at the floor completely dumbfounded as to how things became this way.

"He doesn't deserve this," I whisper.

How could my mom be so cruel? Bygones need to be bygones, they need to move on from the past. When I get back on Monday, I'm going to sit them down and sort all of this out once and for all.

I pause in the doorway and a knot of sadness and guilt forms in the pit of my stomach. His scruffy, unshaven face is uncharacteristically relaxed as he sleeps. It's such a contrast to his usual scowl and furrowed brow. He grumbles in his sleep and turns over, and I realize his bald spot has grown ten times larger since when I was a kid.

CHAPTER THREE

"Wake up bitches, it's time to party!"

This is the first thing I hear in the morning, a classic Serena voice note to Roop and me. I can't help but smile; sometimes I think she's all talk and no action. She's probably going to be the biggest prude out of all of us this weekend.

I have my stuff ready to go. All I need to do is shower, and in about half an hour we will be on the road with our music cranked and not a care in the world.

Okay, I'll admit it: I'm officially excited about this girls' getaway. It's the first time we've done anything like this, even though we've been friends since the third grade. There's nothing like that first little taste of freedom, so I know the girls are even more pumped than I am.

It's a shame Roger won't be there to enjoy all that freedom with me. Apparently, he has a soccer tournament this weekend. I neglected to mention we were going to Whistler since I know that would send him into a spiral of a thousand questions about what we'd be doing and who we'd be with. The only thing "Surrey Jack-ish" about him is his tendency to get jealous for no real reason. Sometimes I wind him up a little to watch his jaw clench and his voice deepen at the mention of me with another guy.

When I pull up to Serena's house, her mom is in the top window, peeking through the blinds with the scowl of all scowls on her face. I give her a smile and a wave, but she just glares at me in return.

My friend's parents and I don't exactly have the best of relationships. I guess I seem like the ring-leader, since I'm always the one grabbing them from their houses and whisking them away. So, of course, they blame me for all the shenanigans we've gotten up to over the years.

"Holy moly, I'm excited to get the hell out of this shithole of a town!" Serena says as she gets into the car. She immediately reclines her seat and puts her feet up on the dashboard.

"Genius, everyone from this 'shithole of a town' is going to be there too," I reply.

"Right. Valid point. Nonetheless, let's get this show on the road," she says, taking her cheap bottle of wine out of her bag and storing it under the seat behind us.

I head to Roop's place, but she's waiting for us two houses down from her own with giant shades on. She looks as frantic and nervous as ever. I assume she crept out of her house in order to avoid running into her brother. Just in case he had a last minute change of heart about letting her go.

Roop throws her bag in, jumps in the back, and lies down so no one can see her as we pass her house. "Drive woman, drive!"

She has a way of making things overly dramatic and utterly hilarious without even meaning to. Her worried nature and paranoid thinking has actually saved our butts from getting busted many times before though.

"Hey Roop, I think I want to invite your brother up. Roger and I haven't been getting it on lately, and since your brother's older (and so much more experienced) maybe he could teach me a thing or two." I tease Roop as she peers out the back window like an escaped convict.

"Ew! Shut up! You're so nasty, Tara!"

"Hey now, don't get it twisted. Serena is the professional undercover hooch of the group," I say, winking at Roop in the rearview mirror. Serena doesn't even feed into my jab. She just throws an empty water bottle at me.

"Whoa! Don't obstruct the driver's view. Can we *not* get ourselves killed on the way up? Who knows, this might be the only time you little ones are let out of your cages."

My tiny broken down Honda can barely handle the fast speeds of the Sea to Sky highway, but I push good ol' Betty as fast as she can go. Serena named my car that after she got her *brand new* Honda from her parents and named it Veronica. I turn off the AC and roll down the windows to let in some brisk BC air. I readjust my sunglasses and smile. Just like that, we're on our way to the weekend of a lifetime. I can just feel it. This is going to be one for the books.

Our road trip playlist is a mix of club anthems and the Spice Girls' greatest hits; Serena and I spend the first hour of the drive singing along at top volume. Roop doesn't join in. She sits quietly in the back seat, one too many furrows in her brow. She's obviously stressed about getting in trouble when we get back, so I try to get her to loosen up a bit.

"So Roop, you want to prove us wrong and do something risky for once?"

She rolls her eyes at me. "How about you stop trying to sound like a peer-pressure advert? Loser."

This is what she always does. She tends to try to get herself out of awkward situations by cracking a joke.

I carry on anyway. "We've got a bottle of red with your name on it. Crack it open for some pre-gaming on the way up." I swerve in and out of traffic because I want to get there as quick as possible so we have more time to get ready. That's usually the best part of a girls' night out any way.

She bursts out laughing, "What am I like twelve? Is that your idea of taking a walk on the wild side?"

Serena chimes in. "Tara, what are you getting on her case for? You're the one who acts so prim and proper. I seriously don't get it. You have it the easiest out of all of us. Why don't you just live *like a white girl?*"

I glance over at her as I speed up and switch lanes to get in front of a super slow moving black sedan. "What on earth does living like a white girl mean? Let's hear your hooch-ology tip of the day."

"You know what I mean! Act like a guy, and not care about being judged for it. Brown guys are so biased. They chase girls of every other ethnicity like getting in their pants is the ultimate achievement in life. But when it comes to marriage, they want a 'pure and untouched' Indian wife. I can't stand their double standards. When I get married, I hope the guy knows all about my raunchy reputation. I don't care, I'm proud of my past and all the juicy details it has to offer," she says, reapplying her lipstick in the mirror and combing out her hair.

"Serena you're totally stereotyping. Not all white girls are like that," Roop says, taking a moment to take her headphones out and finally join in on our conversation.

"Yeah but the ones all my ex's have ever cheated on me with are." Serena shakes her head in disgust. "Anyways...Why do you guys always make things about me? I was talking to you, Ms. Tara. We're only going to be young once. We may as well be wild and free while we still can. I feel like you take yourself too seriously. You place yourself above the rest of us just so you don't have a tough time falling asleep at night. You're just as much of a worry wart as good ol' Roop back there."

"Ouch, Serena. Don't sugarcoat it, tell me how you really feel, why don't you?"

She rummages through her giant TNA bag, then her eyes light up as she says, "Voilà! Found it." She holds up a little bag filled with white powder.

"Are you freakin' kidding me? You brought cocaine? I'm not doing that shit!" I shout, nearly swerving into oncoming traffic.

"No, silly. It's not coke. It's just a bit of molly."

"Oh, because that's *so* much better," I say. I do my best to keep my eyes on the road as I try to snatch it out of her hand so I can chuck it out the window.

Serena always has to add some element of surprise to our outings. I was wondering what it would be this time. Last summer at the beach, she decided to randomly get up and jump off of the pier in nothing but her granny panties. I know - you'd assume a girl as sexually charged as this one would at least invest in a nice G-string or something. She claims guys like it better when you seem unprepared to be seen naked.

I recall the particular lesson of that day like it was yesterday. "Nobody likes a hoe. That's the number one rule. You never let a guy know you've slept with anyone else. They don't want sloppy seconds. You've got to make them think they're the only one you've ever hopped into bed with after one date. Being in your high-waisted floral underwear is like you're unprepared for this 'surprise' encounter, but you just *can't* resist."

Even though she talks a big game, Serena's not as bad as she makes herself out to be. Plus, the poor girl hasn't exactly had a picture-perfect upbringing either. Her parents don't give her the time of day; they just chuck money at her to keep her quiet. But how many of us brown girls have a Brady Bunch family life anyway?

Roop's shrieking voice snaps me out of my thoughts as Serena waves the bag in front of her face.

Roop tears her headphones out again; her eyes become the size of saucers once she realizes what she's seeing. "Serena! What the hell are you doing with that? What if we hit a roadblock? Or the hotel staff finds it? Or what if it's not even what you think it is and you end up *dead*. Then what? Throw it out! Throw it out right now!"

Roop is in full panic mode and has her tiny butt in the air as she's trying to rip the drugs out of Serena's hands.

I can't help but laugh; but why in the world wouldn't Serena wait for Roop to be slightly more intoxicated before she sprung this on her? What kind of reaction was she expecting from Ms. Goody-Goody?

"Okay, just calm down, will you? We'll figure out what to do with it once we get there." Serena gives me a sly smirk and puts the bag back into the inner pocket of her bag.

To be honest, I have no intention of taking the molly. It's not my thing at all - I barely even like drinking. But I've seen Serena on this stuff before, and it's quite the sight to see. If she wants to pop some molly and sweat it out after, she can do as she pleases. She's a grown ass adult, not to mention that this makes things all the more entertaining for me to watch.

It seems like everyone from the lower mainland decided to head up at the same time as us, so traffic is at a standstill. In the car behind us, there's a group of guys, and they're not bad looking. By the looks of it, they've noticed us too, since one of them has his arm hanging out the window even though it makes him look like a complete douche. For reasons beyond my comprehension, decades upon decades of Surrey guys have used this gesture as some sort of mating call. Since it hasn't faded, I assume it must be working for at least some of them.

Traffic starts to break up as we pass by a construction zone. The guys switch lanes to catch up and are right next to us now. I decide to have some fun, so I speed up even more, and then cut them off a little.

"Wow a couple of them are pretty cute, never seen them before," Serena says, springing up and giving them a flirtatious wave.

"Yeah, they're going to look even cuter in my rearview," I speed up and weave in and out of traffic to get further ahead of them.

"Whoa, look at you being all risky and stuff. If I didn't know any better, I'd say you're trying to act hard in front of them."

I roll my eyes at her and say, "Calm down! I'm just having fun. That's what this weekend is meant to be all about, right?"

Everyone enjoys Whistler in their own way. It's a place where two opposite groups from our generation go to have fun. There are the people who take advantage of the great outdoors, and then there are those who live life only to get wasted and make bad decisions.

The village is a quaint little place in the middle of the mountains. It's filled with pathways and rows of shops, which are run by people looking for a change of pace. There's also a few fairly popular nightclubs and bars. They tend to be filled with people like us who come up from the city with the goal of becoming completely obliterated and letting loose. Although the three of us aren't that bad when we're intoxicated, we're certainly not here to partake in any physical activity, unless you count the potential of Serena hooking up with someone.

We finally reach our hotel and get checked in. Of course, the first thing Serena wants to do is stock up on booze. We decide we'll head to the nearest liquor store after we dump our bags in the room.

The place Roop booked for us is awesome, it's like having our own little apartment. We're all giddy with excitement as we run around the place, checking out what it's got to offer. There's a cozy fireplace next to a comfy velvet couch. In the other corner, there's a little nook in the window which overlooks the entire village. I stop for a moment to take in the breathtaking view. The mountains still glisten with patches of snow, even though summer's just around the corner. There's even a second floor where the main bedroom is. Serena slingshots one of her thongs at us from up top, and I throw a pillow from the couch up at her but miss. "Dibs on this bed!" Serena shouts down.

"Yeah okay, we'll all end up crashing in that bed at the end of the night anyway," Roop says.

"Holy shit guys, you can see right into the room across from here! That guy's totally getting a blow-job right now," Serena exclaims, her face pressed up against the window.

"Serena! You're such a perv! Stop watching!" Roop shouts in horror.

I burst out laughing and grab my wallet so we can go grab some food and Serena's beloved booze.

Serena browses through every aisle of the liquor store as if she's a kid in a candy shop. She says she wants to try mixing some fancy drinks for us. All Roop and I care to do is stock up on chips, popcorn, and candy.

"Hey guys, lets Google how to make some crazy shots and play *"Never-Have-I-Ever"* when we get back!" Serena says, trying to get us amped up for our first night here.

"That didn't go so well last time," Roop says.

The last time we played that game was a couple summers ago at a sleepover at Serena's house; Serena got choked because she thought we were lying about not doing any of the nasty shit that she had apparently done. Really, though – she's the one who was probably talking out of her ass. Nobody's going to get that freaky and then brag about it.

When we get back to our room we crank some tunes, lay out all our food and drinks on the table and pig out like crazy. Even Roop lets loose and starts doing a fake striptease on the countertop to Britney's "You Want a Piece of Me."

I love seeing her have a good time. She's usually so reserved and afraid to have fun. It's like she thinks something bad is going to happen if she doesn't remain the mother hen of our group.

We chill for a couple hours, cracking jokes and laughing about the plans we had made when we were kids. We thought adulthood would be this magic ticket into a life of sweet careers and a shared apartment in downtown Vancouver.

The village darkens while we're out on the balcony; when we finish the last bottle of wine, we head in to embark on a tipsy journey of getting ready together. Serena handles her booze the best, so she straightens our hair for us. She claims we'd burn a bald patch into the back of our heads if we did it ourselves. I tease mine up and add a bit of extra black eyeliner to the outer corner of my eyes.

Roop walks past me and jokingly says, "As if you need to accentuate your big-ass blue eyes even more."

I laugh and snap my eyeshadow palette shut, and start loading up my purse with my usual "night out" items.

"You're missing the condoms," Serena says, peering over my shoulder as I'm crouched down in front of my raggedy old suitcase.

Even though I know she's just messing around, I say, "I don't think I'll be needing those, but we can grab some for your whorey ass on the way out."

She shoves me playfully and slips her feet into a pair of six-inch heels; her shoes click across the floor as she walks over to the full-length mirror to check herself out.

Roop and I join her, and after about a million selfies, we collectively decide that we look pretty damn bangin'. The three of us were always dubbed the "pretty ones" in high school. Now that we're a bit older I'd say we've grown into our own looks a whole lot more. Roop's the sweet one, pretty and petite with her hair cut short. Serena's the sexy vixen of the bunch, with pitch black hair and huge boobs. And I suppose I'm the one who looks like I'm not even brown. We've all got our noses pierced, but Serena wears a hoop in hers, even though everyone in Surrey says those are reserved for the "girls with no morals."

"Okay, so before we start this weekend of debauchery, let's go out to the balcony and make a toast," Roop says after we upload the collectively-agreed-upon hot picture of the night to Instagram.

We grab our champagne and stand outside on the balcony. We ignore the hooting and hollering coming from the street below of the guys claiming they can "see right up our dresses" from down there.

Roop clears her throat and smiles at us while tucking her pin-straight hair behind her ears.

"I just want to say I love you guys, and no matter where life takes us, or what happens when we're older, I hope we always stay as close as we are right now." We clink glasses and take a big gulp of the bubbles we found in the mini-bar inside.

"Aw shucks, look at you getting all emotional on us!" Serena grabs Roop and gives her a bear hug, and I join in.

I'm getting teary-eyed thinking how lucky I am to have these two girls as my best friends in a city full of jealousy and backstabbing.

Serena breaks up our little moment of affection and says, "I know I'm a bitch sometimes. And I'm tough on you guys about being such damn pansies, but you guys keep me grounded, and I thank you for that."

Not to be outdone, I drag over the plastic patio chair from the table and climb on top of it as I raise my glass.

"Okay. My turn. I honestly don't know where I'd be without you girls. You guys are more than my best friends – you're my sisters. No matter how fucked up my life got, I've never felt alone because of you two. We've grown up together - now here's to growing old together. Let's make some kick-ass memories."

Just as our glasses clink together, the chairs leg gives out, sending me tumbling to the ground. I manage to hold my glass up and keep it intact.

"Holy crap! Are you okay?" Roop pulls me up, but they're both holding in their laughter.

I can't help but begin to giggle, which causes them to crack too. "I kind of deserved that one for trying to be a hero. At least I didn't fall over the edge of the balcony," I say, wiping the dirt off of my dress.

"At least you didn't spill your drink! Serena says, linking arms with the both of us and steering us out.

"So, you take your little pill yet or what?" Roop asks Serena as we walk down the main strip of the village towards the crowd and music.

"It's not a pill. It's a powder. And no, I'm not going to do it by myself. That's just sad," she says, pouting.

"Well from the looks of it you won't have a problem finding somebody to join you."

The village is packed. It's swarming with people, and most of them look younger than us.

"Alright, where do you guys want to hit up first?" I ask.

It looks like Roop and Serena are thinking the same thing I am: this is actually pretty lame. There's about three places to go and most people are just wandering around staring each other down. It's just like back home, but everyone's all in one place.

"How about here?" I gesture to a place called Gary's. It has the loudest music blaring outside.

We get in easily because there's barely a line up. Surprisingly, it's pretty busy inside despite our initial impression.

"I think we would've been better off just staying back at the hotel. I don't see how getting eyed-up by a bunch of chicks in sluttier outfits than us is going to be fun." Of course, Roop has to be her usual debbie-downer self. You can always trust her to be the one to walk into a place and want to walk right back out two seconds later.

"They probably don't let Indian guys in because they know they're going to be trouble. Guaranteed the ones they do let in will want to fight each other after their third Crown and Coke," I say. I scan the room–it's packed with all girls.

The majority of *apnay* (East Indian people) always have a point to prove. If two groups of guys end up in the same place and they don't know each other, you can pretty much put money down that there will be a scrap between them by the end of the night.

Serena's already at the bar ordering shots. It looks like she's flirting with the bartender, the only guy in the place right now. He's not even that great looking, she must really be bored.

We pull up a couple of stools to join her. She throws back three shots one after another without even offering us one. She probably knows we'll refuse any way.

She spins her stool toward us and says, "This place it pretty cool! I like how it's underground. It's so different from anywhere in downtown!"

She ties her hair up into a high ponytail, which is always a signal she's buzzing. I roll my eyes at her because she can't actually be serious. She seems to really be enjoying herself. Perhaps she indulged in her happy drugs after all.

Her head snaps up, and she looks past me with this super excited look on her face. "Check out the guys who just walked in. Aren't they the ones from the drive up?"

I look over casually so I don't get spotted checking them out. "Yup. Except they look ten notches more lame without their Lexus truck," I reply.

She hops off her barstool and struts on over to them; all the girls in the room glare at her as if they're going to eat her alive. This is exactly what I love most about Serena. She seriously doesn't care about what people think about her. She has more self-confidence than anyone I know.

It seems like the guys like the attention, since all five of them are gathered around her and are pretending to look completely engrossed in what she's saying. A couple of them look like total 'roid monkeys, and the other few look like their dweeby followers.

"They look like trouble," Roop says with a worried expression on her face.

"Roop, everyone looks like trouble to you. If you had it your way we wouldn't even leave our hotel the entire time we're here."

She smiles and nods. "This is true. Fine. Let's go over there."

Serena's already waving us over by the time we down our drinks. Upon closer examination, I see that the one with pierced ears and a tribal arm tattoo looks pretty familiar. I think he used to play on Roger's old soccer team.

He steps forward as soon as we reach them and says, "Hey, you're Tara right? I'm Ryan. You probably don't remember me."

All the sudden it comes back to me and I do remember him – he's a snarky ass. Whatever, I have no intent of making chit-chat with him anyway.

"It's a shame about you and Roger breaking up. I always told him he was a fool for not locking a girl like you down," he says, licking his lower lip and taking a step toward me.

I take a deliberately obvious step away from his nasty breath and cheap cologne and raise an eyebrow at him. "Um, we've never been officially together, and I'm pretty sure that's a requirement before you break up. Not to mention that we're on perfectly good terms, so I don't really know what you're talking about."

He exchanges a look with one of his friends that I can't really read. "Oh, my bad then, guess I got you mixed up with someone else."

"Yeah, guess so," I snap at him. "Let's go, Serena, this place sucks." I tug on her arm, but she completely ignores me.

Oh great, drunk Serena is out to play–the one who never wants to leave unless she's the last person out of a place. She absolutely will not turn down a drink unless it's the one to put her under the table.

"You guys go wander around." She waves her hand at us, still smiling up at one of the 'roidy dudes.

"I thought she was seeing some mystery guy. Wonder why she's acting like a ditz trying to impress these dudes now," Roop says.

"She's seeing someone?" I say, feeling surprised this is the first I'm hearing about this.

"Yeah, I read a couple texts over her shoulder to some guy she's got stored in her phone as the heart emoji."

I look over at Serena as she throws her head back and laughs as if one of them just said the most hilarious thing she's ever heard.

I try to make eye contact with her so she knows we're leaving and call out, "We're leaving now Serena! Text us if you need us."

When we step outside, the warmth of the day has faded away into a chilly night. I take a deep breath in. Even though it's cold, I don't mind that I'm not wearing my jacket. All of the alcohol in my system seems to be hitting me all at once, and I know it'll warm me up soon enough.

"Let's go explore, shall we?" I link arms with Roop, and we step away from the mini-Surrey dungeon of doom.

"It's pretty damn beautiful up here, hey?" Roop says, pointing her face to the night sky with her eyes closed.

I look at her and smile. She seems so carefree right now, instead of tightly wound up and stressed out. Maybe it's just the alcohol, but it's a good look for her.

We walk around for a bit even though we're not entirely sure where we're headed. I just know I would rather be anywhere but in that shithole. We see some girls we went to high school with who I wasn't particularly fond of, but Roop greets them with a big fake smile anyway.

"Jessica! How's it going?" Roop says.

She gives us the good 'ol one over and says, "Roop and Tara? You guys look so different. Where's your third musketeer?"

Different? I think to myself. Okay. And you still look like your miniature hippopotamus self.

"Oh, she's around here somewhere; we just stepped out for some fresh air." Roop replies.

Jessica pulls out her lighter and starts fiddling with it. "I see. Well, we're heading up to this spot with a killer view to blaze. Care to join?"

Before Roop can refuse I say, "Yeah sure. Why not?"

Roop looks at me quizzically and I mumble that we had nothing better to do anyway.

"We're going to the top of the village. Trust me, you guys are going to die when you see how nice it is." One of Jessica's sidekicks says with the excitement of an un-neutered puppy.

"Wow! Like, seriously? That sounds amazing!" I say sarcastically. Only Roop catches on to the way I'm mimicking these dimwits.

Roop whispers to me, "I guess it won't be so bad smoking up after so long. Not to mention that it sure beats watching Serena being felt up by those freaks."

"Yeah, you've got to be wrong about her seeing someone. She wouldn't be acting like that if she was into somebody." The two of them have never kept a single secret from me, so this is kind of weird. But Roop's probably just tripping out. Serena's practically allergic to monogamy. I'm pretty sure it's against her entire belief system.

As we hike up to this surprise spot, my thoughts can't help but drift back to what Ryan said about Roger and I back at that dingy club. I really need to have a talk with Roger when I'm back. This is getting pretty ridiculous.

I'm so lost in my thoughts that I don't realize we're being led way the heck out to the boonies by these girls. I'm surprised they can even walk this distance in the trashy heels they're wearing. A couple of them are just carrying their shoes in their hands like us, though.

"We're here." Jessica says as she sparks up to light the thinnest joint I've ever seen.

I step up and take a moment to take in the view before me. It's unbelievably beautiful. I pull Roop up so she can see it too.

"Holy shit! This is unreal," Roop says wide-eyed and amazed.

It's almost so perfect that it doesn't even look real. How so very lucky we are to have this natural beauty a stones throw away from our homes. The surrounding mountains and the cozy glow of the village shining below are damn amazing. I feel untouchable like this, looking down on everything. It's nice to be away from so much nonsense and just have a moment to myself. Or maybe I'm just getting a second hand high from whatever weed these girls are smoking.

Roop and I both sit down at the edge of the cliff while leaned up against a big smooth rock.

She sighs and says, "Damn. You almost forget how views like this can make you feel, eh?" This makes me turn and look at her with surprise because it's unlike her to be so wistful.

I give her a playful nudge. "Okay, can you not get all emo on me? I'm not going to save you if you jump."

Even though I'm teasing her, I totally get what she means. Ever since I was a kid, I've been drawn to this kind of view. A city view isn't just a cluster of lights; they're individual pieces that are part of a greater whole. I prefer a view like this to one of a natural landscape any day. Each light represents a person, and each of those people has a deeply intricate life of their own. These lives consist of people they love with their entire being and people who love them that way right back. They all have places to go and people to see.

We're passing the joint around now and Roop and I decide to take a toke or two. Each hit has me feeling increasingly nostalgic. Roop's just as quiet as me so I bet she's having some deep thoughts of her own right about now. She breaks the silence after a while.

"What're you thinking about Tara?"

I'm feeling completely unreserved, so I let her in on my thoughts. "Do you ever think about how many stories are unfolding at this very moment? Everyone's just living out their lives. Some people put life into their years and some just watch the years pile up behind them.

I ramble on despite her silence. "Everyone is the center of his or her own universe. No one realizes that we're all just one big grid-map of lights. One day, those lights are going to switch off, and nothing will be left behind."

For a second I feel like Roop's not even listening, since she's just grinning like an idiot and staring into thin air. She turns to me and continues smiling.

"Tara, you're too deep for me. As a matter of fact, you're too deep for all of us. You're an old soul, you know that? There's something different about you, and the best part is you don't even know it...Or maybe you're just mega-high."

We both burst out laughing. When our laughter dies down, we sit together quietly, enjoying BC's finest herbal remedy. Each exhale allows the stress of our mundane lives to drift away and intertwine with the surrounding mountain air.

The rest of the girls are swapping stories about typical nonsense that you'd expect a group like them to be amused by.

"Oh man. Remember that time Gagan was caught fucking Sandeep's boyfriend?"

Another girl (who I'm pretty sure is this Gagan girl's cousin) pipes up to stand up for her. "That was just a stupid rumour that a couple of horny seniors started because they wanted to get in her pants, but they knew they never stood a chance."

Roop and I roll our eyes, I know we're both thinking the exact same thing: these girls have not excelled or grown in any way since we graduated.

"So, you guys still keep in touch with everyone from high school?" I say with a tone that doesn't mask the fact that I find this rather lame.

Jessica's sidekick replies, "No. Not really. We don't keep tabs on people - if that's what you mean. It's just us five that are still tight."

Jessica stands up and wanders over to me. "Hey Tara, how are things going with Rog? Heard you guys went through a pretty awkward phase there for a bit."

They all exchange knowing glances. For the second time tonight, I feel like I'm the only one left out of some sort of inside joke about Roger and me.

Roop interjects because she sees my face twist into an expression that looks like I'm about to push one of these girls over the edge of the mountain.

"Oh no. They still are and always have been just friends. People just like talking shit because they have nothing better to do," Roop says, putting her arm around my shoulder.

One of Jessica's other minions, a dimwit-looking tart with super gaudy blonde extensions, decides to break the obviously growing tension. "Anyways. Forget all that, I heard Simren's parents shipped her off to India because they caught her giving head to some distant relative who was visiting!" She holds her hands to her mouth as if this is the most outrageous thing anyone's ever said.

One of the other girls replies, "What? No way! That's got to be a lie!" Even though it's clear she's as equally delighted with this tidbit of gossip as the other imbecile.

I can't take anymore of how pathetic they sound so I snap, "Is this your guys' idea of passing time? You sit around spreading rumours which someone as sad as you probably made up?"

From the quiver in Jessica's double chin, it doesn't seem like she's taken very kindly to my brutal offering of honesty. She's got a major bitch-face going on now. "Well not everyone's a spoiled brat like you, Tara. It must be so hard sitting in your big house, not having to do shit all with mommy and daddy doing everything minus wiping your ass for you. You can't even face the music about your STD carrying boy-toy."

Something inside of me snaps and I start to see red. I feel like there's steam blowing out of my ears and I don't hear anything after that. My peripheral vision disappears, and all I see is Jessica's fat fucking face that's about to get knocked in. I walk toward her with my right heel in my hand and swing it hard against her head. She whimpers as she falls to the ground with that one solid blow.

Her main sidekick comes at me screaming, "You stupid bitch, I'm going to knock you the fuck out!"

On basic instinct, I grab her by the hair and throw her down. Her extensions are left dangling in my hand. As I turn to walk away she gets up and is about to grab me but not before Roop throws her down again. We're dangerously close to the edge of the cliff. Everything feels like a blur, until I realize I'm sitting on top of the chick, raining down punch after punch. Roop begins to pull me away as she realizes there's blood gushing from her nose as if I've broken it.

Roop looks like she's going to cry. I feel terrible for dragging her into a situation she'd never condone if my life wasn't at risk. I can't believe that the rest of the girls haven't stepped forward to help their friends up.

"You guys are all fucking pansies. Your friend's bleeding on the ground, and you're just staring at me with your ugly mouths hanging open," I say to the lot of them standing there.

Still, none of them flinch, so we walk away. We're silent all the way down, and my hand is throbbing. Roop's shoes are busted open, so she's limping with one heel on and one off.

We get back to the hotel ready to tell Serena about the bizarre scrap we just had, but she isn't back even though it's 3:00 AM. We sit in silence, staring at a blank T.V. screen, feeling extremely sobered up and a little unnerved by what just happened.

Finally, Roop breaks the silence and says, "Tara, what the hell was that? How did we go from talking about the philosophy of life to bashing our high school arch nemesis' face in?"

She looks visibly shaken. This is not her type of scene. She's probably already feeling guilty. I get up and snatch up the remainder of our vodka bottle, and in my best hardcore voice I say, "I didn't choose the thug life, the thug life chose me."

We burst out laughing despite our mental and physical exhaustion. I switch on the T.V. just to get our mind off things – specifically, the thought of what those girls may do to us tomorrow. Everyone knows a scrap amongst people from Surrey is never just that, there's always a retaliation of some sort.

Some point in-between late that night and early the next morning, Serena stumbles in piss-drunk. She looks a complete wreck. Her eyeliner's smudged, and her usually perfect hair's a mess. She just stands there staring at me like she's got something to say.

I break the silence, "Well, well. Look what the cat dragged in." I get up to help her to her room, but she just backs away. She nearly falls over, but she eventually finds her way to the bathroom.

"What's up with her?" Roop asks with her eyes half shut.

"I don't know. She's probably still fucked up off whatever she took. I'm going back to bed; it's too early to play mommy to her."

CHAPTER FOUR

We wake up around noon, but Serena is still asleep in her drunken daze. I try not to make any noise as I get up since I know she's going to be mega-hungover. From the looks of it, she had a rough night banging someone–or banging someone up like we did.

I creep past her to go shower up. Once I get out of the bathroom, I see that Roop's already dressed and on her way out to grab breakfast. From the furrow between her perfectly arched eyebrows, I can tell she's still upset about last night, but I broach the subject anyway.

"Man, I'm starting to understand why guys get into so many fights. When I was punching that chick, it wasn't just because I was pissed about what Jessica said. I was letting out all my rage on her."

"What do you have to be so angry about Tara?" Roop says, digging through her purse for something.

"What do you think? My dad's a drunk, my mom hates me, yet everyone thinks I have it so easy."

She seems surprised that I refer to my family drama, since it's a subject I generally steer clear of. She doesn't try to give me some half-ass superficial words of comfort or tell me my life's not so bad like a fake friend would. She just grabs my hand, squeezes it, and is quiet for a while.

"Dude, I just can't believe you jumped in," I say, giving her a playful shove.

She grabs her jacket and says, "Well, I kind of had to. You're not exactly a pro-scrapper. I wasn't going to leave you on your own. I can be a down-ass bitch too!"

I burst out laughing hysterically. "You did not just say that! Thug Roop in the house! Watch out everyone. This little one is going to become the ultimate good girl gone bad and make us all look like freakin' saints."

I guess we're being too loud for Miss Party Animal because she comes out grumbling with her shades on and her hood pulled over her head. She doesn't look at either of us as she sits down.

"And where the hell were you, missy?" I get up and snatch Serena's glasses from off of her.

She squints her eyes and massages her temples as if the sun is the worst possible thing right now. She doesn't look directly at me but just says, "Oh no. It's not what you think. I wasn't with those guys. I saw some other people I knew, and I was with them. I had a pretty low-key chilled out night. We just wandered around the village and lost track of time."

Roop says what I'm thinking, "I smell bullshit."

Serena doesn't even bother giving a snarky response back. She just carries on acting jumpy and weird.

"Are you holding out on us? Since when are you not ready to divulge in all the juicy details of your life? Come on, just tell us! Who is he? You must have been with someone you actually liked if you're not telling us all about it!" I say with a big grin.

She looks seriously offended now as she stands up and slams her hand on the table. "Is that what you guys fucking think of me? That if I'm not with you I must be with some random guy getting my brains screwed out? Contrary to what you may believe, I do have a social circle outside of you guys, you know."

"Whoa, whoa. Someone's a bit touchy. Since when do you have other friends? You're so full of it Serena. Whatever! Don't tell us. We'll find out sooner or later anyway. People love talking smack around here. We learned that last night. Right, Tara?" Roop winks at me.

I try to match her feigned bravado. "Exactly, some girl will run her mouth until somebody has to shut her up."

Serena looks at us completely perplexed as she slowly sits back down. "Uh, okay. What did *you* guys get up to last night?" Then her eyes land upon my swollen knuckles, and she shrieks, "Whoa! Did you get in a fight?"

"More like she pounced on Jessica Mann and then we both beat up her no-name sidekick," Roop replies, trying to sound even more nonchalant.

"What! Wait. Back up and tell me everything! How did you guys end up with them? I don't believe it. There's no way you or Tara would ever hit someone, let alone *that* fat ass. She could have smothered you to death with her giant cellulite covered ass." Serena says, finally loosening up a little.

"Okay. First of all, why's everyone always selling me short? I can stand up for myself. I am *not* a doormat. Let that be known," Roop says, flexing her non-existent muscles. "I'm the new and improved Roop."

"Yes apparently a Roop who beats people up on the top of mountains in a drunken stupor," Serena says through her laughter.

Then she holds up her perfectly manicured hands up to the both of us for a high-five. "Oh man. Good fucking job girls. We all know that girl had it coming to her." Then she perks up and re-tightens her ponytail, "Anyways, fuck all that, let's figure out what we're doing tonight."

"What do you mean, 'we?' You mean, how are *we* going to start off the night together, only to have you tell us to scurry along ten minutes later?"

"Oh come on! Let's go grab food, I'm freakin' starving!" she says, heading inside to avoid our questions once again.

We grab a twenty-piece nugget combo at McDonald's, despite Roop's protests to get something a little healthier. As we walk back to our hotel, I see a guy through the window of a coffee shop; his back is turned, but the set of his shoulders looks familiar.

"Can't be him," I mutter, shaking my head.

"Can't be who?" Roop asks.

"Oh, nothing. I really need to get my head in check. I thought I just saw Roger."

Serena's eyes dart around, and her jaw tightens. She picks up her pace and pulls me along to catch up. "Let's go take a nap. I'm not going to have the energy for tonight unless we crash for a bit."

"Same here," Roop says.

I link arms with the both of them, happily humming to the music of the shops along the way.

After we wake up from our power nap, we wander out to the balcony again to people watch. The village is buzzing with way more people than yesterday. I see a ton of faces I recognize, with the addition of excited teenyboppers everywhere. I check my phone for the hundredth time to see if Roger has texted me yet. But nope. Nothing.

We don't spend as much time getting ready as last night. I hold up my glass of cheap wine to make a toast. "Here's to tonight being nothing at all like last night."

"Sounds like a plan!" Serena and Roop say in unison. We clink glasses with one another, down our drinks, and head out.

I push my hair up to make sure the tease doesn't fall out. "You okay Serena? You've been really quiet all day."

"I'm just tired. Maybe we should just have an early night tonight."

Roop and I exchange a puzzled glance. Serena Rai wanting to cut a night short? Something's definitely up. Oh well. When she wants to spill, she will. It's not like her to keep secrets. If she has something to say, everyone usually hears about it.

"So guys, I overheard my brother and his friends talking once. They said there's a crazy rave here," Roop says, trying to act all cool and "in the know how."

"Honey, if your *brother* knows about it – it ain't cool."

"Hey! What's that supposed to mean? He was cool back in his day!" she snaps back at me.

"Hmm, a rave huh?" Now this has caught Serena's attention. "That sounds like a nice change of pace. Let's do this," she says with a smirk.

While wandering the outskirts of the village we see a group of people we know. Serena asks them if they know anything of this supposed 'Lost Lake Rave.' Turns out they do. It seems like everyone but us knows about it. Once we head up to the main road, we see a giant mass of people headed toward it. Just like that, this night has taken a turn for the better.

"Well, we're definitely not dressed for something like this," Roop says.

There are a lot of people in all sorts of funky clothes. But most of the brown girls have stuck to their usual "black on black" attire. I see a group of Asian girls in colourful tank tops, miniskirts, and flower headbands.

Everyone seems around our age or younger. I don't see many guys, but whatever. That's not the prerogative for tonight anyway. When I get back, I'm making things official with Roger. There's no need to complicate things by making the mistake of hooking up with some random.

I'll leave that kind of wild frolicking to Serena. I'd say Roop too, but we all know that ain't ever going to happen. It's hard to believe she's still a virgin, but she is. The poor girl thinks she's going to meet some *apna* Prince Charming who will sweep her off her feet and make all the waiting worthwhile.

Serena pulls us away from the crowd to a wooded area. I stumble as I try to keep up. There are tangles of branches scratching up my legs and poking into areas they really don't need to be.

"All right guys, don't act like little pussies now. This is the perfect time and place for this," Serena says, and her eyes light up. She opens the locket on her choker necklace to reveal her little bag of molly.

Completely out of the blue, Roop grabs it, spills a bit into her drink, and gulps it down.

"Whoa! What the heck Roop? I thought I would have to give you a spiel about not wasting your youth before you even considered taking it," Serena says, completely gobsmacked.

Roop checks her reflection in the forward camera of her phone as if she's suddenly going to look different after taking a hard drug for the first time. "Fuck it. Where has being a straight arrow gotten me? Absolutely nowhere. I have a reputation as clean as a whistle in a city filled with filth. I *still* haven't earned my family's trust or respect. I may as well do whatever I want for once."

She's on to something. Why be so prim and proper when it feels so good to be bad? Even though I have a knot in my stomach about what I'm about to do, I take a cooler out from my bag, throw a bit of the powder into it and drink as much as I can in one go. Serena throws the rest in and throws back the remainder of my drink.

We all carry on walking as if nothing happened. Roop breaks the silence and asks an obvious lingering question. "Hey guys, can we just make a joint decision about what we're going to do if we see Jessica here? I really don't want to get chucked in the ice cold lake during a sneak attack."

"Man, they aren't going to do shit. Those girls get in fights left, right, and center. They probably have ten other people to get revenge on before they even think of you." Serena says.

"We did mess them up pretty bad, though." Roop replies.

"Stop worrying. You're killing my buzz. Drama-free okay? That's the goal of tonight. For it to be *drama-fucking-free*," Serena says, smiling with her eyes closed and her face pointed toward the cloudy night sky.

We walk for what seems like ages, but I can't really be sure because everything's gone hazy.

Roop stops dead in her tracks and just stares into space for about a minute before speaking. "Guys. I can't feel my face." Her drawn out way of speaking combined with her panic-stricken expression makes Serena and I burst out laughing.

Serena snaps her fingers in front of Roop and nudges her to keep on walking. "You'll be just fine my dear. Just soak it in. Let it happen. Let molly make you her bitch."

I giggle at this a little more than I would on a sober mind. Everything's just a bit more vivid and intriguing at the moment - especially Serena's jokes.

Roop still looks pretty disoriented. "I don't know man. I don't like it. My legs feel like JELL-O."

I assure her she's going to be just fine. I had a feeling she was going to regret her spur of the moment decision pretty quickly. She's gone from scared to paranoid looking. She keeps checking over her shoulder every couple of steps and suspiciously eyes down anyone who passes by.

She was like this the first time we all smoked weed. I can picture it just like it was yesterday. It was the summer we turned 14. The three of us crouched in the corner of Roop's balcony in the middle of the night, giggling away. It was one of the rare times we were allowed a sleepover. We thought we were so cool rolling a blunt with some bunk weed we stole from her brother.

Roop quickly went from the ringleader to all-star trip artist when she became convinced the smoke was going to cause her lungs to collapse. She also thought it was going to trigger a random bout of psychosis.

When I ask if Serena remembers all that. She just shakes her head and laughs. "That girl needs to learn to *relax*."

I laugh and nod my head. "How about we make the mission of the night for her to loosen up and have fun for once?"

"Sounds good to me!" Serena says seeming like her usual chipper self after that strange emo mood she was in.

I turn to look at Roop, who's grinning like an idiot and pointing straight ahead. I follow her gaze and see giant speakers, with house music blaring through them. There's a huge sea of people who look more fucked up than the three of us combined.

There are people doing keg stands and guys shotgunning beers. There are girls in tutus and coordinated leg warmers prancing around in a circle like they're at some sort of wild séance. The thick smoke from the bonfire in the dead centre of it all rises and twists up into the sky.

Serena glances around and then changes the direction she's leading us. "Let's go down this way instead. I think we should do our own thing tonight. I'm not in the mood for mingling."

I try to see who she saw that made her suddenly turn from party starter to uncharacteristically introverted in a matter of seconds. But I just see a group of brown guys in the distance. A couple of them look like the same guys she so eagerly ditched us for last night. One of them is wearing the same letterman jacket that I got for Roger for his 21st birthday.

Upon closer examination, I realize that he kind of looks like him too. But it's probably the chemicals I just pumped into my bloodstream playing tricks on my brain.

"You ladies look like first-timers. Come join the party. There's no need to be shy." I turn to see a guy who looks like he'd be the mastermind behind a school shooting. Perhaps I'm being too quick to judge, but the long scraggly hair and black trench coat aren't helping his case whatsoever.

Serena rolls her eyes at him. "Scram. You're blocking our view."

At that very second, we hear a loud crackle and pop in the sky. Roop jumps and screams, "Holy shit! Gunshots! We're all going to die."

The guy laughs and as he turns to walk away he says, "It's just some firecrackers sweetheart. You brownies should be used to it. Don't you guys blow shit up for a living?"

"What the fuck did you just say? You ignorant piece of shit!" Serena pushes past us and gets right up in his face.

"Truth hurts honey. It's not our fault all *you people* have taken over half of BC." A girl with an equally horrendous sense of style seems to appear out of no-where to rush to this guy's defense.

"As much as I'm enjoying this lovely chat with the KKK wannabes over here. Let's get the fuck out of here – too much trash in this place," I say, gesturing to the assholes.

When I turn around, I see that Roop has wandered toward the bonfire. She keeps stomping on forward as if she can't hear us calling after her. I feel like the molly hasn't affected me too much. The trees are greener, and the air is more intensely crisp, but other than that I feel the same.

"Oh no. Why has the dimwit gone and stood right next to Jessica Mann?" Serena says.

Just as I look up, I see one of the minions point toward Roop and whisper something to a very bruised up Jessica. Her right eye is swollen shut. Then I spot her friend, who looks even worse, and I feel a huge pang of guilt.

A look of recollection and subsequent rage crosses Jessica's face as she charges toward Roop. We run towards them, but it's too late. They've got Roop circled.

"Quick! Get down" Serena tugs on my arm hard enough to dislocate my shoulder.

We squat behind a tree a couple feet away so we can rush them when they least expect it. It's the only chance we have at this point.

"Hey! It's you guys! Roop says, stumbling towards them. "I know you guys. Whoa. What happened to your face, dude?"

"This is nothing compared to what I'm going to do to you and that bitch Tara when I see her."

Roop begins to wave her finger in the air while staggering toward Jessica like a drunken baby giraffe. "I'm not telling you where she is! You big fat bully!"

I start to get up to help the poor girl out; clearly, she won't be able to hold her own if they actually jump her. But Serena pulls me back down once more.

One of Jessica's friends starts reasoning with Roop. "Look. We have nothing against you because I know you're just a pussy-ass follower doing what you were told. But if you don't tell us where to find her, you'll be the next best thing to punching her perfect little face in."

A crowd begins to form to see what the catty shouting is all about. Just as one of them throws Roop to the ground by her hair, we jump out.

"Hey, fatass! We're over here," Serena shouts.

Jessica stomps over and takes a swing at Serena. She backs up and manages to dodge it, but it catches me on the left cheek. The sting of the blow causes my knees to buckle and I drop to the ground. I feel someone kicking into my side with all their might. It feels like someone's stabbing me in the stomach. I curl up in a ball trying to protect my head as they continue to kick me. I have absolutely no idea if Serena and Roop managed to get away or not.

"Get off of her! That's enough!" I hear a guy's voice shout, and someone lifts me up. I can't tell who it is through the pain, but he sounds just like Roger.

"What are you all staring at?" He shouts to the crowd. "Haven't you seen a fight before? Scram! Carry on with whatever you lame-asses were doing."

The crowd disperses, and I see Roop and Serena leaned up against a tree with blood trickling down the sides of their faces. The guy wanders off back to his friends before I can see who it is; he says something to them and leaves through the woods.

Another guy from their group says, "Damn. You guys look fucked up. Let's get you girls back to the village."

We quietly oblige. We're all feeling too rough to even care how embarrassing this whole thing is.

"Now I really can't feel my face," Roop says as we sprawl out across the bed.

I guess the whole chivalrous act is over, since Serena's clearly having the moves put on her out on the balcony.

I hear her attempt to get rid of these douchebags. "Well thanks for all your help, but I think we're just going to pass out. Time to try to forget the last 48 hours before we head home tomorrow."

I pull the covers over myself, trying to block the ringing in my ears out.

Just as I'm drifting off to sleep, I hear someone say, "Roger saved your asses. You owe him one, but you can repay me instead. What you playing shy for?"

Am I just tripping out again? At least now the blows to the head give me a valid reason to be hallucinating.

I stretch and feel a crack in my shoulder as I get out of bed. Those girls fucked us up good. I go to put a pot of coffee on for us before we hit the road. Serena's already on the balcony nursing her emotional and physical hangover. I wonder if she's been out there all night. She doesn't even hear me open the sliding door and just continues to stare blankly at the glorious mountain range before us.

The morning chill is a bit too intense for my cuts and scratches, so I grab a blanket and cozy up to her. I don't think I've ever seen her look so serious or withdrawn.

"Enough of this crap Serena. Out with it. What's going on? You've been off since our first night here," I say, looking directly at her miserable face.

She bursts into tears, grabs a hold of my arm and buries her face into it and begins to sob the loudest I've ever heard anyone cry. She looks up at me with her puffy, bloodshot eyes and says, "You're going to hate me. I'm going to lose you forever."

CHAPTER FIVE

It's been three days since the discovery. Every time I open my eyes from another failed attempt at sleep, it all comes rushing back. Each time it runs through my mind everything feels like the first time I heard it. I'm still in shock. I can't believe the two people I trusted more than anything in the world have betrayed me like this.

My fluffy white duvet covers are no longer a source of comfort. Now I feel like I'm being suffocated by a reality created by lies and deceit. Who knows how long it'd been going on for?

I hear a knock on my door and then Roop walks in looking very concerned. "You weren't answering any of my calls, so I thought I'd come see how you're doing."

She sets a box of Krispy Kreme donuts down on my dresser. As tempting as that is, I just don't have much of an appetite right now.

"You know, I expected my phone to be buzzing off the hook since Whistler. But nope. Neither of them have the decency to even apologize," I say sorrowfully.

"Maybe because it's one of those mess ups that there's no words for."

I pull the covers back over me. "Ugh, just thinking of them as a *'them'* makes my stomach turn. I can't believe he did this to me. I can't believe *she* did this to me. Roger and Serena were screwing each other's brains out right under my nose."

Roop climbs in next to me, into my iron rod double size bed.

"I know, Tara. It hurts, and it sucks. But I'll help you through this. It can only get better from this point on, right?"

I tell Roop I'd rather just sleep the day away. She gives me the "you shouldn't be alone" and "just come out with me" speech but quickly gives up. Before leaving, she pauses to tell me I've only got a week to wallow in my misery.

I get out of bed and run a hot shower. I curl up in a ball in the corner of my tub and hold myself as the water pours over me. I can't believe that the entire time in Whistler I thought I was only imagining that

I was seeing Roger. Turns out it *was* him. That's who Serena spent the first night up there with. I was also right about thinking it was him who pulled those girls off of us during the scrap. I feel so betrayed, but even more stupid. It's humiliating to think all his friends and probably half of Surrey knew about the two of them and I didn't.

After a couple more days of moping around the house, I realize that perhaps my parents honestly do not care about me whatsoever. They've barely acknowledged my miserable appearance other than a few inquiries about why I wasn't going to my classes. I don't even care to sort their issues out anymore.

How could I attempt to fix someone else's life when mine was in shambles? It'd been happening right under my nose the entire time. Roger and Serena were hooking up at the same time he and I were. Maybe even on the same night. As soon as I left his place, she probably swept right in for round two.

"How am I ever going to get over this?" I say to myself as I fumble with my keys to lock up the front door on my way out.

Roop told me if I don't leave the house today she was going to drag me out kicking and screaming.

Just as I'm about to head toward my car, I stop to follow the sound of a commotion going on near my neighbour's house. When I go to get a closer look, I see my dad waving his hand around and shouting. The usually friendly Fijian lady who lives in the next-door basement suite seems equally animated.

"I know you took it! You drunk! You're the only one who saw me leave my key under my doormat!" I run over because my dad is going beet red, and all the neighbours are poking their heads out their windows.

My dad looks at me more furious than I've ever seen him and says, "Tara, she's saying I stole her jewellery stash from under her kitchen sink. I wouldn't even assume she has anything to stash. Look at her for God's sake!"

"You bloody Punjabis. You take over our town with your monster houses, fancy cars, and useless businesses. All this criminal activity is here because of *you people*," she says, shoving her manicured finger into his chest.

"Okay, lady. Let's calm down a tad, shall we? As you said yourself, we're well off enough to not need to go around committing petty crimes. I'm sure you've simply misplaced your stuff. And believe it or not, it's possible someone else, *of any ethnicity*, may have taken it. Why do you assume it's my dad?"

"Everyone around here knows he just freeloads off your mom ever since his family ripped him off. The walls are pretty thin around here, you know!"

My dad stomps past me. He charges into our house and slams the door. I leave our neighbour standing there and follow him inside.

"Don't listen to her, dad. She doesn't know what she's talking about."

"No Tara. They're right. They're all right. Your mother, the neighbours, and the whole rest of the world. I'm a useless waste of space. You'd be better off without me."

He storms off before I can even reply. It's best I give him time to cool down; he's just being melodramatic.

I sit sipping my peppermint tea, watching a group of young girls who look fresh from India. They're laughing about how wrong the *gori* barista got their traditional names. I wonder what it must feel like to be as young and carefree as them. I can't handle all the crap going on in my life right now. Things just possibly couldn't get any worse at this point.

My phone buzzes so I check my texts.

ROGER: *hey...r u free to talk?*

There it is. The first message from Roger. My finger hovers over the delete button. Perhaps I should just be done with them for good. My stomach drops at the thought. I suppose I could give him a chance to explain…

    TARA: *there's nothing you can say to make this better.*

His reply pops up instantly.

    ROGER: *i know tara. but at least hear me out. u only heard one side of things.*

My fingers answer before my brain can.

    TARA: *unless you tell me my two best friends weren't actually fucking behind my back…nothing you say is going to make sense to me.*

What's wrong with this fool? He fucks off for like a week when he full well knew what I'd be going through. Then he reappears with some weak attempt to reach out to me. Fuck the both of them. I don't need them, or anyone for that matter. I just need to get the fuck out of Surrey.

I leave my drink unfinished and grab a couple of light reads from my favourite author. I chuck my phone in my bag, think about going home, but decide to head to the beach for a run to clear my mind. I've got my runners in the trunk. I'm always prepared for a refreshing run. It's the only thing that helps me switch off. I just focus on where I am in that moment and block out the rest.

The beach is packed with happy couples, and I can't help but want to shout to them to save themselves before they get their hearts broken. Most of these dudes are probably just in it for the lay.

I finally get to my favourite stretch of the beach. There's a paved path that runs along the ocean; it's usually fairly quiet in this area, except for the push and pull of the waves. I throw my headphones in, take a sip of my water and begin my run. Each time my feet hit the ground I feel like I'm getting farther away from my problems.

I breathe in the fresh ocean air. God, I love it here. I couldn't imagine living anywhere other than the coast. It's a wonderful place to be, but it's so easily taken for granted. The quiet hum of nature is exactly what I need to cleanse my mind. For the first time in days, I feel myself resurfacing. I can finally think straight again.

I slow down my pace because there's a freshly married Indian girl with her wedding bangles up to her elbows in my path. She's walking with who seems to be her husband and an older woman.

Yikes. What a fairytale newlywed sight to see. The typical "dip" trio.

"Hurry up Sukhjinder. We have to get home in time, my uncle and his family are coming over for dinner."

Judging from the dude's authoritative tone, I'm assuming this wasn't a "love marriage."

The poor girl scurries along obediently. A slow smirk appears on the woman's face. I suppose that confirms that she's the mother-in-law. How pleased she seems as she realizes she's still in the power position with her son. At least *that's* not my life.

I turn onto my cul-de-sac and see Roger in his car a couple houses down from mine. It was the spot he always picked me up from, because it's a safe distance from my house. He gets out as soon as he sees me pull up and pleads for me to talk to him. He looks like an absolute mess. He's got a scruff of a beard coming in. His eyes are bloodshot, and he's uncharacteristically in sweats on a Friday evening. He's usually quite pulled together and would be ready for a night out on the town around this time.

He stands right in front of me and grabs both of my hands. He squints his eyes the way he knows I love and says, "Please Tara. Just hear me out. We can't stand what we've done to you."

Despite the fact that it makes my heart flutter hearing him pronounce my name the Indian way–by rolling the 'r'–I still feel so much anger toward him.

"*We?*" I reply. My eyes brim with tears that threaten to spill over and make me look even more pathetic than I already do.

"Do you know how weird it is to even think of you two as a couple? How would you feel if I was fucking one of your "boys?" You were my person, Roger. The one who made all the bad go away. Now you're the one causing it. I just don't think I can deal with this. I need to get the hell out of this city, away from you and everything related to you," I say and turn to walk away.

He grabs a hold of me and pulls me into his arms. I muster all of my strength to keep from sobbing into his chest. It's so hard not to melt into him and fall back into the comfort of his presence.

He pulls back but keeps a hold of my hands. "Didn't you see this coming, though? Things were so off between us. One second you're with me and the next you're mentally a mile away." He's stuttering, trying to spit out the words. I can tell he's scrambling for just the right way to make this all better.

He carries on despite the look of extreme rage on my face, "I never meant for this to happen. It was just a couple of random moments of weakness Tara. Serena opened up to me about all the fucked up shit her uncle did to her when she was little. Did you know about all of that?"

I don't know if what he's saying is true or not, but at this point, I really don't give a shit.

"No. I did not. But how did that lead to you sleeping with her? You know what, fuck it. Screw her brains out until your heart's content." I shake him off me, but before I leave, I ask, "I just want to know one thing. How did it feel to lead me on? You didn't even allow me the decency to stop throwing myself at you every chance I got."

He lowers his gaze and shakes his head. He knows he fucked up.

"I can't bear losing you," he says without looking up at me.

"You already have."

He calls after me even though I'm already walking toward my house. "I'll always be your guy, Tara. Whether you want me to be or not, I'll always be there for you."

I run up to my room and allow the sadness to seep into my soul once again. I crank my heartbreak playlist saved for every fight with Roger. Except this time it feels a whole lot different than the normal bouts of bickering over nonsense. After bawling my ass off while venting in my journal, a sudden surge of anger comes over me. I dig out every letter, note, and photograph having to do with Serena or Roger and rip them to shreds.

Later on that day, Roop and I meet up for a quick bite to eat. She's been pestering me to hang out ever since I put myself on lockdown mode. I think she's just making sure I don't revert to my old self-harming ways.

"I just think it's funny that Serena had him come try to explain. She doesn't even have the balls to come talk to me herself." I start complaining to Roop before even properly saying hello.

Roop nods along as she takes a bite of her burger. "I know what you mean," she replies absentmindedly.

"You're still talking to her, aren't you?"

She takes a deep breath in and says, "Well, yeah. Whatever happened is between you two." She pauses and finally looks up at me. "I don't want to get in the middle of it."

I'm caught completely off guard, even though this is so very characteristic of Roop. Of course she'd take a neutral stance towards this mess.

"So you three are just going to carry on as if it's okay, and I'm just supposed to go along with it? That's fantastic. I literally have no one now." I chuck a twenty down even though I didn't touch my food and storm off.

I get home to the same old shit. It's either thunderous arguing that people could hear from their high rise apartments downtown, or secretive whispers referring to something about me.

I hear my dad say, "She doesn't need to know. Why do you want to hurt her?"

They must've heard me come in because suddenly their voices go super quiet, and I can't make out what they're saying anymore. I'm sick of all the secrecy. That's it. I'm opening *the box* tonight.

"The box" is this top-secret wooden chest my mom has hidden in our basement closet. It's under a pile of blankets reserved for "guests." But ain't nobody going to visit this dysfunctional home.

I remember the day Serena and I discovered it. We were playing a make believe game of detective. I think we were about nine years old. I climbed into the closet under the stairs but soon started freaking out. I felt something that must've been a spider crawl up my leg.

"Serena! Get me out of here. I can't find the light switch!" I screamed with absolute horror.

She ripped the closet door open and pulled me out. She was in hysterics, while I was frantically jumping around and swatting my legs.

"Hey, what's that?" She asked once she was over her laughing fit.

She was pointing to a giant pile of blankets that seemed to be all too strategically placed in the corner of the closet. I poked my head into the closet and crinkled my nose at the smell. It was a nasty mixture of moth balls and boxes of old incense sticks from India.

"Not sure. Some of my mom's old stuff is probably around there," I said, not really all that interested in checking it out.

"Well, isn't that what this game is all about? Maybe we can discover why your mom is such a *bitch*."

This is what drew me to Serena in the first place. She seemed so cool and ahead of her years. She used words I wouldn't dare to say. She was always so sure of herself. Ever since we were teenagers, every guy wanted to be with her and every girl wanted to be her–Roop and I included.

"All right, Sherlock. Let's check it out." I knew she wasn't going to let up.

As we were pulling the chest out, my mom came storming down, wondering what we were doing in the dark. She saw what we were about to do and became absolutely livid.

"How dare you to go into my personal things! You can't go rummaging through stuff that's not yours." She yanked the chest away from us furiously. "Get out! Both of you get out right now. Serena, I'm calling your mother to tell her what a bad influence you are."

That day she scared the living daylights out of the both of us. In Indian culture, a threat to phone home is as good as saying we were being shipped to the motherland. We ran upstairs and waited out the screaming match, which was occurring between my parents.

My father tried rationalizing with my mother. "They're just children, Jindi. Why do you have to overreact to *every* little thing? Of course she doesn't know the truth. How long are you going to blame her for everything? It was of no fault of hers! She's just a child in all of this."

My mom has always been horrible to me, but that was the first time she ever yelled at me that badly. I didn't understand why she hated me. Back then, I desperately wished that I could've been better so she'd be happier. These were the thoughts that consumed my childhood. I obsessed over how to make my own mother love me. I eventually settled on just accepting it was all a crock of shit. The older I grew, the more I convinced myself that I didn't need love from a woman like that.

The first time I spoke to anyone about it was the night Roger and I first snuck out together. We sat atop the edge of a little cliff overlooking the city. We used to call it "the spot." It was our little place that barely anyone knew about. I remember opening up to him about my mom while resting my head on his shoulder as he traced circles on my hand.

"She barely likes herself so obviously she couldn't love me either. She probably sees me as a summary of each of her negative qualities. I'm a huge reminder of all of the bad things in her life. That has to be it. What else could it be?"

I turned to him; he stared off into the distance with a furrow in his brow, I could tell he was listening intently.

"Maybe she's just tough on you to make you a stronger person."

I sighed and snuggled in even closer to him, "Yeah, maybe. Who cares, though? When we grow up, we're both going to move somewhere amazing and leave all this shit behind." I beamed at him and waited for him to confirm that he wanted the same thing.

Even at that age, I wanted nothing more than to just be with Roger forever. As I eagerly awaited his reply, he simply smiled and squeezed my hand even tighter. Then he began gathering up our chips and pop so we could head back.

I stood to brush the dirt off the back of my jeans, and Roger grabbed me by the waist and told me to look up. "Look, Tara, It's a *taara*."

A shooting star, my namesake, streaked across the darkened sky. I stood there and wished for a better life, one in which I was actually loved and wanted. I wanted to belong, like the stars belonged to the people they shone down upon.

Tonight is the night I solve the biggest mystery of my life. I'm going to find the answers to all the questions making up this giant void inside me. It's time to figure out why my bitch of a mother hates me so. Typically I'd consult my besties about this, but since they've now entered the *frenemy* zone, I think I'll ride this one out solo.

"I don't need anyone or anything," I say aloud to myself.

I wait for my parents to fall asleep and then I creep into the basement, shining the light from my phone so I can see. I don't dare switch on the light or make too much noise. I can't risk being busted once again.

I cautiously crack the closet door open. No matter how many years have passed, I think I'd still react the same way encountering a spider.

I crawl to the back corner of the closet and pull off all of the old dusty blankets. I bring my shirt up over my nose. They smell musty, like they've been left untouched ever since the last time I was down here. When I move them aside, I see that the chest is sitting right there, just as it was nearly a decade ago.

"You'd think she would've at least thought to re-locate it," I mutter as I reach down to drag it into the hall.

It's got a lock on it, which takes about five seconds to pick with a bobby pin. Good thing Serena taught me the perfect flick of the wrist for it.

My hands feel clammy, and my heart races as I'm about to finally open the damn thing. Just as I'm about to spring the lid open, I hear a massive thud from upstairs. Seconds later, I hear a bloodcurdling scream that sounds like it's coming from my mother. I throw the chest back into the corner of the closet and run up the stairs as fast as I can.

What I see next is something I know will be engrained in my mind forever. My father lies on the floor at the foot of the stairs, blood pooling around him.

I stand in the hallway completely frozen and just stare in shock at my mother screaming for me to help.

"Tara! Come quick. Hurry. *Hai rabba ah kee hogaya?*" *Oh god, what has happened?* My mom screeches at me to help in a voice I don't recognize.

Finally, my frozen body unlocks to allow enough movement to get to them. My legs feel like they weigh a thousand pounds and everything's happening in slow motion.

I nearly slip on his blood; there's so much seeping out from the back of his head. My mom sobs into his chest, banging her head with her hands and yelling in Punjabi. I kneel beside him, unsure what to do. All I can do is notice every detail with horror. It's all etching itself into the depths of my subconscious.

He shakes violently; white foam oozes from of his mouth and then his body abruptly stills. The blood seems like it's reached every corner of the room.

"He fell down the stairs, Tara. Call 911. Don't just sit there!"

I grab my phone and call for an ambulance. A high pitched sound rings in my head. I don't even know how I'm explaining what's before me. As we wait for them to arrive, each moment stretches into an eternity. I feel freezing cold and burning hot at the same time.

They're here within minutes, but it's too late. Just like that, my whole world has been blown apart from the inside out. My father is dead.

CHAPTER SIX

I've been trying to keep myself as busy as possible with funeral preparations and gathering pictures for the memorial slide show. I have alternate bouts of crushing grief and complete numbness. At times it feels like I'm operating on autopilot. We have a steady flow of visitors coming and going all day long. There's people I've never seen before sobbing like one of their own has left them. Then there's our neighbours who are more curious than anything. Even my mother's empathetic co-workers come to pay their condolences.

I have a digital frame playing on a loop with all the pictures I had with my father in them. There aren't many. We don't have a whole lot of happy family memories. The sight of his lifeless body lying in our foyer has been burned into my brain like a scene out of a horror movie.

My mother is convinced what happened couldn't have been an accident. Sure he was a drunk, but never a clumsy one. He must have taken matters into his own hands to permanently quiet his emotional turmoil. I suspect he must have overdosed and then flung himself down the stairs. Nothing else explains the foam.

Roop has been glued to my side ever since it happened. I think she'd even follow me into the bathroom if I allowed it. I think she too knows my father took his own life, and she's worried I might follow suit.

Someone taps me on the shoulder, and I turn around to face Serena. I burst into tears as we stand there sobbing into one another.

"I wasn't sure if you wanted to see me," she says, her shaky voice riddled with guilt.

"I just can't believe this is happening."

I don't have any room in my heart for anger or sadness about anything other than what has happened to my dad. The details of last week seem so trivial compared to what I'm facing today.

"I'm here for you. Whatever you need to do just tell me and I'll get it done," Serena says, handing me a tissue.

"Thanks, Serena. But I feel like I should handle all of this on my own." I look over to my mom, who's now in a complete stoic trance. She's barely responding to people's sympathies or half-hearted hugs. Her eyes are even more hollow looking than usual. She's so still I barely see her blink. The theatrics surrounding her don't cause her to waver one bit.

"I think she feels even more guilt than I do," I say to Roop and Serena.

"I can't even imagine what she must be going through. Despite all the ups and downs, they were still husband and wife," Roop says as she picks up empty teacups. She's been keeping herself busy serving chai ever since the guests began to pour through the front door.

Roger tentatively walks in and heads straight toward us. I feel a knot fall deep into the bottomless pit developing in my stomach. The irony of him bringing me white roses nearly makes me laugh. I always told him they were my favourite kind of flower, even though they're considered inauspicious. Every now and then he would slip single white roses into my bag as I was leaving his place. I suppose that stopped a while ago, though.

He's been by a few times since it happened. He got here immediately after I called.

"Thanks, Roger." I take the roses and set them atop the growing pile of flowers that I know will wilt and wither as they remain neglected.

"How are you holding up?"

I pause and just stare at the three of them for a moment. This is the first time we've all been in a room together since I found out about Roger and Serena.

I swallow hard and try not to look them directly in the eye; I know I'll break down crying again if I do. "Everything just feels like a surreal nightmare right now. I'm kind of just going through the motions. Just gotta keep moving. Don't want to slow down, or it'll all sink in." I pause and then whisper, "I'm afraid I won't be able to handle it."

An elderly Indian woman catches our attention when she begins to sob unnecessarily loudly. She's on about the *dhokha* my father's family betrayed him with. She says it's understandable how he couldn't possibly bear living with himself any longer. I clench my jaw and muster all my strength to keep myself from going over there and giving her a piece of my mind. How dare she turn this into some sort of entertaining tidbit of gossip for everyone to take away with them.

Then there's talk of who will take his ashes to India. My mother speaks for the first time since the accident; without looking up, she says "Tara."

It's the night before the funeral and Roger sneaks into my room. He climbed the vine fence, which is surprisingly sturdy for having been rotten from years of gutter water flooding onto it. He hoists himself in through my window and sits by me on my bed. I just got out of the shower, and I pull my robe tightly around me. Roger tugs on a lock of my wet hair; his eyes linger, and I feel inappropriately vulnerable to be sitting near him like this. It's silly because he's seen me a lot more exposed before. He attempts to break the awkward silence between us, speaking in a hushed voice so my mother doesn't hear us.

"Tara, I know I fucked up. But please just hear me out, you're leaving in a couple days, and I just can't bear the thought of being so far away from you when things are so fucked up between us," he pleads. A floorboard creaks, and he pauses.

"It's probably just the rain hitting the roof; Mom's been asleep for a couple hours now, don't worry." I avoid responding to his outpouring of feelings, despite the fact it made me feel an uprising of butterflies. I suddenly feel hopeful of the possibility that we might still be able to smooth things over.

"I want to salvage what's left of us and give this a real shot. Serena and I were just a fling, just a one time thing Tara. You know that." He reaches out and grabs my hand, but I pull it away.

"I don't want to think about any of that. You can't just come at me with all of this just because you feel sorry for me because of dad," I say. But secretly I want him to pull me into his arms and stay the night.

He looks down at his phone, and I see that his mom's calling him. "I told them I was going to put the garbage out. I better get back."

He stops and stares at me long and hard before reaching out and resting his hand on the side of my face. I close my eyes and momentarily allow myself to melt into him. He's still my sole source of comfort, and I need some sense of love and support after everything I've just been through.

"Be strong tomorrow. I'll be right there with you the entire time."

He gives me a kiss on the top of my head before he leaves back out the window. I stand there watching him until I can't see him anymore. It's taken my dad passing away and a secret affair with my best friend to make him see what he had with me. I wish I could erase the last two weeks of my life and go back to being a dumb girl in love with a guy too self-absorbed to appreciate it.

The funeral home is packed. I even see our crazy neighbour who was shouting at my father only a short while ago. It's like they've created a mannequin version of my father and placed him in a coffin for us to say our goodbyes. Roop, Serena, and Roger stay close by as I deliver the eulogy honouring the brighter parts of my father's life. I want people to know he was more than just another drunk Indian man lost in his own mistakes. I manage to keep my composure, for the most part, until I see how so very torn apart my mother is. She can't bring herself to press the switch on the incinerator, so I walk over to do it. It makes me feel like I'm on the other side of that glass myself.

My mother collapses into me, sobbing and squeezing me with all of her might. Just as soon as the procession is over, she switches back into her regular unfeeling and detached self.

On the way home, she doesn't so much as flinch to tell me that she was serious about me taking the ashes to India all alone. I fight with her about it, and even Roger tries to reason with her about how it doesn't even seem safe for me to travel there alone, but she is adamant that it must be me. I try to question her about why she can't come with me, but she doesn't budge. She has her mind made up, so that means I am indeed leaving.

Once we're home, she reverts to ignoring me as she busies herself with loading the dishwasher and dusting each item on our mantelpiece about a hundred times. It's like she's in a giant rush to be rid of the both of us. She even had all of my things packed for me.

Roger came back to the house with us, so he offers to drive me to the airport. Under normal circumstances, my mom would've never allowed him to hang around so much. But in times of tragedy I suppose the "no boys" rule doesn't really apply.

Roger keeps glancing over at me, checking in to see if I'm okay. I'm sure he finds this just as bizarre as I do, and he's worried for my well-being. At least s*omeone* is.

"You know, I'm pretty sure it's not even safe for me to go to Kiratpur straight from the airport all by myself."

We're not meant to take any detours along the way to this final resting place for Sikh souls.

"Aunty, if you just wait a week, I'll be done my exams and I can take her," Roger offers hesitantly. We both know my mother would much rather ship me in a UPS box than have him take me.

"Your father's relatives will meet you there." My mom completely ignores Roger and responds to me robotically.

"Say what now? I thought we had sworn off any communication with them years ago?" I suddenly feel suspicious about why she's actually sending me to India.

"Well, this is a special circumstance, and as you said, I can't risk the chance of anything untoward happening to you–a girl of marriageable age."

I clutch my carry-on bag, which contains the airplane safe sealed container of my father's remains.

It seems like it weighs a ton, but it's not as heavy as the weight of this responsibility. I take a deep breath in and try to inhale strength to ease my nerves.

The religious master of ceremonies at the funeral made things quite clear. He offered many bits of explanation of this passage from life to death, which did set my heart at ease a little.

As Roger speeds up to take the exit for the departures area of the airport, I bitterly say, "You hate me. I always suspected it, but now I know it to be true. You're sending me away because you can't stand having me around."

My mom's face twitches slightly, and she swallows hard. It seems like she's holding back the urge to cry, but I know she won't break.

We pull up to the airport drop-off zone, and Roger reaches over and pats my hand. My mom cringes at this offering of comfort. With zero compassion or care, she says,

"We're here. Let's just part ways now. There's no need for a long drawn out goodbye."

Roger turns the engine off and stares down at his phone. I'm sure he feels awkward to be caught in the middle of such an intimate moment between my mother and me.

"You're not even going to bother walking me in? Wow. Maybe I shouldn't even bother coming back,"

I say to her as I get out of the car. I slam the door as hard as I can behind me.

Roger hops out and grabs my suitcases. I see my mom shake her head as he asks her something, most likely if she's sure she doesn't want to come in to see me off.

The lump in my throat becomes a pit in my stomach. I grab my purse and begin marching toward the airport entrance.

"Hold up! I'm coming with you, Tara," Roger calls after me. He quickly grabs a trolley for the luggage that I accidentally left behind.

I turn around to look at my mom one last time. A single tear rolls down my cheek. I can sense a strange finality to this moment between us. Now I'm certain that my mother doesn't care for my existence whatsoever.

As Roger and I wait in line to get checked in, I look directly at him for the first time in a while. I can see the uncertainty and sadness in his eyes. Even though he makes a terrible boyfriend, I do have to admit he's been a wonderful friend throughout all of this.

Once we reach the departure gate, things begin to feel extremely tense and hurried between us. Our usual chemistry has been replaced with an uptight absence of comforting words.

"Tara. I just need you to know...Just know that I love you." He struggles to get the words out. He looks into my eyes with so much pain that I break down crying.

"How did things become this way, Roger?"

He grabs a hold of me and hugs me as tight as ever.

"We'll make it through this. You're my girl. You'll always be my girl. I was just too dumb to see it."

I look up at him through bleary eyes and try to freeze this moment. How so very long I've yearned for him to want me back the way I've always wanted him.

I try to let go and move from his embrace, but he just carries on holding me, running his fingers through my hair. Then he grabs my face in both his hands, leans his forehead against mine and says, "I promise you, I'll fix it all. We'll be together in a *real* way. I'll make it real for you, I promise."

I can't help but smile as I wipe the snot away from my nose with the sleeve of my hoodie. I've been wanting hear that he wants me to be his 'forever' since the moment I met him. It only took a whole lot of crap to get him to say it.

I pause just before heading into security. He stands there frozen, watching me leave. I try to memorize the way he looks watching me walk away. Even though it's not forever, I never thought there would be a time where I would leave him standing somewhere alone and not go running back to be with him one last time.

The never-ending flight feels like absolute torture. The random bouts of turbulence make my stomach turn every which way. Or perhaps I'm queasy from thinking about all the uncertainties waiting for me at my destination. Not to mention everything I'll have to deal with upon my return.

I wish so badly that my Aunty Pyaro could've been alive to receive me in India. I haven't even stayed over at a relative's house before, let alone flown across the world to go live with them for a week. I have no idea what I'm headed towards.

A solid three movies, four nasty in-flight meals, one stop over, and what seems like ten thousand nervous thoughts later I find myself standing in Gandhi International Airport. I'm here. I'm in the place I will put my father and my unanswered childhood questions to rest.

The infamous smog of Delhi hits me hard as soon as I step out of the crowded airport. I've attracted the stares of many, just because I'm a foreign girl travelling alone. Even the airport security who seem they're on the verge of nodding off into the folds of their turban look at me with disdain.

I stop to search my bag for cough drops, or a scarf to cover my mouth and nose. Even in the wee early hours of the morning, the mixture of heat and air pollution instantly constricts my airways. I nervously pace back and forth as I stand by the long row of sleeping rickshaw drivers. It's where my mother instructed me "my family" would be waiting.

I'm approached by what seems like hundreds of eager people looking to help me out in anyway possible in return for a buck, or rupee, or two. Endless sex trade abduction scenarios flash through my mind as these yellow teethed, greasy haired fellows approach me one after another.

I clutch my bag and try to switch my phone on. Oh shit, perhaps there isn't a driver coming. It's entirely possible that mother has dumped me here to fend for myself. I desperately wish Roger was here with me.

Just in that moment of sheer panic, I spot a man holding a sign that says TARA KAUR with a star under it. I head on over toward him and ask if he's related to the Sidhus.

He replies, "Rajin send me. You go his hotel."

I have no idea who the heck Rajin is and why I'm going to his flippin' hotel, but I guess I just have to jump in with both feet to begin this journey. I breathe in and out as deeply as the thick air allows.

"Please be nice to me India, I have a lot banking on you right now," I say aloud to myself as I follow the man into his broken down three-wheel rickshaw.

CHAPTER SEVEN

The advanced modernity of Delhi surprises me. I was picturing rows upon rows of straw huts with herds of cattle travelling between them. I stare out the clear plastic window of the "vehicle," which feels like it's going to fall apart. My eyelids feel heavy with exhaustion, but I'm completely taken in by the vibrancy of this complex city. Hotels line the first portion of the journey, with intermittent slum-villages in between. Each red light brings hordes of children and other homeless people banging on my door. They plead for something, anything. When I reach into my bag for some change, I'm roughly advised by the driver to simply ignore them.

In broken English, he tries to reason with me. *"Kya fada hai?" What's the point?* "Not feed all. Why feed one? Heartbreak both sides."

Truth be told, I'm too afraid to open the door anyway. It feels like the length of a whole other plane ride before I get to the spot where I'll meet my relatives.

Along the ride, there are no beautiful landmarks or natural sights to see. But that doesn't matter. From what I've seen so far, India is truly magnificent. I suppose that's why it's referred to as "God's country."

The spiritual energy here is unreal. Not to mention the loud, symphonic street noise coming from every angle. As the sun begins to rise so do the inhabitants of this country's unbelievably crowded capital. There's a melodious blend of individuals habitually yelling as their only form of communication and the various horns of many different modes of transportation. There are motorbikes, rickshaws, delivery trucks labeled "TATA," and some regular cars too. What's difficult to bear is the simultaneous pleading of the hungry plaguing nearly every inch of every street.

Even though the style of driving here is rather daunting, I honestly can't remember the last time I felt this exhilarated and *alive*. It's like there's a tangible buzz in the air, and I just love being part of it. For moments at a time I nearly forget the purpose that brought me here. We slow down as we approach another cluster of hotels, which aren't quite as nice as the ones I saw earlier.

Mesmerizing rows of street merchants sell colourful sarees and bangles. They're all competitors, yet they buzz about from stand to stand consulting one another like colleagues. I once overheard a class-mate who had just returned from wedding shopping in India. She was telling her friend about how all the marketplace shop owners have a hushed collective agreement to raise the prices of merchandise when selling to a foreigner. Just watching the banter and flow of movement amongst the merchants makes me feel like even more of an outsider than I already do.

We pull up to a crumbling, shoddy looking build-ing and come to an abrupt stop. The driver pulls open his glove compartment, takes out some green leaves, pops them in his mouth, and begins to chew like a camel.

"Try some *paan*, good for teeth." He offers me some, and I can't help but cringe at the thought of putting something out of his palm into my mouth.

I simply shake my head in response, but I think he sees my disgust and then grunts, "Eight hundred rupees."

Before I can reach into my bag, a neatly put to-gether young man walks up to the rickshaw, hands the driver a couple of crisp rupee bills, and says something in Hindi. The boy then proceeds to grab my bags.

I get out and say, "Oh no, no. I got these."

Another person looking for a handout, I guess.

He pauses, looks me up and down, and says, "I'm your cousin Rajin. I've been instructed to take you where you need to go."

"Oh! I'm so sorry. I was expecting a group of people. Are *Thaya* and *Thayee* waiting inside?"

"Your Aunt and Uncle won't be joining us. The highway has been closed for the day due to protestors against the recent election outcome. Two rooms have been booked. We'll stay here and depart first thing in the morning."

His robotic way of speaking is a little disconcerting. It's not exactly the warm welcome I was expecting. I detect a British accent mixed with an Indian one, which he is trying desperately to mask. I must admit his English is surprisingly good. He must have attended a swanky Indian private school.

He looks like a well-polished fellow. His hair is spiked slightly to the side with practiced perfection. His crisp white dress shirt is the perfect contrast to the royal blue sweater vest he's wearing on top. He has the face of an innocent child with a hint of mischief. Like he's hiding one too many secrets he's learned from eavesdropping.

As he holds the door open for me, I notice that his eyes slant upwards a little, just like mine.

"I hope I'm not disrupting you from your regular routine. I really appreciate you doing all of this for me."

He hoists my suitcases onto his head, and I follow him into the hotel lobby - if that's what you want to call it. The stench of urine in the entryway is enough to make me want to go running back out of the place. Two frightening looking men stand behind the front counter, eying me up. I look around in every corner of the place trying to see if there's anyone waiting to grab me and throw me into the back of a trunk.

There's a ripped up mattress and a starved-looking dog tied next to it along the wall leading into a corridor. I'm assuming just around the corner, is where the ever lovely guestrooms are. The walls and ceilings are stained with numerous suspicious brown spots. There's a bucket catching drips of muddy water falling from the half rotten roof.

I look at my new-found cousin with hesitance and distrust. Before I can open my mouth to say there's no way in heck I'm staying here, he says, "Sorry. This is all that was available in the area. There's some big conference going on. Most of the five star places have no vacancy right now. Father would be livid if he found out we were staying in such a place. But I assure you, it's safe. My friend has stayed here with his cousins from abroad many times."

I don't want to seem like a snob, so I lie. "I guess it's fine. I mean people stay in worse places on Euro trips, right?"

He accepts the room key from one of the creepy guys at the desk. Rajin stands in front of me and throws the guy a couple more crisp bills. The man behind the counter twists his moustache into a point between his dirty thumb and forefinger. Then he mumbles something to the "receptionist" who's nearly salivating as he looks at me.

Rajin snaps his fingers in front of the man and says, "Have you fools never seen a pretty girl before?"

More terrible thoughts of being chained to a metal bed frame in a sex camp run through my mind. I tell my brain to cool it. This kid seems decent enough. He wouldn't put us in harm's way; I'm probably just being my usual paranoid self.

The room's not as bad as I had anticipated. There's running and relatively clear hot water - so there's my first pleasant surprise. My next move is to pull the dresser up against the door, so it can't be forced open. Rajin and I agreed we'll head out after getting some rest.

I hear a bang in the hallway and jump at the thought of one of those big-bellied men coming into my room. I pull the curtain shut and stand completely still with my eyes closed for a moment. I block out all the street noise and try to absorb everything that has happened in the past few days.

I breathe deeply and turn to face myself in the mirror beside the condemned-looking bed and say, "I can do this. I can be alone and be unafraid."

I unroll my neatly packed towels onto the bed trying to cover as much of it as possible. They create a cushy barrier between the probably-bug-infested mattress and myself. I sit on the edge of it, but fatigue gets the best of me. I grab a couple of t-shirts from my bag, stuff them under my head, and fall asleep.

"Hello! You alive in there?" Rajin bangs on the door and I realize I forgot to set an alarm on my phone.

I look at my world clock app and realize I've been knocked out for nearly half of the day.

"Yes, sorry! Coming!" I shout back, feeling rather disoriented from the uncomfortable sleep.

I look toward the nightstand where my father's remains are. It dawns upon me that I wasn't meant to stop along the way to Kiratpur. Shit. I already broke rule number one.

Rajin clears his throat and says something again. I can barely hear him over the rumbling sound of some machinery next door.

I open the door and peer at him. I must look like a crazy mess with my eyes half open. I think I see a faint smile when he repeats himself. "Let's head out soon so we can get there before dark."

I wonder if he hung around the hotel this entire time or wandered off to explore the streets of Delhi.

"Okay. I'll meet you in the lobby in ten," I say to him and shut the door so I can pull on my jeans and a fresh TNA hoodie. Despite the warnings that India's supposed to be scorching hot this time of year it was a bit brisk this morning.

I hear him walk away, and I begin to feel guilty that his family forced him here for me. I'm sure he wasn't too thrilled about having to escort his estranged cousin to put her question mark of a father to rest. I wonder if my father was made out to be as horrible as his was to me.

We've been on the road for a solid hour. Neither of us has said a word to one another yet so I decide to break the silence. "You know Rajin, I think I'm getting used to the chaotic flow of traffic here. These moments of near head on collisions don't faze me anymore. I guess I can trust that these drivers have enough experience to avoid crashing every five minutes."

Rajin simply smiles back and only removes one of his headphones to half-heartedly listen to what

I'm saying. I carry on despite his apparent lack of interest in speaking to me.

"His personal hygiene skills are, however, rather questionable," I whisper, fanning my face with my hand.

I try rolling down the window to get some fresh air, but that only brings in the equally revolting stench of cow dung and smoke. We're not even halfway into our eight-hour journey, and I'm already yearning for this day to be over.

Rajin twists his face into a disapproving expression. "So, your mother never came. That's a shame – but I suppose I'm not surprised. I can't blame her for never wanting to step foot on this land again."

"What do you mean?" I ask him. "What happened the last time she was here?"

He clicks his tongue in a rather feminine way and then finally turns to face me. "You really don't know, do you?"

"Know what? Don't tell me that *even you* know all about my family secrets."

He just laughs and pops his headphone back in, as if to suggest it's not important enough to let me in on what he knows about my past.

I yank his headphones out a little aggressively and say, "Well, that's why I'm here. To find out why my mother is so miserable and what my existence has to do with that." I nudge him playfully then say, "You can tell me. I won't tell anyone you did."

He simply replies, "It's not my place."

"Well, I have a right to know."

"*Well.* Ask someone else then."

I don't press on any further because the annoyance in his voice shows that this conversation is over.

I rest my eyes for a while. My neck feels sore from being hunched over and crushed between my luggage and the car door. You would think for such a wealthy family they would've arranged for some proper transportation for such a long journey.

I nod off for a huge chunk of the journey and spend my few waking moments soaking in all the various forms of life I see on the way. Women with their children strapped to their backs as they use sharp objects (which have no business near a baby) to tear into the concrete road. A group of *hijras* readjust their sarees as they form a circle around a couple of school boys, clapping and dancing to make them nervous. Then there are the rows of sleeping children and dogs, all mixed together like one life has zero precedence over the other.

It's unbelievably sad how much suffering will plague each of these children's lives. Two little boys chase one another, wearing tattered clothes and giant smiles. Rajin waves his hand in front of me.

"Hello? Earth to Tara. We're nearly there. It's just before sunset, we might be able to make it home before dark." My stomach drops and I clutch the bag holding my father's remains even closer to me. The driver pulls up toward the dirt road leading up to the river. I can see people standing at the shore in the distance. This must be the place. This is what I've come here for. I've finally reached where I will set my father's soul free for all of eternity.

Rajin leads the way toward the serene body of water into which I'll pour the ashes. Once we reach the shore, I take out a scarf and cover my head with it. My hands tremble uncontrollably as I take the urn out of the sealed container. Despite the fact I don't think anyone is on the receiving end of my prayers, I close my eyes and repeat the one piece of *gurbani*, that my mother taught me as a little girl.

"I can do it if it's too hard for you." Rajin steps up beside me and places his hand on my shoulder. My throat tightens to the point where breathing becomes painful.

I shake my head and take a few steps forward so that I'm just about by the water. A few feet away, another weeping family has come to see one of their loved ones off too. I plant my feet firmly on the ground. I clutch on to the urn so tightly that all the blood in my body rushes to my head. My brain knows what I have to do, but my body just won't move.

"I must do this on my own," I say aloud, mostly to myself. I'm trying to summon the courage to say this final goodbye to my father.

As I stand frozen before the eerily calm body of water - which holds the tears, ashes, and memories of so many, my mind drifts back to one particular childhood image.

For some reason, all I can picture are my father's hockey trophies. I remember the way I would catch him with his thoughts a lifetime away when he gazed at them.

He was a dreamer. Now it's time to set him free to reach those dreams. I don't know what led him to falling so deep within his own sadness, but I'll find out and set it right. I will do right by him, even if he's not here to see it.

"Goodbye, Dad. I hope you find your peace now."

My insides feel torn apart, and no matter how strong I'm trying to be, I can't help but allow a few tears to slide down my cheek. My body quivers again as I pour the ashes into the river. It's done. He's completely gone now. A sense of peace and calm takes over me.

Rajin guides me back to the car as I sob and wipe the tears from my face. We have a short but silent ride up to my father's village – where Rajin lives.

As we pull into the entrance of our *pind* (our village), I roll down the window to get a better look.

I'm instantly hit with a whiff of the most intense smelling cow-manure I've ever smelt. There's no more diesel and dirty rain to fill my lungs. Endless farmland and all the smells and sights that go along with it surround me.

There's a railway crossing here; my father used to tell stories about it. I can picture my father as a carefree child playing in this very spot. He and his sister used to walk along the tracks on the way to school. When I asked him about the danger of a train hitting them, he just smiled and said jumping off at the last second was all the fun. His older brother (my thaya) used to shout at them for taking that route to school.

From Pyaro's stories, I gathered that my thaya was more of a father figure to my dad and bhua since their parents passed away when they were young. Also, my dad's brother was nearly ten years older than him. I think their fear exceeded their respect for him most of the time.

It's unfortunate that family ties were broken because of a battle over land. How could they share so much animosity over money? As I'm pondering this, we pull up to a massive house. It sticks out like a sore thumb amongst the shack-like homes. There are even a few clay homes, which is the type of place I expected myself to be residing in during my stay here. Boy, was I wrong.

"We're home," Rajin says.

"Wow, beautiful place. Even back home this would be considered a mansion."

"Does our well to do home in a poverty stricken place abide by your Canadian standards?"

Oops. "That's not what I meant. I'm just happy to finally see where my dad grew up."

"Well, he sure didn't grow up here. My dad tore that tiny shack down decades ago. He built this with the fortune he made around the time your father left for Canada. Or so I'm told, anyway."

A small framed middle-aged woman comes out to greet us.

"*Sat Sri Akal* Tara! You're finally here. I'm your Aunt Bhindi; it's so nice to meet you." She has the same British-Indian accent Rajin has. Like they're trying hard to mask the fact that they're born and raised here.

"It's nice to meet you as well." I manage to squeeze out, even though her bear hug is cutting off my air supply. For such a tiny woman, she sure is strong.

Her royal blue chiffon dupatta falls beautifully around her and is pinned in an elegantly graceful way. She's by far the classiest and most well-put together Indian woman I've ever encountered. I wonder if I should have my head covered as well. Perhaps my dad's side is ultra-religious in addition to being mega loaded.

"Follow me. We mustn't be late for tea. There is much to discuss now that you're finally here!"

She pushes me along into the large foyer, and I need a moment to take it all in. I turn around to grab my bags but the house servants have already swept all my belongings away, as well as any traces of the dirt we may have brought in from our travels.

I stand in the entryway with my mouth hanging open. The extravagant wall tapestries make this place seem as if it were the home of the wealthiest family in all of India.

There is floor to ceiling white marble stretching from the front entrance to the far back wall. There's a nearly hidden glass door, which seems to lead to the back garden. A gigantic water fountain marks the middle of the grand entryway. A friendly-looking lab wags his tail at me excitedly, but my aunt tries to shoo him away.

"Sorry about Johnny. We don't get many visitors so when we do he gets very excited."

"Oh, what a cutie! I always wanted a dog, but mother never cared for them. You're a good boy aren't you?" Just as I bend down to pet him, I hear a man shouting in the distance. The closer he gets, I realize that his angry shouts are directed at me.

"Oy! You just put your father to rest. Now you're petting a dirty animal. Has your mother taught you nothing over there?" A tall, angry-looking man stands towering over me, looking down with complete disgust.

He's a rather large and unpleasant looking fellow. His moustache is curled upward at the tips and the only thing protruding farther outward than his nose is his extremely large belly. He has a tightly wound red turban on his head.

"Rajin *ka Papa,* she was just saying hello," my aunt says. She addresses the man, my uncle, as "Rajin's father" and covers half of her face with her dupatta as she speaks. She keeps her gaze downward the entire time he stands before us.

"Sorry Thaya Ji. He's just so cute, I couldn't help it."

Aunt Bhindi gestures toward his shoes. When I don't move, she opens her eyes a little wider at me, and Rajin whispers that I'm meant to bend down and touch my uncle's feet as a greeting. It's meant to be a blessing of some sort, but I've only ever seen this in Hindi movies or my mom's television shows.

It makes me feel queasy. But I do it anyway. I'm only here for about six more days, so I can tough it out and accommodate their silly and borderline sexist customs.

He grunts in response and touches the top of my head. There you go! An elder of my family has blessed me. No more misfortunes will come my way now. *Yeah right.* I can't help but roll my eyes at how this day went from bad to worse when I walked into this seemingly backwards-thinking household.

"Rajin, put her suitcases in the room across from ours," Thaya says, picking his teeth and admiring his reflection in the oversized mirror next to us.

Rajin silently obeys his father's command and heads in through the equally magnificent corridor. The servants follow, hopefully not to unpack my things for me. I follow behind as I feel the short time we've spent together has made me feel a little more comfortable with him than my too-eager aunt and slightly frightening uncle.

The walls are lined with more intricate rug tapestries and oil paintings depicting the Mughal raj over India. There are interwoven images of bloodshed and suffering all over the place.

"Interesting choice of decor," I say to Rajin as we enter the guest room.

"Ah yes. Father has a way of making every corner of this home unpleasant. It's like you're never meant to ever quite feel at ease, with or without him around."

"Yeah, he seems like a pretty intense guy," I say while picking up and examining a silver candelabrum. I carefully place it back down on one of the three wooden dressers in this gigantic and lavishly decorated guestroom.

"You have absolutely no clue what kind of person that man really is," Rajin says with such disgust that I begin to feel even more concerned about my stay here.

I am essentially under a stranger's roof for the next few nights. I wonder how I'll cope. At least I'm going back to my real life soon. For poor Rajin, this is his reality. There's no escape.

"It seems like your dad runs a tight ship around here. But I'm sure I can manage to keep my head down and my mouth shut – for a little while anyway. It seems like that's what's expected of women in this place. Am I right?" I ask, searching for my toiletries bag in my suitcase.

"You'll see soon enough." Rajin says with a grim expression, before leaving the room.

I can't help but feel like his open-ended comment meant a little something more. It almost sounded like a warning.

CHAPTER EIGHT

As I lay in bed awake in the middle of this warm Punjab night, I feel every inch of my body pulsing with mental and physical exhaustion. Since I arrived to the village and parted ways with what was left of my father, the strange chilliness has left the air, and has been replaced with a thick, constricting heat.

Everything that happened over the last few weeks is playing on a loop in my mind. I'm randomly stricken by the image of my mother embracing my dead father, the lakes with so many souls floating amongst it, and Roger's face as I walked away from him.

A few more hours of tossing and turning brings a bit too much light streaming into the room. My head pounds from being up all night, so I draw the thin lilac curtains shut. That's when I notice that the windows have bars on them. I've heard that only people who need to fear for their safety are most defensive of their homes. Perhaps my uncle has more to him than I initially believed.

I can hear my aunt and uncle bickering about something. I spring out of bed to eavesdrop on the heated conversation occurring downstairs. For a moment I feel as though I'm back at home listening to the usual squabbles between my parents.

Their voices get louder, so I can clearly make out what they're saying now.

"You will give it to her today. There's no time to waste. The Gill family won't understand a delay. I've given them my word, and that's final."

"But Jeet, she's only just arrived here. Look at everything she's been through. Let the poor girl have a moment to grieve."

"Since when do I need to say something twice around here? Get it done, Bhindi. *Today!*"

I tiptoe to the door and open it just a crack. I try to hear more of what they're saying, but the conversation seems to be over. It's obvious they were talking about me. What do they want to give to me, though? More importantly, who the heck are the Gills? Perhaps I'm finally about to be let in on some family secrets.

After quickly getting changed and skipping the oatmeal breakfast the servants left just outside my door, I decide to confront my aunt and uncle head on. My uncle doesn't even acknowledge my presence when I walk into the drawing room. He just walks away in a huff. My aunt can't seem to make eye contact with me either, but she offers me some towels and soap for a bath. She seems all jittery and odd.

"Your bath has been drawn for you and is ready whenever you are," she says nervously.

"Wow. Thank you. Talk about the royal treatment. I sure could use some R and R right about now."

"R and R? What's that?" She says with a hushed voice so my uncle doesn't hear her.

"Rest and relaxation."

"I know what it stands for, dear. I just meant that not a lot of that goes on around here," she says with a raised eyebrow. She says something to the servant staff, who hurry off to complete whatever task she commanded. Just as I'm about to leave the room she says, "Tara, could you meet me upstairs when you're done getting ready? Let's go to the shops today." She pauses and then adds, "Also, I have something important I need to discuss with you."

"Sure. Sounds like a plan. I'll be up soon."

I'm too curious about my aunt's nervous tone to enjoy the tantric oils or perfect lukewarm temperature of my rose petal-infused bath. I use my feet to shut off the running water of the claw foot tub and jump out onto the plush rug.

I throw the jeans and tank top I had on before but add a scarf since we're going out, and then rush on up to find my aunt. She's standing outside of her bedroom having a servant hold up a mirror as she powders her perfectly pointed nose.

She looks like the poster woman for an Indian housewife, with her oversized sunglasses and a blanket shawl draped across her shoulders. At first glance, you would never guess she was born and raised in India.

"The driver should have the car ready. Let's get going. I have a few items I need to pick up from the jewellers," she says, placing a deep purple dupatta over her head and tying it around her neck. She looks more like Audrey Hepburn than any Punjabi woman with a *chunni* back home.

As soon as we begin making our way to the *shehr* (the city) I'm hit with the reality of India. The disparity between the rich and the poor is undeniable. There's little middle ground. The walls of this home enclose us into the illusion that there's no poverty or suffering in this place. It feels like you're in a whole other world. In my aunt's case, it seems as though that world is one of the rich housewives of Punjab.

"So what do you do?" I ask her trying to make conversation.

"Well, despite my years of higher education, I do not have a high status career. All of those years of study went down the drain as soon as my marriage was arranged. My days consist of managing the servant staff and my social life. I hold *great* pride in being one of the original founding kitty party organizers in this area." She says that last bit somewhat sarcastically.

"A kitty party? I'm sorry, I'm not familiar with those." Whatever it is, it sounds a bit dodgy to me.

"Oh right! Sorry. I suppose I shouldn't assume you know the goings-on of an Indian housewife. I'm sure westernized women such as your mother have no time for any nonsense like that," she says with a hint of bitterness.

She clears her throat in the most lady-like manner possible and says, "A group of us housewives got together for a gossip session once. We decided to make it a regular thing. So we all bring food and take turns hosting while we discuss our television serials and the real life drama of everyone in the neighbourhood. It's rather fun. Perhaps you will join one someday."

"Oh, I don't think they have those back home. But I do enjoy hanging out with my friends. Sounds about the same as that," I respond politely as I gaze out the window of our fast-moving vehicle.

I'm getting a pretty clear image of what this lady's all about. She seems superficially happy on the out-side, but appears to be completely numb and miser-able on the inside. I can definitely relate to that. But something tells me she's had a lot more heartache and grief in her years than I have.

"So first we will go to Sector 17 in Chandigarh to collect my latest purchases. I needed a new jewel-lery set for my friend's daughter's wedding ceremony coming up. They were just sizing and getting it all shined up for me."

"Yeah sure, no problem. I'd love to get a feel for what a day in the life of my thayee is like," I say. I smile reassuringly, and genuinely mean it. I could use a little mundane distraction from reality in the form of retail therapy. Even if the purchases aren't for me.

We pull up to a massive three-storey complex. The windows have bars going across them in every di-rection, and I can see why. Directly outside of it is a crowd of beggars and hijras. They flock around foreign visitors and look for any bit of pity someone may take on them.

I watch as one well-to-do looking man raises his hand to a little boy who's tugging on the back of the man's trousers. The little boy sticks his tongue out at him and runs away as fast as he can.

Everyone's going about their day, moving in and out of the stores like wealthy Indian robots. It's as if they don't see the people who cannot afford to even dream about stepping foot inside of the plaza.

As we're about to walk through the entrance, the same little boy comes up to me and offers me blessings of having many *munde* (sons) in my lifetime. He's most likely been told to say such things by those teaching him the tricks of the begging trade. I pat his head and offer him whatever change I have in my pocket. He doesn't even reach out to take it from my hand. Instead, he says, "*Budda bill de.*" Meaning, give me a bigger bill. I suppose he thought what I was giving him was a joke.

These individuals move from person to person, repeating the same phrases and hoping for a substantial amount of cash. It's like an occupation and craft of its own. I suppose the problem of poverty in India is more layered than I initially realized.

A transgender woman starts saying things in Urdu that I only catch bits and pieces of. Once we step inside, I ask my aunt what she was saying.

"She was saying you have eyes like the stars, hair like the night sky, and skin as glistening as the moon. She was quite taken with your beauty. As would be so many of the eligible young men here," she says with a wink.

"My gratitude to you, and her. No need for any young men, though." I respond with nervous laughter because I can see where she's going with this.

"You'd make a beautiful bride Tara. Absolutely stunning! Let's just see what bridal sets they have. You can try some on for fun!"

Despite my protests, we spend the next hour trying on breathtaking pieces of jewellery. Sparkling diamonds fused into solid white gold are being laid out in front of me as if I'm truly getting married. I try on each one my aunt picks out, and for a moment I feel like I could actually get used to this. Maybe her life isn't so bad after all.

I look at myself in the mirror with the heaviest piece in the entire showroom tightly clasped around my neck. I look years older than I am, and I just love the feeling of the cold metal against my chest. The earrings weigh a ton, but I would sacrifice my earlobes for their beauty in a heartbeat.

"I wish I could have them all," I say dreamily as I stare at my reflection – along with everyone else in the store.

"Ah yes, me too. But not even all our family riches could justify buying this place out," my aunt says, loud enough for everyone to hear.

From the way the employees are waiting on her hand and foot, I can tell she's a regular in this swanky store. Surrounded by the rows of jewels, under the crystal chandeliers, and sitting perched atop a velvet cushioned chair, she's completely in her element. She's been ordering the staff around without sounding bossy or rude. This is totally her thing, and I can see why. It feels pretty awesome to have people tending to your every need while been showered with beautiful gems.

We spend the rest of the day browsing in different clothing and jewellery stores. Somehow, she manages to drag me to the bridal section in each place we visit. I'm her pretend bride for the majority of the day.

She's decided that fuchsia looks best on my fair skin tone, with gold embroidery to bring out my light-coloured eyes. She also recommended for me to have my hair dyed blonde. In her words, this would make me look like a complete *gori*.

Ah, the tendency for all Indian women to wish for themselves and their daughters to look white. It's pretty sad if you think about it. The lengths they go to in order to appear a different race from their own. My exceptionally light skin tone is what sets me apart from others in my culture. At times I've resented it. I feel it's the first and only thing people notice and classify me by. I'm one of the lucky white ones. Yay me.

Halfway through the day, we break for lunch at a slightly questionable all you can eat buffet. Not to my surprise, my aunt's lunchtime conversation topic of choice is marriage. More specifically, mine. I try to brush it off and continue to enjoy my seriously tasty *aloo chaat* (potato and yogurt appetizer), but her comments are starting to get a little too weird. Maybe it's just her way of keeping occupied. She's probably trying to keep amused with the only topic that brings any excitement to women her age in this country - marriage.

What a joke. That's the last thing on my mind right now. When we get home, I'll have to break it to her that I'm not even with anyone, let alone ready to get married. Imagining Roger dressed as a Punjabi groom in a *sherwani* and turban makes me nearly burst out laughing.

That must be what my aunt and uncle were on about earlier.

They probably want me to get married soon and invite them to the wedding so they can apply for a visa to visit Canada. Too bad, so sad. Not happening. Not a chance.

I could barely keep my eyes open on the ride home. But the blaring headlights coming straight at us, paired with the heavy rainfall made for an interesting journey. I would nod off momentarily only to be jolted awake by the sound of a horn or vehicle buzzing all too close by. Two servants pull the gates open for us. Once we're parked, I peel myself out of the seat and head inside, feeling exhausted.

"Tara, could you meet me in the drawing room? I have something I need to give to you."

"Aunty, could this wait until morning? I really don't think I can keep my eyes open any longer. The jet lag has finally caught up to me," I say, yawning and rubbing my eyes like a two year old – but that's honestly just how tired I feel right now.

"All right dear, first thing tomorrow then. Goodnight." She gives me a hug and begins to walk away.

"Oh, I almost forgot. I got these for you when you weren't looking. I just couldn't resist."

She hands me a glass case with the biggest diamond earrings I've ever seen inside. Each one has got to be at least three carats in size.

"Oh my goodness, these are beautiful! You seriously shouldn't have. This is too much Thayee Ji," I say, but I can't peel my eyes off of them.

"They remind me of what you are. A beautiful sparkling diamond. Just like a star. And exactly like your name…Tara, the shining star, how perfect." She beams at me as she unscrews my tiny studs and pops the new ones into my ears.

"Wow, I appreciate this so much. Thank you."

"No problem, sweetheart. You deserve it after everything you've been through."

I stare at my reflection with my new bling for ages once I get into my room. I can't believe I own something so beautiful. Maybe I was quick to judge my aunt and uncle after all. It's so generous and kind of her to get me such an extravagant gift on our first day out. I'm sure whatever she has to tell me isn't that bad. They're probably the type of people who just take a little time to warm up to.

I sleep for a few hours until my biological clock tells me it's time for lunch. Really, it's about 1:00 AM, but I decide it's time to go explore this palace of a home. It's too beautiful to not want to wander around and see what else is in this place.

After a few minutes of tiptoeing around various rooms and corridors, I find a winding staircase which leads to the roof. Nearly every house in India has a roof-top balcony. This particular house towers over the rest. I can see the entire village from here. I shiver when I peer over the edge, despite the fact it's a sticky hot night. I try to swat away the mosquitoes which have swarmed around me. I close my eyes and take a deep breath in after finding a seat. I'm nearly used to the smell of farmland, so it doesn't bother me as much as when I first arrived.

As I look up at the stars, I realize how so very different my life has become since the last time I gazed up at the night sky. I remember what it felt like being atop a mountain with my best friends on a carefree road trip. I'm in a completely different universe now. How crazy is it that life can change so much in just a single instant?

The twinkle of the stars is so much brighter here without any city lights interfering with their shine. The quiet of the night is such a contrast to the vibrant buzz that fills the air during the day. You can actually hear your own thoughts here. Compared to the life I've put on hold back home, life here seems relatively stress free. There's no drama or complications. No angry mothers, cheating boyfriends, or lying best friends. Just a simple and peaceful existence.

I'm completely lost and absorbed in my thoughts when I hear the faint call of someone coming from behind me.

"Tara? Is that you?" A shaky, eerily familiar voice calls out to me. I turn around and nearly collapse from the shock of seeing the person standing before me.

"This isn't possible. How is this possible?" I choke out between sobs as I run towards her.

"Sweetheart, it's me. It's your Aunty Pyaro. I'm okay, and I'm here. I'm here with you now. Everything's going to be okay," she says and pulls me into a massive hug. I'm instantly thrown back to the early years of my childhood.

CHAPTER NINE

We talk until the sun rises. The first dawn breaks, and we don't even notice. I just can't believe she's really here in front of me. I mourned her for half of my life, and now here she is, alive and well.

"Tara I know no matter how many times I explain to you what happened you won't understand why I had to leave you. But I'm just happy we're together now. That's all that matters."

"Me too. I still have so many questions, but I just want to enjoy these few days we have together. I don't want to waste it being angry with my mother for keeping you from me."

"Don't blame your mother, Tara. There's much you don't know. So much happened when you were younger, and before you were even born. That poor woman has been through a lot."

All Pyaro could tell me was that she had to disappear from my life because those were my mother's wishes. I just don't understand why my parents had to make me believe she was dead and gone. Why did my mother feel the need to cause me so much pain and suffering?

I'll get my answers now. Pyaro Bhua will help me solve this lifelong mystery of what makes my mother the way she is.

"We better get back to bed before your thaya finds out we were up here all night. I'm sure you've found out how he is by now," she says, standing up and offering me a hand.

"Oh yes. It seems he still thinks this is the 19th century, and all women are subordinate to men," I say as I dust off the back of my pajama pants. "He needs to wake up and get off of his high horse. Aunt Bhindi seems nice, though. We had a great time yesterday. I wish you could join us today. She has some big meeting planned in which they both have something to discuss with me." I link arms with her as we walk back inside.

"Yes. I know all about that. Oh my dear girl, don't worry. I'm here for you now. I'll help in any way I can, but you're going to have to be strong. Okay? Just how I taught you to be when you were little." My stomach twists into those all-too-familiar knots in response to her cryptic warning and worried expression.

We hug goodbye, and I head back to my room. Even though it's nearly morning, I fall into the deepest sleep ever for a couple of hours. It's the best sleep I've had since I got here. By the time I wake, the seemingly invisible maid staff have laid out an outfit for me.

It's a traditional Punjabi *salwaar kameez*. I've worn many East Indian clothes before, but never anything quite as beautiful as this. The blush pink fabric is completely covered with the most exquisitely detailed antique embroidery I've ever seen. There's a beautiful and equally heavily embroidered net dupatta laid out next to it.

I hold the outfit against myself and look in the mirror. It's absolutely gorgeous. I wonder what the need for me to be so dressed up on a Friday afternoon is for, though. Perhaps we're having guests over.

Next to the clothes, there's an equally beautiful pair of thick antique gold bangles with emerald stones lining the outer rim. These must cost a fortune—they couldn't possibly be for me as well.

I see a note, which reads: *Please wear this and meet us downstairs at 1:00 PM. Love, Your Aunty Bhindi.*

Oh, wow. It really is all for me. I put on the impeccably ironed suit, and it's a perfect fit. How on earth did they guess my measurements so accurately? I love the way it's tight around my waist and gradually swoops out at my hips. It makes my frame look even more petite. The bangles slide on easily; they're super heavy but stunningly gorgeous. *Today must be my lucky day,* I think to myself.

I play some music off my phone while I do my hair and makeup. I straighten my hair and leave it all to one side. It's grown quite long–it's just at my waist now. Perhaps I'll chop it all off once I get home.

When I'm ready, I head on downstairs. Based on the uproar of laughter and chatter I hear when I get to the bottom of the steps, it seems I was right; there are some people over.

"Tara, come here for a moment," Pyaro Bhua calls from the hallway just outside the main sitting room.

She looks exceptionally nervous. She takes my thick-bordered dupatta and covers my head with it.

"There are some people here who are very excited to meet you."

Her lips quiver as she says this and she's beginning to look a little sweaty.

"Oh, okay. Do I know them?"

"No, but they've heard a lot about you, and it'll only be a quick meeting. Then we can spend the day together!"

Why's she talking to me like a five year old?

"Okay…sure. Let's go in."

I walk into a room filled mostly with men. There are two women sitting beside my thayee. The three of them chatter excitedly like a group of teenage girls. The older gentlemen are having the standard Indian drink of whiskey in the same crystal glasses my father always used at home.

There's one guy about my age looking straight at me, eyeing me up and down like a piece of meat. And then I realize exactly what this is. It's a marriage proposal. Live in the making. I've walked into my own arranged marriage meeting.

"What the hell is this?" I whisper angrily to her.

"Just go with it dear. I'll explain later."

"There's nothing to explain! Get me out of here now!" I reply, a little too loudly.

I catch the women's attention. One of them stands up to greet me. She looks like an Indian mannequin. She's clearly had one too many cheap Botox injections. She reaches out to give me a half-hearted pat on the back as her lips curl into what I think she intends to be a smile. It makes her look entirely terrifying. Her hair's coloured a deep red, and she's wearing perfectly ironed and pleated dress pants with a beige button up blouse. She's the only woman in the room with her head uncovered. Yep, she's certainly the little perv's mom.

I can't believe I've walked into an actual Indian drama scene, and I'm the star. This has got to be some sort of joke.

Rajin walks into the room, and as he's passing by me, he says, "Told you things were going to get interesting."

"You knew about this?" I say to him. Every ounce of me wants to bolt out of the room at lightning speed. Actually, scrap that, I feel like immediately booking a flight home and never coming back here again.

As I stand there with steam practically blowing out of my ears, I realize that now *everyone* is staring at me. The tension in the air is nearly tangible. Things are starting to become rather awkward.

I feel livid that these so-called family members think they have the right to take my future into their own hands.

Pyaro takes my arm and sits me down. She motions for the staff to start the next round of snacks for our lovely guests. The three women whisper something to one another and then smile at me approvingly.

Oh great. They like what they see. Of course, it doesn't matter that they don't know a single thing about me. They expect me to be a silent and obedient wife to the stone-age looking goof sitting across from me.

My 'suitor' clears his throat and attempts to make conversation, "So Tara, your uncle says you just arrived here a few days ago, what do you think of our country so far?"

His teeth are so disgustingly crooked and yellow it nearly makes me gag. His hair is slicked back with what I can only assume is baby oil. His *mommy* must've massaged it into his scalp last night before tucking him into bed. He's wearing a button up checkered shirt with brown khakis, which are much too short for him. I can see a thick coat of fur on his legs poking through, above his tennis socks. I think he has some sort of tattoo on the inside of his wrist. He's a complete mess of a guy, that's for sure. I can't fathom how they thought this to be a suitable match.

"Yep. Just got here. I'll be going back in a few days, though," I say through tight lips. I can't bring myself to make direct eye contact. All I can do is stare at that greasy head of his.

"Well, you probably haven't seen *everything* this country has to offer. It is *Incredible India* after all. There's a side to it you only get to know by staying a while. What's the rush to get home?" He's trying to give me some serious bedroom eyes, but upon closer examination, I realize he looks like he's completely high off his rocker right now.

"Well." *You fucktwat.* "I'm only here because my father died from the heartache of the horrible marriage he had with my mother. I don't really believe in love, or marriage for that matter. In fact, I've been toying with the concept of becoming a nun," I respond with a deadpan expression.

The women collectively gasp, and Rajin coughs to cover his laugh.

My would-be suitor runs his fingers through his nasty hair before speaking again. "Ah, yes. Of course, you're feisty. You're western born. But even wildest of horses can be tamed."

Did this guy just seriously refer to me as a fucking animal? What does he mean 'tamed?' Now I really feel like I've stepped into a time capsule into the past. I roll my eyes at him. Looking away is the only thing that keeps me from gagging.

"Tara, you will treat our guest with respect. This isn't the way our family handles such situations. Apologize immediately!" My purple-faced uncle snaps at me.

"Apologize for what exactly? You've completely blindsided me with all of this. I'm out of here." I get up and storm out of the room.

I expect at least Pyaro or Rajin to follow me, but no one does. It seems like it's been hours since I began hastily throwing my things into my suitcase while only taking a break to scream into my pillow. I stop pacing back and forth for a moment when I hear the guests getting ready to leave.

There's happy banter and laughter as everyone bids one another farewell. Instantly, a surge of rage begins to boil up from within. I rip the gold bangles from off of my wrists and chuck them against the wall.

Did they think they could buy my obedience? Bribe me into some business transaction of a marriage? What a joke!

I feel my anger coming to a boiling point, and I kick the first thing I see. My handbag goes flying across the room and all the contents scatter across the room. I see a picture of Roop, Roger, and Serena and I. I must've missed this one during my "must eliminate all traces of Roger" phase.

It's a photograph from our high school graduation. From the carefree smiles on our faces, it's clear we thought we were on top of the world at that moment. We look so young and innocent.

I hear a knock on the door, toss the picture aside, and shout angrily, "Who is it?"

"It's Rajin. Can I come in?"

"Yeah, fine. As long as you're not harbouring any more secrets for your dad," I reply sarcastically.

He comes in and takes a look around at the aftermath of my temper tantrum. He sighs, and then begins to gather my things and put them back into my purse.

"Thanks. You don't have to do that, though," I say, softening at his attempt to help.

"Well, it's the least I can do. You have every right to be angry with me for not telling you about all of that. It was pretty ridiculous, and I would be angry too if I was in your position."

"They have another thing coming if they think for a second that I'd just peacefully agree to whatever they arrange. I mean, they barely know me, and they have the audacity to set something like that up?"

"I know it seems crazy, but there's so much you don't know. You walked into this home blindly, and that's not fair. Your mother should've prepared you," he says as he examines the photograph of my friends and I.

"Wait, what? Are you telling me my mom knew about this? No way. She's capable of screwing me over in so many ways, but she wouldn't go this far."

"Tara, there's so much about your mom's life that you don't know about. I think you need to talk to Pyaro Bhua about it."

"You all keep referring to some *big family secret*. But no one's telling me what it is. You're younger than me, and even you know. Out with it. Tell me everything."

"I only know because I listen. You do a lot of talking, but you never stop to take in what's around you. You need to look past the surface and think maybe everything isn't what it seems. Maybe your mother doesn't *hate* you like you think she does. Perhaps she just hates what happened to her."

"What happened to her? What are all these elusive references to the past you all keep making? Nothing is making any sense! I want answers, and I want them now. I'm going to find Pyaro."

As soon as I step outside the door, I see her standing there with an apologetic look on her face. I scowl at her and stand before her with my arms crossed like a little kid.

She takes a step toward me, but I back away. "Tara, I tried to warn you. So did your Aunt Bhindi. We thought they were coming tomorrow, but your uncle called them over today. I'm so sorry you had to walk in on that as if it were a big set-up. Next time we'll give you more time to prepare."

"What do you mean *next time*? There will be no next time. I'm *not* getting married. I'm not even ready for that type of commitment yet. And what makes you think I'd want to settle down here? I have my mom to take care of. She's all alone back home. I need to call her and let her know she was right about all of you."

"Sweetheart, she's the one who gave us the go ahead on this. She just wants what's best for you, we all do."

"So you're trying to say she knew about this too? No. You're lying. You're not how I remember you at all. I can't believe you'd do this to me!" I back away from her, feeling completely betrayed and on the verge of tears.

"Just come for a walk with me. We need to talk. It's time you know the truth. Let's go for a stroll about the field. It's beautiful out there, and you haven't even seen it. We'll have privacy to discuss things. There's something you need to see."

She reaches into her sweater pocket and pulls out an envelope with my name on it. It looks like some sort of letter. I decide to see what this is all about and follow her outside.

Despite the terrible start to my day inside the house, it's a beautiful day outside. The fresh air helps cool my anger a little. There are rows and rows of corn in the field; it seems to be the main crop my uncle harvests. There's a mud hut in which Pyaro tells me our servants live. Their makeshift home is surrounded by a herd of cows and a couple of black goats.

As uneasy as it makes me, I suppose it makes sense that a conniving, manipulative family like this would be okay with people living amongst animals on their property. Two little girls, who must be the servant's daughters, are playing in the dirt without a care in the world, right next to a pile of cow dung. They don't seem fazed by their surroundings in the least, while I'm gagging from the putrid smell.

Once I get back, I'm going to be more grateful for my comfortable life. I guess I've had an entitled and spoiled upbringing. Even considering the emotional trauma plaguing the last few weeks of my life.

Pyaro Bhua must notice my look of dismay. "It always struck me as odd too. Seeing them living amongst the fleas and garbage while we look down at them from our big home. But truth be told, they're actually happier than we are."

"Yeah, funny how that works. Sometimes a simple life is the best one," I respond.

I eye the letter clutched tightly in her hand. "Can I please have that? It says my name on it, so I assume it's for me."

"Yes, that's why I brought you out here. Your aunt and uncle don't know I'm showing you this, so please don't tell anyone."

I sit on a few haystacks a little up the way and open the envelope. Inside, I find a typed letter signed by my father.

Dear Tara,

If you're reading this, it means I've gone through with something I've been battling for a long time now. I had to let go of you and everyone else. I had to set myself free. I want you to know I didn't do this because of you or your mother. I know you wanted to see your mother and I happy but she just holds too much against me, and I don't blame her. There is much you don't know Tara. Your mother has seen a lot of pain and heartache in her time. All of this is my fault. For that, I will never forgive myself. I cannot live like this any longer. That's why I must say goodbye now. I just need to know that you'll be okay when I'm gone. That's why I've contacted your aunt and uncle in India and made arrangements for your future. It's my dying wish that you go through with the match they see fit for you. Despite what I've said about them, they know what's best for you. You must trust that. They are well-established and well-connected people. If you wish for peace to be brought to my soul, I'm going to need you to marry the man they find suitable for you. Please be the strong and brave girl I raised you to be.

Love always, your father.
Jagmohan Singh

My hands shake and my head spins. I'm holding in my hands his final farewell, and his final wishes. And what a final wish it is.

"I don't know what to do with this. How can he ask me to throw my life away here? These people barely know me. How could they possibly know what's best for me?"

I feel this immobilizing pain and pressure as I hold my father's letter in my trembling hands. The reality of losing him is hitting me ten times harder knowing I have this hanging over my head now too.

How can I deny him the one thing he's asking of me when I am the reason he isn't here right now? I could've saved him if I'd just taken the time to discover what was hurting him so deeply. If only I wasn't so consumed in my own meaningless drama. Now here I am with a chance to make all of that up to him. I can set things right by just listening to him for once.

"I need some time to process this," I say, folding up the letter and putting it in my pocket.

CHAPTER TEN

I'm completely absorbed by crushing waves of anxiety as I wander the endless land surrounding the village. My feet begin to ache, but I'd rather go anywhere but back to that wretched home. I read the letter over and over about a thousand times, wishing for the words to somehow rearrange to give me a different message.

I carry on walking among the fields until my heart becomes numb and my tears run dry. I walk until the sun sets and the twilight fades. Suddenly, I take a look around and realize I really shouldn't be alone in the middle of a field in the dark.

I hear a rustle in the bushes, and at first, I think it's an animal of some sort. Then I hear footsteps and heavy breathing directly behind me. I think someone's been following me this entire time. I turn around to confront the intruder, and before me stands the guy I was being set up with.

"It's not safe for a girl to be out so late at night all by herself," he says, taking a clumsy step closer to me.

His dweeby attire has now been replaced with a cut sleeve shirt and tattered sweatpants. He takes a swig from an unlabelled bottle of dark brown liquor then begins digging into his pocket for something. He pulls out his phone, flicks the light on and shines it right into my eyes. Before he tucks it away again, I notice that his bare arms have rows of track marks on them. I knew something was completely off about this guy. I read about the Indian drug epidemic once. Based on his delirious expression and nearly incoherent speech, it seems like he's coming off a bad high right now.

"What're you doing here? I thought you and your family left ages ago," I say nervously. I begin to walk backwards, so I can keep an eye on him. I glance around, hoping there's somebody within earshot, but we're in a very secluded area. There's tall grass all around us, and it's becoming darker and darker by the minute.

The more he closes in on me, the scarier he gets. His eyes are like saucers. He keeps scratching at the corners of his mouth and licking his lips.

I reach behind my back to pull a sugar cane out by its root.

"I stuck around because I wanted to speak with you more. You're very beautiful, you know. I could make you the happiest girl in all of India if you let me." He grabs my wrist and tries to pull me in towards him.

I yank my arm away and try to run, but he grabs me from behind. "I was still talking to you, you dumb bitch. Where do you think you're going? You foreign whores are all the same. You think you're better than us because we're born in India and you're not."

The angrier he gets, the more he slurs his speech. He nearly drops the bottle he's holding.

His grip on my arm becomes increasingly tighter. I need to get out of here quick. I try to think back to my karate lessons but my legs have gone numb, and my stomach is doing flips. I don't know how to get away from this disgusting excuse for a man.

"Look, we can talk tomorrow okay? I never turned you down. How do you know what my answer was going to be? I just need time to think things through…." I plead with him, because from the revolting look on his face I can tell what he's going to try next.

"There's no need to play hard to get with me. I bet you're a real bad girl back home. You probably fuck every guy you meet. Let me show you what a true Jatt Punjabi is like."

He lunges at me, grabbing me by the hair and pushing me down in the dirt. He grips me by the wrists and holds me down. I scream as loudly as I can, but I'm miles away from home; I don't know if anyone will hear me. He muffles my screams with a hand over my mouth, and I bite it with all of my strength.

He slaps me hard and shouts at the top of his lungs. "Who do you think is going to come save you? You have no one. That faggot cousin of yours isn't here. Your uncle wouldn't care what happens to you. He just wants the Canadian visa that we promised him. You're going to be my wife. I can do as I please. Stop fighting it and take what I give to you."

He forces me to touch his crotch and leans down to try to undress me. When I resist, he punches me in the side. Just as he's about to get my shirt over my head, someone grabs his arm and twists it behind his back. He lurches, trying to stand up and shake his arm free.

It's Rajin; he grabs the bottle from nearby and hits him hard against his head. The creep drops to the ground immediately. After the blow, there's blood everywhere.

Rajin holds his hand out to me. "Let's get you out of here."

Rajin swiftly walks me into my room, everything seems a haze. "I can't believe he attacked me. He's the exact type of guy I'd *never* agree to marry," I say, curling up into a ball on my bed. My heart still feels like it's going to beat right out of my chest.

Rajin pulls the covers over me and pats my head. "I should've warned you about Deepa. I know what he's all about. He's been making my life hell ever since I can remember."

"Deepa. That's his name. I wish you hadn't told me. I don't ever want to see or be near him ever again," I say, fighting the urge to burst out crying.

Rajin nods understandingly and hands me a couple of tissues and a glass of water.

"What did he do to you?" I say. The trembling sensation in my limbs begins to settle a little.

"It's a long story. But it all begins with the fact that my father was dying to have a son pretty much as soon as he was married. It was the only way he could ensure his riches stayed within his immediate family.

The only problem was my mother was declared barren within the first year of marriage. So he started searching elsewhere for a son to be produced for him. But that plan didn't exactly work out as anticipated. Many years later I miraculously appeared. But you know what they say, "karma is a bitch." That's what father must've realized anyway - when he caught me in my room with another boy."

I'm taken aback by his candid openness about himself. He becomes a little uneasy at my silence.

"Rajin, I don't judge you or see you any differently okay?" I reassure him. "You can tell me anything. I'm your big sister." I give him a huge hug and I start to feel more sorry for him rather than for myself – being gay in India under the roof of a strict, masochistic father can't be easy.

"Nothing you do or say can make things right Tara. You don't know what my father did to me. Or rather, what he got that creep he's trying to marry you off to, to do for him." His voice breaks off, and he begins to cry silently.

"What did they do Rajin? We'll make it right together, I promise." My heart is breaking to see him so upset.

He looks up at me with bloodshot eyes and says, "He had the love of my life killed - right in front of my eyes. My dad took everything away from me because he thought that would *fix* me. All it did was change the way I viewed him. I vowed to never think myself a part of this family again. As soon as I get the chance, I'm moving out of this place. I need to get away from here and try to start over. I can't ever be free here. Trying to begin anew is the only thing that'll bring peace to my poor Sunny's soul. He's dead all because of me."

I grab him and hug him as tight as I can. The pain of a close loss is one of the most difficult things to bear. To have to actually witness it–I can't imagine what he must be going through. He's just a kid, and he's hated for who he is. I have to help him in any way I can.

"How can I get you to Canada?"

He clears his throat and dries his eyes on a crumpled handkerchief. "Well Tara, that's where you already were meant to come in. Dad has made an arrangement with the Gill family to get us to Canada as permanent residents within a month. Apparently, they're in tight with some high ranking authority in the immigration agency. In return, the Gills wanted their son married to a foreign-born girl. They asked around, and we were the only ones with such a connection. A Canadian born, blue eyed-beauty was their specification–you fit the bill exactly."

"Wow. I can't say I'm surprised." I take a deep breath in trying to process everything I've just learned. "So what you're saying is that I'm just a pawn for the 'greater good'?"

He nods, and I shift my weight uncomfortably, feeling like this entire family has played me all along. But I can't help but want to help Rajin before I return home. I ignored my father's request for help, regardless of how indirect he was, and look what happened. I can't let that happen to one of my own again. Rajin has *no one* on his side. Perhaps I was meant to come here to help him out of his giant mess of a life.

"Look, Rajin, I don't blame you for wanting to go through with this. Trust me, I understand the need to break free. I get what it feels like to be hated by your own kin. I can't promise you that I know exactly how you'll get to Canada. But I do promise you this – I'll get you there somehow."

I can tell he's hesitant to say what he's about to say next, but he grabs my hand and says, "Tara, there's more. I don't think that letter they showed you was really written by your father. My father fabricated that whole guilt tripping 'death wish' request as a way to ensure you agreed to everything. I'm so sorry I didn't tell you all of this sooner."

As I sleep, everything that happened seeps deeply in to my brain. My fear of this disgusting stranger who attacked me turns into rage. As do my feelings toward my conniving snake of an uncle.

I'm starting to think that my uncle is the real reason my father's dead. After all, it was him who tricked my father out of what was rightfully his. He's the one who sent my father into such a deep downward spiral that he never recovered.

I don't know *exactly* what happened between them all of those years ago. But I do know I must bring peace to my father's name and do right by Rajin too. I owe them that much. I won't be stifled by fear any more. I'll fight back strong, and I'll fight smart. They won't win this battle as long as I'm alive.

"Darbaja kholo!" Open up! *"Usee Rajin Sidhu di talaksh karn aaye hun."* We're here to question Rajin Sidhu about an assault. The infamous Punjab Police yell thunderously, banging their batons on the front door.

It's been two days since the incident with the creep. My flight home was meant to be today, but I postponed it. I hear more banging and shouting at the front door. *"Punjab Police! Darbaja kholo nei ta usee thor du gay!"* Open this door or we'll break it down!

My uncle shouts outside Rajin's room to find out what this is all about before he lets them in. He knows that once they're in, anything's fair game. It's a pretty well known fact that there's no rule of "innocent until proven guilty" in this country. An allegation of any kind from a member of high society is as good as a conviction. It doesn't matter if there are two sides to a story. Whoever has the most pull with the government wins. Unfortunately, as I learned last night, that power definitely belongs to the Gills.

They must've sent the police here to get Rajin once they saw the bloody state their drunken, drugged up son came home in. I begin to panic thinking about the possibility that the sick fuck may be dead. We *did* just leave him there. I was just hoping his lack of retaliation meant that he decided I wasn't worth the trouble of pursuing. Rajin's nowhere to be found, so I head in to the foyer to sort all this out.

"We need to speak to Rajin Sidhu. We have a warrant for his arrest."

"He's not here right now. What's this regarding?" My uncle asks the chief, who's poking his baton into different corners of the room. He looks like your typical Indian pig as he wanders about the place as if he owns it, eyeing everyone down suspiciously.

"Nice home. All from farm work? *Shaad tuhadi family di investigation karni parigee.*" *Perhaps I should launch an investigation into this family.* His broken English and pompous attitude matches his large and in charge appearance. He yanks his brown coloured trousers back over his gigantic belly and lets out a belch.

"Is this about something which happened to Deepa Gill?" I step forward and ask.

"Tu kohn ah? Tenu kee pata Deepa nu kee hoya. Ohnu kisay ne marn di koshish keeti si. Sanu lugda oh jera kusara ithe rendha ah ne ah sub kuch keeta. Ohnay jaroor Deepa teh badla lena huna."

He was brutally assaulted by someone on your land. We have reason to believe the young gay boy who lives here is responsible for this malicious act of violence. I'm sure he must've wanted to plot some 'revenge' against him for quite some time now.

"I was with him that evening. We were nowhere near Deepa. He was at our house earlier, but he went home after that. Interesting that you'd look into the assault of a *besharam umlee* (shameless skid) like

Deepa, but ignore the murder of a young boy like Sunny Singh." A collective gasp echoes in the room at my bold statement and perhaps the utterance of Rajin's lover's name.

I carry on despite the angry looks on the officers' faces. I don't know if they're catching everything I'm saying, but I know they can tell my tone isn't one of fear like everyone else in the room. "If he stuck around, someone else who has a problem with him must've found him wandering around here drunk. He seemed rather inebriated when he left," I lie, trying to keep my voice calm and steady.

"Who exactly are you, anyway?" One of the junior pipsqueak officers asks from behind his large, round boss.

"Sorry, I suppose I should've introduced myself first." I hold out my hand to him, he stares at me in return. "I'm Tara Sidhu, visiting from Canada. My uncle was arranging my marriage to Deepa. Why would Rajin attack him if our families are about to unite as one?"

My uncle looks at me with surprise. A satisfied smirk spreads across his weathered face. He seems pleased that I've accepted my fate as a mere pawn in his ploy to emigrate out of India. I'll let him think whatever he wants for now. My main concern is getting Rajin out of this mess. After all, he's only mixed up in all of this because of me.

The better-spoken of the officers tries to appear more intimidating than he is and interjects before his pompous superior can speak, "We'll be back for Rajin if we don't hear from him within twenty-four hours. Also, we'll need to bring *her* in for further questioning." He gestures toward me and purposefully knocks a vase to the ground. The mirrored vase lands on the hard marble floor with a loud crash and breaks into dozens of tiny pieces.

The older officer grins at the subordinate officer's complete disregard for proper police etiquette. I wonder if the younger one started off straight, but soon learned the only way to survive in India's uniform is to abandon your morals.

Once they leave, everyone turns to stare at me. It's clear they want answers; my mind races to piece together one heck of a cover story.

Just then, Rajin walks through the back door. "What's going on? Why's everyone just standing here?" He asks while looking around at our pale and panicked faces.

My uncle begins speaking in a breathless rant before Rajin even fully steps foot into the room, "The *police* are looking for you! Let me guess, you went after Deepa because of your allegations against me. I never did anything to your *little friend*. What happened to him was an act of God. It was completely out of my control." He shrugs and folds his arms across his chest.

Rajin stomps his foot and chucks his keys hard against the wall. "Just stop, okay! Stop lying! The world is your stage, you just pull your puppet strings as you please. So what if the fucking police were here? Pay them off. Do what you do. It's not like you haven't been accused of murder or assault before," Rajin says and turns to escape to his bedroom.

My uncle slams his hand on a nearby table and shouts at him in a deafening voice.

"Get back here now! We're not finished discussing this. I want to know what happened. Why have both of you been so quiet? Did you think attacking him would stop this *rishta* from happening?"

I stand in front of my uncle and face him head on for the first time since I arrived. "Deepa attacked me. He came at me in the field when I was alone. He was trying to force himself on me. If Rajin hadn't got there in time…God knows what could have happened." I glare at him searching for even a miniscule ounce of sympathy within his eyes.

But there isn't any. He doesn't seem fazed in the slightest. This man truly is a shell of a human. How can I be related to such a cruel individual?

He shakes his head at me dismissively. "Deepa comes from a respectable family. As crafty as your mother you are! Simply making up lies to get out of this union. Well, guess what? You will *not* tarnish my reputation like this. You're a daughter of this household Tara, and you'll start acting like it *now.*"

"Excuse me? I'm *not* your daughter. My father's *dead.* Remember? He died from the pain of betrayal that originated with you! I don't know exactly what happened, but now I know he was right. You're an evil snake. All you care for is personal gain. You don't care who you stomp on in the process, as long as you get to the top."

His eyes become glazed over with unrecognizable anger as he raises his hand to me. My aunt Bhindi throws herself in between us and pleads for him to back away.

Just then, the phone rings. It's the Gill family. My uncle solemnly listens to what they have to say, hangs up, and pushes past us, leaving us standing there in agonizing anticipation about what they said.

We each disperse into our separate corners of the home. I spend the rest of the day venting my thoughts into my journal. I flip back over my last few entries. I used to think my biggest problem was my two best friends hooking up. Now I'm dealing with a domineering, nightmare of an uncle while being forced to marry a rapist.

There's a knock on the door, my aunts and Rajin poke their heads in. I get up and swing the door open, gesturing dramatically for them to enter. The three of them sit stoically on my bed and look at me with bleary, bloodshot eyes. They look as though they've just seen a ghost.

Rajin breaks the silence and begins to talk, his voice shaky. "The Gills have given us an ultimatum. They said they have a way to pin every single offence my father's ever committed on me. That means money laundering, kidnapping, extortion, and this assault - which would be the least of our worries at this point. I could be given the death penalty Tara."

My aunts sob into one another's shoulders, using their dupattas to dry their eyes.

"What! They can't do that. That's straight up blackmail! Those are all lies, complete lies. If anyone should pay for those sins, it should be your father, *not* you. You're *nothing* like that man!"

"They said there's only one way that they're willing to drop it all...."

"Well? What is it? What do they want? Money? Just give them whatever they want!" I say, but my insides quiver with anticipation.

"They want you, Tara. They want this wedding to happen straight away - this weekend. That's their demand."

CHAPTER ELEVEN

I stand in front of a bronze-framed mirror in my aunt and uncle's bedroom. It's the crack of dawn, everyone else in the house is just waking up. But I've been up with knots in my stomach all night. I take in every inch of my appearance.

This is a moment I daydreamed of since I was a little girl. A lump catches in my throat, and I swallow hard, trying to push it down and keep composure. None of those imagined scenarios of beautiful red bangles and perfectly applied bridal make-up included a forced marriage and my dire desire to be a runaway bride.

I'm a sparkly disco ball of a *dulhun* (bride); each stone shines bright on my traditional crimson red wedding outfit. The weight of the dupatta on my head is no less heavy than the burden to carry this through.

I spoke briefly last night with my mother. She sounded ecstatic. She said she'll be coming next week to see how I'm settling in with my new family. She's clearly overjoyed for having the nuisance of an unwanted daughter finally removed. Little does she know this marriage is all a sham. I'm only going through with this to ensure Rajin's safety. Once the coast is clear, the both of us will escape to Canada and leave this circus of a life behind.

"Tara, are you ready?" Rajin pokes his head through the door, and from his puffy eyes and pale skin I can tell he didn't get any sleep either.

I can't muster a reply. I just stand completely still, staring at myself, absorbing the surreal reality of this situation.

"You don't have to do this. We could find another way. How are you going to be okay with those people? Even if it is only for a few days…."

"I can handle my own. Don't worry about me, Rajin. You saved my life. Now it's my turn to save yours."

He takes a quick look around and then takes something out from the back of his trousers. He holds a shiny silver pistol out in front of me.

"Take it. Just in case. I can't send you there without knowing you have some way to protect yourself."

I grab the purse Pyaro Bhua gave me last night and shove the gun in there without a second thought. He's right, I won't be able to fend for myself if Deepa tries to force himself on me again.

Then I switch back to autopilot and readjust the heavily embroidered dupatta so it sits just right on top of my hair bun. Although I look like an airbrushed bride out of a magazine, I feel like a prisoner walking toward my doom.

Other people move me in the direction I'm meant to go and help me get through the day. In order to keep from breaking down, I keep my gaze lowered and face covered. The sheer red fabric of my dupatta is meant to create the illusion that I'm a timid bride, but really, I'm just trying my very best to not bolt as fast as I can in the other direction.

My uncle makes several futile attempts to get me to smile for the photographer, he eventually gives up. During the *lavan*, I'm mentally a thousand miles away while my life is being linked to this strange family. It's not just Deepa I have to deal with, it's his entire family too.

Weddings in India are just like everything else here – rushed and chaotic. There are so many faces, food, and so much gaudy décor that once the reception part of this charade begins, I nearly forget this is my wedding. Each time I'm hit with a wave of panic,

I tell myself to suck it up. The last time I ignored someone's misery, they ended up dead. I owe it to the memory of my father to see this through, no matter how bizarre it may be.

When it's all over, and the guests begin to disperse, I notice that Deepa's stuck-up looking mother doesn't look as thrilled as when I first met her. His sister (who I didn't even know existed until this morning) hasn't stopped glaring at me the entire time. Then there's Deepa's father, who's the only person whose presence is even more intimidating than my uncle's.

All in all, I'm in for an interesting few days. I just pray I can use my new marital status to pull some corrupted governmental strings. I must get Rajin to Canada as quickly as possible. Then I'll be on the first flight back to my dysfunctional but *safe* life back home.

As soon I switch from belonging to my family to Deepa's, the shift in everyone's attitude is unbelievable. There's no need for false pretences and forced smiles any longer. Now the in-laws bark orders at me. It's clear that they think I'm going to be their own personal robotically-obedient daughter-in-law.

Deepa has a heavy load of make-up on the left side of his face. It must be a feeble attempt to cover up his bruise from last week's incident. He hasn't spoken to me at all. Perhaps he's just as unhappy with all this as I am. I only hope he remains this quiet and withdrawn until I leave.

I gaze out the window in disbelief that I've really gone through with all of this. It's by far the gutsiest and most outrageous thing I've ever done. I nearly let out a laugh at the thought of my friends' faces when they find out – if they find out. I've got to make it out of here alive first.

"Well, why are you just standing there? Do you think your bags are going to get into your room themselves?" My temporary mother-in-law barks at me.

I didn't even notice we've arrived outside their lavish home; they're all standing outside, waiting for me to follow. It seems like they have double the number of staff as my uncle. Each of them seems to flinch when Deepa's mother speaks.

One of them rushes to help me out of the car, but bitch-face shoots them a death glare and holds up her knobby manicured finger, "You will *not* spoil her. She'll serve this home just as you do. This girl thinks she can seduce my son and then accuse him of untoward behaviour. There's no need to give her an improper impression of what her life's going to be like here." I clench my jaw and quietly oblige. My new sister-in-law leans against the front door with her arms crossed, watching the whole process. She's clearly amused at having someone new in the house to get bossed around.

The room they've given me smells like a mixture of stenches I didn't even think possible. It's a putrid combination of body odour, mildew, and God knows what else. It needs a good clean, and there's barely any space for me to put my things. I stare at the un-made bed and don't allow my mind to go there. I haven't quite figured out how I'm going to get out of *that* yet. I'm going to be in such close proximity with a guy who tried to rape me. My stomach does a flip as I realize I may not be as brave as I thought I was.

The only bright side to all of this is that Deepa is staying in an adjoining room. Thank my lucky stars he had the decency of providing me with my own bedroom. I scan the room and nearly jump out of my own skin when I realize there's a figure sitting on the sofa near the back wall.

"Make yourself at home. This space is yours now. We can change around whatever you want."

I squint my eyes and reach for the light switch.

When I flick the lights on, I see Deepa sitting there, looking completely at ease. It's a vast contrast to the dummy who was moving along side me earlier today, and even further from the aggressive fucker who attacked me last week.

His sympathetic approach must be some sort of mind game.

"I think I'll spend the day tomorrow clearing some space in here. For now, I just need a break – and some solitude, if you don't mind." I try to keep my voice calm and steady. I don't want him to catch on to the fact that I'm afraid of him, or that I'm faking nice either.

"That was an exhausting day. I felt like a dog being told what to do. Sit. Stand. Go here. Go there. It's all just a big production for everyone's amusement. It doesn't matter if the bride and groom are exhausted by the end of it all," he says, kicking his feet up on the foot of the bed and lighting a cigarette.

I cringe at his reference to us as a real couple. He removes his red turban and chucks it on the table before him. Then he begins to unbutton his shirt. I quickly turn around and start fiddling with the zippers on my suitcase. Oh shit. He's already undressing in front of me – I'm completely fucked.

He gives me an all-knowing look and then says, "Don't worry Tara. Nothing like that will happen until you're ready. This room is yours, I'll sleep some-where else. I was coming off a bad trip that night in the field. I'm trying to get clean. But every now and then shit like that happens. I'm taking over as head dealer now, so I can't be rocked off my own stash anymore. Get what I mean?" He flicks on his lighter, lighting up the most clumsily rolled doobie I've ever seen.

He offers me a toke, but all I can do is stare at him. I'm completely flabbergasted by his 180-degree change in behaviour. Not to mention the fact that he's a dealer–the *mentally deranged and addicted to his own stuff* kind of dealer. It's almost like he has a split personality or something. Oh man, this is creepy.

He carries on because he can tell I'm not sold on his peace offering. "Look. I'm sorry for what happened. It was a one-off situation, and I shouldn't have done all that shit. It was wrong of me, and I'm sorry. It'll never happen again."

With that, he leaves through a door leading to his room and closes it behind him. I'm left completely dumbstruck at this surprisingly easy first encounter with my "husband." I glance at my purse holding the gun Rajin gave me. I start to feel like maybe I could tell Deepa the truth after all. I could try to persuade him to get me the contact information for the immigration officers.

I'll have to suss out the real situation for a day or two before I decide. I turn and stare out the window at the endless land. One of the safety pins holding up the weight of my *lengha* snaps, and it nearly falls to the ground. I hope I can get out of this place – and get out alive.

Deepa's mother's shrill commands and high expectations awaken me. She makes a point to say that no one prepared for my arrival because they were hoping I'd be a no-show. I decide to start cleaning up the room, hoping to give the impression I'm here to stay. Plus, I really can't stand this filth any longer.

"Do you have a mobile phone?" Deepa barges into my room with a huge bag of stuff in tow.

"No, not one which works here," I say, instinctively pulling my sweater closer around me. I'm not sure which Deepa's out to play today.

"That's what I thought. Well, I got you one. Oh, and here's the keys to your car as well." He chucks a pair of keys on to the bed in front of me.

"My *car*?" I ask, completely shocked and confused.

"Yes. You don't want to be relying on others for rides, do you?" he asks. There's a hint of a smile at the corner of his mouth—he knows he's caught me off guard.

"No, I guess not," I say, not knowing whether to reach out and grab the keys from him or run and hide in the bathroom. This is all becoming too strange.

Before I can walk away, he places the phone and keys in my hands and closes my fingers over them. Feeling him touch me again sends a shiver down my spine, the exact opposite of the kind I'd get when I was with Roger. The big goofy grin on his face makes me wonder if this guy's actually certifiably insane. The servant announces there's a phone call for Deepa so he leaves to answer it.

Just then his mother walks in and sees me with a pair of keys in one hand and a phone in the other.

"What's all this?"

"Deepa got me a phone...and a car."

"What? He didn't mention anything like that to me. You just come in here and start making demands on your first day? You western born girls think you deserve everything. Well, that's not how our family operates. You have to fit in to *this* family now."

"And how exactly am I meant to do that?"

"You work for what you need, and give more than you take. But most importantly, you exist for the good of the family, not just for yourself."

"I see. Is that how you were when you lived with your in-laws? Didn't see any of them yesterday," I snap back, feeling quite annoyed with how entitled this woman is.

She takes a step in toward me and sticks her finger in my face. "Listen up, girl. You will not disrespect me. If you think that kind of behaviour will be accepted here because of your light skin and eyes, think again. My son listens to my every word. He won't take well to you speaking to me in that tone of voice. And you know how things go when he loses his temper, don't you? Or need he remind you of your place again?"

"So you admit it. You know about the attack. What kind of woman are you?" It doesn't really surprise me, but at the same time, I'm disturbed by how evil this woman is.

"I'm the type of woman who knows when a girl needs to be controlled before she gets out of hand." She looks me up and down with a snarl.

"You're a bitch." The words come rolling out of my mouth before I can stop myself.

She slaps me hard on the face, grabs the phone and keys from my hands, and storms out. I keep myself from bursting into tears by making a silent vow to put this woman in her place before I leave.

I go to the kitchen to find something cold to ease my stinging cheek. Mina, Deepa's sister, sits up on the countertop, swinging her feet and texting away on her phone.

"Yikes. Let me guess…you were reamed out by Reema."

"Yeah, something like that." I hold a glass jug of milk to my face to soothe the pain.

"So what's your deal any way? I know it wasn't love at first sight with you and my brother." She inadvertently accuses me of being a gold-digger, I can't help but feel annoyed by this.

"Well aren't you clever," I say, examining my cheek in the reflection of my face on the stainless steel fridge.

"Doesn't take a genius to figure out this is all nonsense. Why would someone from Canada marry a random they just met a few days ago? Seems a little odd."

She eyes me up and down as she re-applies her deep purple lipstick. She doesn't wait for me to answer, though; she just hops off the counter and saunters out.

Probably off to her college to hoe around in secret. Girls here are no less skanky than the ones back home; they're just better at hiding it. She'd be a pretty girl if she carried herself better and spoke with a little tact. More specifically, if she had a mother who could teach her a thing or two about social etiquette.

I hear someone clear their throat behind me, and I jump at the sound. When I turn around, I see a dark-skinned servant looking nervous as ever.

"Yes?" I ask him with an encouraging smile.

"Hello, ma'am. Ms. Gill has informed me there will be a dinner party tonight. She instructed us to set out what you're meant to wear. It's something from her wardrobe. Nisha will assist you to get ready."

The poor fella spends his days being bitched around by the wicked witch of Punjab – I don't blame him for being a jittery mess. Man, I can't *believe* that cow. She slaps me and then expects me to look all chipper and happy for her lame event – wearing *her* clothing.

"Let her know I'm fully capable of getting ready myself, thank you."

He stares at me blankly as if I've just said something in pig Latin and scurries off.

173

I wonder who'll be attending this dinner party. Couldn't they let me have a day's break after the wedding? I have a feeling it's just going to be one thing after the other with these people.

From the looks of it, this home sits in the middle of a gigantic parcel of land. Winding, interconnected pathways that are lined with big mango trees surround the house. I inhale the dewy air. Regardless of how spectacular the rising sun looks across the horizon, I'm overcome by a wave of homesickness. I want to be in my own house. I'd give anything to be headed to class or curled up with a good book by my fireplace.

Most of all, I miss my friends. I can't imagine how shocked they're going to be when they hear about all of this. They probably won't believe me. I think I'll give them a call tonight. I just need to get my phone back from that stupid cow.

Just then I feel a tap on my shoulder. "Madam, Ms. Gill requests your presence in her dressing room."

"What is it now?" I snap at a young, scared looking girl, who I can only assume is Nisha, but I begrudgingly follow behind her.

When I enter Deepa's parent's master bedroom, Reema doesn't even look up to address me. She continues to blow on her fingernails as her servant moves on to painting her toenails.

"Tara, your family will be attending the formal post-wedding dinner party tonight. There will also be some other guests there, including some of my closest friends. I don't care for silly traditions like a new bride not being allowed to help with housework for a certain time period. So I expect you to be assisting with the preparation."

"Will Mina be helping as well?" I ask her, fully knowing what the response is going to be.

"Mina will be helping in her marital home when she gets married. Look, Tara, the sooner you accept your new life, the easier it will be for you. If you resist what's expected of you, well then there are *different* ways to make you adjust a little quicker."

"Are you threatening me again?"

"Consider it whatever you want. Just know I don't have much patience when it comes to girls like *you*."

There it is again. A reference to the kind of person I am, when she doesn't even know me. It's like she's chalked me up to be this blood sucking wench just because I was born somewhere other than India.

My phone and keys sit on the counter behind her. I move as slyly as I can and grab the phone when she's not looking and head back to my room.

After a couple hours of dusting, organizing, and setting my things out, the place looks pretty decent. Even though I have no intention of staying here more than a week, I've always been the type of person who needs to sort my environment out in order to get my mind straight. It helps distract me, allowing me to feel as if I can control at least a small part of my life.

I think I'll give Rajin a call. He must be so worried about how I'm doing here.

He answers after the first ring.

"Hi Rajin, it's Tara."

"Tara! How are you? Are you okay?"

"Yeah, I'm actually doing alright. I mean Deepa's mom is a total *you know what,* but other than that I've just been staying out of everyone's way."

"Don't worry Tara. I'll get you out of there as soon as possible."

"I'll have the conversation with Deepa tonight after you guys come over. He's been surprisingly nice to me, so maybe he won't mind helping to get you a student visa or something."

"I have my fingers crossed Tara. My stomach's been doing flips thinking about you stuck there. Be careful, okay? Don't let your guard down. That entire family makes my dad look like a saint."

"It's only for a short time. Then I'll be out of here, and this will all be a distant memory."

I hear someone chuckle behind me. A smug looking Mina is posted up in the doorway, grinning ear to ear. I quickly hang up and slide the phone into my back pocket as casually as I can.

"Oh hey Mina, need something?"

She tosses up the plum she's eating, catches it, and then takes a big bite. She stares at me and smirks. "Nope. Just checking in on you. But I see you have everything all figured out."

She walks away whistling before I can even begin to make up some sort of explanation.

"Well, I'm completely fucked now," I say aloud to myself and flop down on the bed.

CHAPTER TWELVE

So far this brutally dull party is just a bunch of fake, useless banter. The women are all dressed in typical Chandigarh style clothes. Each of them have different coloured tunics on with tights underneath. They look like they're desperately trying to shed their Indian roots and shove themselves into the image they have of "the women of the western world."

The queen bee of them all, Reema, sports a bright pink bedazzled top with giant diamond hoop earrings. Her shirt is uncomfortably tight – both for her and for the eyes of all the guests. She might've been able to tighten the loose skin on her face but she clearly needs a round or two of lipo on her body. That's the only way she could keep up with her equally botched plastic friends.

She's been serving up her best performance of kindness all night. No wicked mother-in-law wants to be openly viewed as one. In public, they always attempt to appear like a saintly peach.

She even sits perched up on the arm of the chair I'm on. I resist the urge to gag as she pets the side of my head while telling her 'kitty friends' that she can't wait to bring me to their monthly get-togethers.

Her cunning nature *is* rather amusing. She's a real natural; I could learn a thing or two from her. At the beginning of the night, I nearly fainted when she grabbed a tray from my hand in front of everyone and said, "Oh no, sweetheart. Your *mendhi* (henna) *just* darkened. How could I allow you to get your hands dirty so quick? Have a seat, dear."

I manage to get a minute alone with Rajin to let him know my blunder about Mina finding out the truth.

He pauses and gazes into space as if in deep thought and then says, "Hmm, well I doubt she'll tell them now if she hasn't already. Chances are she'll hold it over you for something. I know girls her type; she doesn't actually care for her brother or anyone else in her family. She'll use this information for personal gain at some point. Just butter her up and hope for the best. Plus, you could always deny it. They have no proof."

"You're right. She didn't rush off to mother dearest, so it must be fine."

"You sure you want to bring it up with Deepa to-night? He's been downing one drink after another with his buddies on the balcony."

"Has he? Oh great. Substance abuse followed by rage seems to be this guy's thing. I don't know what to expect from him when he's out of it."

Rajin takes a look around and lowers his voice, "Keep that gun I gave you close by, and call me if he comes at you in any way, okay?"

At least I have someone who cares about me. I'm glad Rajin and I have become friends. I can tell from the look on his face he's genuinely worried about my well-being. That just makes my quest to free him from this place even more warranted.

"I promise." I feign a reassuring smile.

"Tara, come in here. I have someone I'd like you to meet." This is the first time my "father-in-law" has directly addressed me. I head in to the room he's seated in, and I'm met by two beady-eyed men eagerly waiting to greet me.

"These are the Patel brothers. They went to school with your father," Deepa's father says. He plops a couple more ice cubes into his crystal glass, causing the liquor to nearly overflow onto the faded area rug.

They simply nod their heads hello, and a burly rosy-cheeked woman who's accompanying them stands to introduce herself as one of their wives.

"It's so nice to make your acquaintance *beta* (dear child). Your father was a big star in our school. His early demise is so sad. Please don't hesitate if you need anything. Absolutely anything at all."

"I will. That's very kind of you Ms. Patel."

She carries on her bubbly chatter. When my aunt excuses herself, Ms. Patel suddenly becomes very serious, and she hands me a slip of paper.

"Here's my number, darling. Call me when you can."

There's a sense of urgency in her voice, I nod, smile, and accept the piece of paper. I fiddle with it in my palm and drown out the remainder of the evening's mind-numbingly dull conversation.

Deepa's piss drunk by the end of the night. He keeps hiccupping and telling me how pretty I am. I shove him in the direction of his bedroom and luckily he leaves me alone without much resistance.

I feel for the gun inside my pillowcase, confirming it's still there, and look around for a quiet corner to call home. I settle on crouching in the closet and lay down some pillows to sit on.

As I dial Roger's number, I think of how many times I called him arranging to meet up or to discuss my day with him. Now I'm about to tell him I'm married. Even if it's all bullshit, it's still pretty unbelievable.

He picks up after a few rings, and his familiar scratchy, sleepy voice puts a knot in the pit of my stomach.

"Hey Roger, it's Tara."

He clears his throat, and I can tell he's suddenly sprung wide-awake. He begins to shout into the phone.

"Tara?! I've been worried sick about you. Where the hell have you been?"

"I'm fine, Roger. Things have just been a little crazy. That's why I took a bit to call." I try to sound as collected as possible.

"What do you mean, crazy? You can't just disappear on me like that. I've been harassing the crap out of your mom, but she keeps giving me the run-around. Why aren't you back yet?" He demands to know.

"Well, it's kind of a long story. You got time?"

"I kept thinking that something bad had happened to you. I even contemplated coming to find you myself. Are you still staying with family?"

"Well, yes, I am with family. Just not *my* family."

"What do you mean?"

Here goes nothing.

"Roger, I got married."

He begins to scream so loudly into the phone that I have to hold it a little bit away from my ear.

"Is this some sort of a joke? You *what*? What do you mean you got *married*?"

"It's complicated." I can't help but feel slightly amused with his shocked reaction.

"I knew something was wrong. I just knew it. Your aunt and uncle forced you into something, didn't they? That's it, I'm coming there."

I hear shuffling, and I can just picture him pulling his jeans on from a pile of clothes next to his bed while fumbling around in the dark looking for his keys.

"There's no need for that. It's a fake marriage." I say knowing this is only going to confuse him even more.

I hear some groaning coming from the room, Deepa must be waking up.

"Look, I got to go. My *husband* might hear me."

"Husband...riiiiiight. I don't buy any of this. I know you need me, but you're too damn stubborn to admit it."

Just as he hangs up, a shadow forms over me. "Who are you talking to? Why are you hiding in the closet?"

Deepa staggers toward me and grabs the phone. He presses buttons at random, but it's clear he's too drunk to even read the screen. I try to slide it out of his hands, but he grabs my wrists and pushes me against the wall.

His face is an inch away from mine, and he looks me dead in the eyes and says, "Don't think you can get things shit passed me. I know what you're about. I can be your best friend or your worst enemy. Behave yourself." He forcefully kisses me and tries to shove his tongue way down my throat; I manage to push him off of me and run into the bathroom.

I crouch down with my back against the door, trembling at the disgusting invasion of my body and the close brush with his alter ego.

When I poke my head out to see if the coast is clear, he's passed out face down on the bed. I don't want to risk waking him so I leave him be. I grab my phone from his hand. On the inside of his arm, there are several more marks. They look like fresh injections.

No wonder Deepa's parents were in such a rush to marry him off. His outburst has definitely helped me confirm I can't confide in him after all. I'll have to find my own way out of hellsville and devise a new escape route for Rajin. Perhaps Mina's going to be the ally I need to get out of here.

I leave Deepa lying on the bed, half of his limp body dangling off the edge. I go into the main living room and curl up on the couch there, replaying the strangely satisfying conversation I had with Roger. My mind quickly reverts to Deepa's anger which is coming to a tipping point. I really need to get out of here before something terrible happens.

Halfway through the next day, I remember the strangely intense way Mrs. Patel urged me to contact her. I think now's as good a time as any to find out what she could possibly want to tell me.

I send her a text instead of calling to avoid the chance of being overheard again.

TARA: *hi mrs. patel. it's tara. how are you?*

Her reply pops up on my screen instantly.

MRS. PATEL: *hello dear, i'm fine thanks. when r u free to meet me? there's something i'd like to discuss with you in private.*

TARA: *i can meet next week. right now isn't a good time as i'm still on new bride lockdown mode. you know how it is.*

MRS: PATEL: *oh yes, i remember that time well – revolted by your new role as a DIL and scared to step on anyone's toes. take care and call me if you need anything.*

I stare down at my phone with a furrow in my brow. Why's this lady being so kind to me? What could she possibly wish to speak to me about? I guess only time will tell.

"You discover his little secret yet?" I jump and turn around to face Mina. She's becoming annoyingly good at sneaking up on me.

"Which one? There seem to be many."

"You and I could work together, you know. I think I've got you figured out. Perhaps if you can help me with something...we can work out a deal."

She sounds like she's reading straight off the script of one of the poorly produced Indian drama's she's always glued to. Does this girl even realize how cliché she is?

I run my finger over the sore spot on my wrist where Deepa's hands were last night. Then I pop in another piece of gum, trying for the umpteenth time today to rid myself of the disgusting taste of him.

I stare at her dead on, hoping she doesn't catch on to my vulnerable state. "Why bother offering? You and I both know I don't really have a choice in the matter. You clearly have the upper hand. You have some pretty damning information about me. I know your mom would just eat that discovery right up." I lay everything out straight up.

"Yeah I know, but I don't blame you for wanting out. I wouldn't want to be married to a drug addict, wannabe gangster either."

"So, you know he's an addict?"

"He's been like that since he was 15 years old," she says without a hint of sympathy for her brother.

"Hasn't anyone tried to get him any help?"

"That's where you come in. My parents believe getting married means you're magically cured of anything that's ever been wrong with you," she says with a humourless chuckle.

Deepa walks in, and a smile spreads across his face. "Friends already? That's nice to see."

He looks pleased by the two of us playing nice with one another. It's almost as if he doesn't remember our extremely unpleasant exchange last night.

"Oh yes, I can't wait to braid Tara's hair and have her paint my toenails," Mina responds sarcastically.

Just then the servant walks in to announce the arrival of a guest.

"Who is it?" Deepa asks him.

The servant bows and avoids direct eye contact. In a quiet voice, she answers, "It's Tara's mother. She just arrived from Canada."

I don't know what's been more amusing – watching my mother pretend to be my best friend, or Deepa's mother doing the very same thing. With their shared, secret dislike for me, I expect them to get along wonderfully.

The odd thing is that Reema acted super strange when she saw my mother. I even overheard her whispering on the phone to one of her friends that the *"besharam"* (shameless) woman is here. What sort of dirt could she possibly have on my mom? I wasn't even aware that they knew each other. I'm realizing that there seems to be a lot about my mother that I don't know about.

"She has no shame coming back here. She claimed everything that happened was all against her will. I think she wanted to climb the family ranks to inherit more. Such an actress that woman is. I don't even want her around my husband, Pooja!"

I walk in on yet another one of Reema's gossip sessions. I'm sick of hearing her bash my mom like this, so I confront her.

"What do you have against my mother? The reason you don't like me is obvious—I threaten your relationship with your deranged son. You're worried he might not jump to your every command any longer if another woman replaces you in his life. But my mom just got here. I'd appreciate if you didn't spread rumours about her."

Her eyes sparkle and then shrink into a squint. Her lips curl back, and she throws her head back and cackles like a movie villain.

"Ha! I knew it. They never even had the decency to tell you about true lineage."

"What are you talking about? You're absolutely full of crap. You're a sad, sad woman. You know that? Grow up."

She continues smiling and shaking her head at me as if she's so very full of pity for me. Satisfied with her revelation, she returns to her phone conversation as if she's got a whole new batch of gossip to dive into.

I walk out and pretend that nothing she said fazed me. Truly, though, I have this uneasy feeling inside that whatever she knows about my mother is enough to damage our relationship even more.

When I step out for a breath of fresh air I see my mom sitting on a bench near the front gate, staring off into space.

I wave my hand in front of her face when she doesn't notice me. "Earth to Mom. What are you thinking about? You seem a world away."

"Oh, hi Tara. I didn't see you there. Come sit." She pats the empty space on the crumbling seat beside her.

This home and property could've been something spectacular if only it were better kept.

I sit down on the opposite side of the bench, leaving a giant gap of rotting wood between us.

She slides on over next to me. "Oh come on Tara, I don't bite. No need to be so melodramatic. What are you mad at me for now?"

"Are you kidding me? I thought I was coming here to fulfill the duty of saying goodbye to my father, but you had this all planned out from before, didn't you? The fake letter was probably all your idea too! Do you know what kind of guy you've sealed my fate to? He has a split personality and he's a ticking time bomb. I'm completely fucked without a way out."

She ignores me dropping the F bomb because she can see I'm upset, and she knows I'm warranted to behave this way after everything I've been through.

She takes a deep breath and places her hand on top of mine. Slowly, she begins to explain. "Your dad expressed his hopes for you to be married within a month of his passing to me a few weeks before he left us. I thought this to be the perfect opportunity for you to start over. Your life back home wasn't getting you anywhere. Those friends, that boy—it was all holding you back. I told your aunt what to say, and she wrote it down. Plus, I'm sure Deepa's not that bad. Look at your father. I stayed with him, didn't I?"

I stand up and shout, "You guys worked together to fabricate all of this? You hate them, but not enough to keep them from ruining my life?! And don't you dare try to spin this that way! Dad wasn't a drug addict. Dad wasn't trying to rape you one second and then befriend you the next. He was a good man. *You* are just too selfish to even see that."

"*Selfish?* That's what you think of me? Tara, you have no idea what I've been through."

"Yeah Mom, *you're* the victim in all of this. Of course you are. You know what? I don't know why I even bother at all. I'm out of here."

I get up, and storm inside, slamming the screen door shut behind me. It might keep the insects out, but it sure doesn't keep the monsters inside under control.

A long hot shower is exactly what I needed. Even if I must keep my flip-flops on. I wouldn't dare touch the nasty discoloured bathroom floor. After towelling off and trying to shake off another typical encounter with my mom, I throw on a pair of my nicest jeans. Then I spend an hour curling my hair. I've been sporting a high, slicked back pony-tail or braid since I've got here, and I almost don't recognize myself with my hair down. I wing my eyeliner perfectly and take a look in the mirror. I can nearly hear Roger say, "Damn. You look bang-able."

That's about as romantic as his compliments got.

I head out without informing anyone I'm leaving and walk to the edge of the driveway to wait for Rajin. He asked me to go somewhere with him for the day, but I don't know where. I don't mind the mystery though, I could use an escape from the *fuckery* that is my life.

He shows up at the exact time he said he would, he looks pretty excited. He's wearing a deep purple v-neck, a pair of khaki shorts, and has his hair gelled to the side. I've never seen him so in his element.

"Are you ready to have an amazing day?"

"Um, I think so… I kind of need to know where we're going first!"

"Okay, I'll give you a couple hints. It's an annual event put on for a cause that means a lot to me…especially this year." He glances over at me and hands me a pair of pink-rimmed sunglasses, matching the ones he's wearing. "And we're going to have a blast!"

"That wasn't very informative, but sounds good to me!" I slide on the glasses, roll down the window, and look at myself in the side mirror. Feeling fresh air and not being around people who make me want to vomit feels good. I wish I could've just came here for a normal visit. I'd be home by now with is the addition of a new friend and some strange memories of family I'd probably never see again.

CHAPTER THIRTEEN

I t takes half an hour to reach our destination. There are rows upon rows of booths; people in brightly coloured clothes and face paint hand out flyers from them. Hundreds of people are swarming around, with some of them holding up lit candles to the sky. Leading up to the main hub of the area are several individuals holding up signs and shouting into their megaphones. I try to make out what they're saying, and then I spot a sign which reads: *GAY PRIDE WORLDWIDE – THAT MEANS YOU TOO INDIA!*

"A gay pride parade? Is that what this is?"

"Sort of. The government wouldn't allow us to get away with an actual pre-organized parade. So we just throw this together via text and word of mouth gets the job done. The location changes every year, it's shared an hour prior to ensure the police don't come shut it down. It's more of a memorial to honour those who lost their lives due to violence and prejudice against the Indian LGBT community."

"So you're here for Sunny." I grab his hand and squeeze it because I know this must be hard for him. I can't imagine losing the person I'm closest to. Although, at the moment, I don't really know who that would be.

"Yes, for Sunny...and for myself. I lost myself when I lost him. Everything had escaped me when I saw him take his last breath. My happiness, my hopes and dreams, and my will to live were all gone. My dad didn't realize that killing him killed a part of me too. The miniscule part that cared for him, as his son, is gone. It made me see him for what he really is. Now I just want to be my own person and get the hell out of this place."

"I know what you mean. Don't worry. I'll get you out of here," I say, trying to reassure him despite the fact I'm started to feel a little trapped myself.

I look around, and all I see are tons of people holding pictures of their loved ones. They lost their lives simply for being who they are. People are here in solidarity for those who can't be themselves— especially in a strict, prejudice-filled country like India.

Until now I never knew anyone who was gay. I can't say I've ever had a problem with it, but I do feel guilty for not sticking up for the kids who tried to hide who they were for fear of being targeted.

I've always heard the three letter F word thrown around in social settings. At the school, mall, even on a night out – everyone I know (myself included) use this term without realizing how hurtful it might be to someone who has it as a label hanging over their head.

"I'm glad you brought me here. It feels good to be a part of something that doesn't have to do with my Indian drama of a life."

"Let's get our faces painted and wander around," Rajin says excitedly.

"Okay!"

It's different from any memorial I've ever been to. There's music, dancing, and tons of people handing out t-shirts and stickers with different slogans on them. I find myself bobbing my head and smiling back at the exuberant individuals brave enough to be a part of such a cause.

Rajin stops dead in his tracks, staring directly at this one guy who's wearing a t-shirt with a picture of a handsome young boy on it.

"That's Sunny," he says with a deadpan face and shaky voice. He doesn't tear his eyes away from the man, or his t-shirt.

"Go up to him? Maybe it's a friend of his?"

The guy looks as though he's in his mid-twenties. He has a baseball cap on, and he's wearing perfectly fitted khaki pants. The shirt with Sunny's photo on it is tight around his chiselled arms. His looks don't match his wardrobe at all; he seems like the kind of guy who would normally be in a business suit. He leans against one of the booths, handing out flyers. His composure and picture-perfect face makes him the best-looking Indian guy I've ever seen.

Rajin snaps his fingers in front of my face and says, "Um, hello? I can't just walk up to him. Sunny never told anyone about us. What if he's another ex-boyfriend? We weren't exactly exclusive at the time he was killed."

"If you don't want to go up to him, I will. We can't just stand here staring at the guy all day," I lie–he's got a face I could stare at for forever and a day.

He sees me approaching and smiles. Holy smokes, just when I thought he couldn't get any better looking his facial features arrange in an even more alluring way. When I come face to face with him, he's almost too pretty to stare directly at, I'm completely intimidated and too wracked with nerves to say a single word.

"Was that your boyfriend?" I blurt out before I can stop myself.

From the sympathetic look on his face, I can tell he's noticed the deep flush in my cheeks. If you can see a brown girl blush, you know she's got it bad.

He hands me a flyer with another photo of Sunny on it; when our hands brush against one another, I feel that electric pulse that's only described in romantic movie scenes. The ones depicting the kind of romance that you yearn for in your younger, more hopeful years.

He breaks into another huge smile when I nearly jump back at his touch.

"No. He was my brother. He was killed a few months ago. Did you know him?"

"My cousin did." I turn around to call Rajin over, but he's no longer standing behind me.

"He was right there a second ago. I don't know where he's disappeared to," I say, looking off into the crowd.

He holds out his arm for me to take and says, "Let's go find him. I'd love to speak to a friend of Sunny's."

We walk in silence, and I feel like a giddy schoolgirl in unbearably close proximity to her crush.

"Were you two close?" I ask him, realizing how moronic it is to be crushing on a guy whose mourning his brother – especially under the circumstances that I'm here.

He looks over at me and then says, "I went away for school when my brother was little. My parents and

I had a falling out. I guess I left him high and dry to fend for himself. I was in England when I heard. I barely even knew anything about him or his life… and now he's gone." His voice catches and he loses composure for just a millisecond. Then he clears his throat and nudges me, "How about you? What's your story? Let me guess, you're an American girl visiting family."

I manage to stay focused despite how weak in the knees his direct gaze and sexy British accent make me. "Canadian girl trying to make her way back home, actually. I can definitely relate to family drama, though."

We walk around for a while, and then finally sit down on a bench, enjoying a couple of pistachio *kulfis*. I figure Rajin must've met up with some friends – I'll give him a call in a bit.

Before I know it, we're deep into conversation about my current predicament. He's absolutely bewildered as to why I would oblige to such a thing – and to my attacker, no less.

He's one of those people who hold direct eye contact as they speak to you. It's as if he can see right into your soul, then reach into every nook and corner without even trying. I almost don't hear what he's saying. I'm so absorbed by soaking in every moment with this amazingly normal, attractive, and mature guy. I'm fairly certain he wouldn't cheat on me or beat me over the head with something either.

He stops and puts his hands on my shoulders and pulls me to directly face him. His eyes crinkle in the most sincere expression I've ever received, let alone from a stranger.

"I just don't get how you can sleep near the guy who tried to force himself on you. That's not just moronic, it's unsafe. You've got to get yourself out of there. No matter what they said they'll do to your cousin. Your safety matters too, you know."

The feeling of him touching me and pulling me in so close sends a chill up my spine. I've never even connected with anyone like this before, not even Roger. Speaking with this dreamy stranger is effortless and dangerously consuming.

I smile playfully and say, "You seem awfully fired up about someone you've only just met. For all you know, I could be a horrible person who deserves an ill fate."

A group of rambunctious, inebriated teens walk in between us, hooting and hollering.

His hand falls to rest on the small of my back to guide me out of their way, "I know a good heart when I see one. I could spot that sparkling smile of yours from a mile away. You need to get out of that place, Tara. If you don't, I might have to come get you out of there myself."

"Oh no. I don't need rescuing. I have the situation quite under control," I say, even though I absolutely do need help.

"Oh yeah, and what happens when the bastard gets high out of his mind and comes at you again?"

"Then I grab the nearest sugar cane and run like hell?" I say with a smile.

"This isn't a joke, Tara. Look where we are. This is India. People don't mess around here. Pride is a big thing. What do you think will happen to you when they realize you've been playing them this entire time?

"I'll be long gone by then."

"I hope not too far. We've only just met," he says with a half-smile that sends a thousand butterflies into motion in my stomach.

Even though it's completely inappropriate, I can't help losing myself in his eyes. He's one of those people with a face so perfect you're suddenly reminded of all your own flaws.

I try shaking these thoughts out of my head, but I just can't stop grinning up at him like a lovestruck idiot.

Yikes, better get away from this one.

"Well, it was really nice meeting you. I think I better head back to the car now, Rajin's probably waiting for me there. If he's been gone for this long, then he must not be in the mood to talk."

"Sure, that's understandable. But pass him my number, okay? I really want to get to know more about what happened to my brother. The police might not find it a priority to figure out what happened – but I do."

"Will do." I say, handing my phone to him to punch in his number.

He asks for my number as well then gives me his phone.

When I hand it back to him, he looks down at it and says, "So you're what people's wishes and dreams are made of."

"I'm sorry?" I say, feeling confused and bashful at the same time.

"Tara, a shooting star," he says, while moving a stray piece of hair away from my eyes.

Now I'm certain I'm the deepest shade of red my skin tone allows, and I say, "Yup that's me. Sorry, I'm so rude I haven't even asked you your name."

"It's Dave. Dave Dhillon."

"Nice to meet you, Dave."

He holds his hand out, and when our skin connects I swear I feel the spark again. The one people describe when you finally meet *that* person. The person who's the one you didn't even know you were looking for, but shows up completely unexpectedly. The one who's a summary of the pipedream man you've been creating and chasing your entire life. Here he is in the flesh, standing right before me. Dave Dhillon.

No, no, no Tara. This isn't the time or place. Get a grip.

"Take care of yourself, all right Tara?"

Oh man, there it is again. The way he says my name that makes me want to hear it over and over again.

"I will. You too."

I walk away, dumbfounded as to how I ended up with a number at a gay pride gathering. What are the chances I would connect with the brother of the person whose memory brought me here in the first place? Serendipity? I think so.

I guessed correctly; Rajin sits on the ground with his back against the door of the car. He has his head down and he seems pretty upset.

"Rajin? You okay?" I kneel down beside him and rub his back.

"I don't know. Seeing his picture like that. I just wasn't expecting it. There are other people mourning him too. Not just me. But I'm the one who caused his death. If he never met me, he'd still be here. I killed him, Tara." He breaks down sobbing.

"No, no. Don't say that. Don't ever think that. What happened was *not* your fault. It was the doing of a small-minded and heartless man. You're a good person Rajin. Don't ever forget that," I say, hugging him tightly.

"If I'm so great then why did I ruin your life too? Why did I drag you down with me?" he says in between sobs.

"Maybe I was meant to come here. So you could save me, and then I could save you. That's what this is all about. Forget everything else."

"Okay," he says gloomily and stands to get into the car.

We chat about random stuff for the majority of the ride, but just as we're about to pull up to the dirt path leading to Deepa's house, he asks me who the guy was.

"He was Sunny's brother. He wants to have a chat with you. I'll text you his number when I get inside."

"I never knew he had a brother," he says quietly.

"He said he was out of the family loop for the last couple of years. He's actually from England. He seems like a nice guy."

"Yeah, easy on the eyes too." Rajin finally looks up at me and cracks a knowing smile.

"Really? I didn't notice," I say sarcastically and hug him goodbye before heading inside.

I walk in to a room filled with suffocating silence. Everyone's eyes are on me as I try to tip toe my way across the cold marble floor. I don't even make it half way when the thunderous sound of Deepa's father slamming his book down on the coffee table stops me dead in my tracks. He stands up and places his hands on his hips like he's ready to launch an inter-rogation, much like the ill-equipped police officers did in the Sidhu house a few weeks ago.

"Where were you?" He demands.

Reema answers for me. "She was off doing God knows what with God knows who. I told you she was trouble. There were plenty of suitable local girls for our son. Why did you have to tie our family's name and reputation to *her*?"

Something inside of me snaps, and I just can't carry on the good girl act any longer. "Whoa. Lay off, lady. Now I can't even go anywhere with my family? Am I a prisoner to this home?" I ask.

"Tara, don't you dare speak to my mother that way." Deepa finally speaks up in the presence of his parents. Of course it's in defense of his cow-face of a mom.

"Right. So I'm not allowed to stand up for myself, but it's okay for everyone to treat me like a second-hand family member?"

"Get out of here before I do something unthink-able to you." He charges toward me and threatens me in a way that I know means business. It's the same look he had the other night. His eyes are more than bloodshot, they're filled with fury and rage. He's un-steady on his feet, but he's as frightening as a tiger on the hunt deep in the Indian jungle. I have no idea what he's going to do next, since he's probably high or drunk again, or maybe a wonderful combination of both.

I try to hide my paralyzing fear. As casually as I can, I back away from him. "Uh oh," I say, "I set off his temper switch."

Mina chuckles from the corner of the room. She must be pleased she's not the center of attention for once.

The other day she told me what she wants in return for her silence about my secret. She wants me to help her marry her boyfriend. Her father isn't a fan of his family and is expecting to arrange her marriage to the person of his choosing. I told her what I need from her is to get me in contact with whoever I can pay off to get Rajin out of here.

Whether she's going to come through for me is a different story. I guess it's all in God's hands now. It's interesting that I've only recently found myself asking "God" for favours now that I'm in such a dire situation. I need for his existence to be real so badly that I don't care to question it anymore.

Deepa's mother whispers something to him that sends him from the room in a huff. I take that as my cue to get the heck out of here before things really get hectic.

When I get out of the shower, I hear the doorknob rattling.

Deepa bangs on the door and shouts, "Get out here right now, you slut! I knew you were a lying whore. You think you can treat me this way and get away with it? Is this how you thank me for my hospitality and kindness?"

He kicks the door open and barges in, even though I have nothing on but my towel.

"What are you talking about, Deepa? I haven't done anything." I try reasoning with him.

He throws my phone at the wall and screams ferociously.

"You're so fucking innocent, right? Who the hell is Roger then? Why's he sending you countless text messages telling you he's on his way to *save you*? You think you had something to be saved from before? Well, now I'll really give you a reason to play the damsel in distress."

He lunges at me and slams me against the marble bathroom counter, holding my wrists down and breathing furiously inches from my face. His breath is hot and stinks of the darkest of liquors. He has a fresh line of track marks on his arm.

I struggle to get the words out; his weight is suffocating. "Deepa, I know about your addiction. I want to help you. You're not thinking straight. Just please let go so we can talk this out."

He grabs my hairdryer from the countertop and smacks it hard against my face. I swear I hear my cheekbone crack. Blood gushes from my nose and I fall to the ground from the pain.

"Please, Deepa. Stop. Don't do this," I cry, curling up in a ball on the floor. My towel has fallen off, and I pull it to try to cover myself as best as I can.

He delivers one agonizing kick after another to the side of my naked body, shouting at the top of his lungs. He keeps calling me a two-faced slut. The ear-piercing yelling begins to fade, and I drift off into unconsciousness.

A pool of blood surrounds me when I awaken. My entire right side feels numb and paralyzed. I'm shivering from head to toe, lying naked on the floor. I slowly get up and face myself in the mirror. I have a huge red welt on the side of my face. My left eye is swollen shut, and there's a trickle of blood running from my nostrils to my mouth. I can't even break down crying. I just fall back down to the floor, gasping for air, holding myself and rocking back and forth.

I think back to the last time I felt like this. Like I just couldn't catch my breath even though I was sitting still. Like I couldn't take anymore. It was the time my mother told me she regretted my existence. That was when I decided I'd rather not be a part of this world anymore.

My thoughts begin to spiral out of control. Maybe killing myself is the only way out of all of this now. I can't help Rajin. I can't even help myself. I'm a worthless void of a being. I'm not anyone's hero. I want to end it all, just like my father did. At least then I'll be far away from all of this.

While crying uncontrollably, I scramble around the bathroom searching for a razor blade or some pills to take. I can't find anything, and I let out a guttural cry that the entire village must hear. I slap myself, trying to regain composure. I feel like one of my back teeth has been knocked loose from the attack. Waves of pain suddenly roll through my body and every single inch of me quivers.

I take a deep breath in and realize I can't leave this world without saying goodbye to Rajin and my mother. I need closure with them before I can be done with all that my life has become.

I swear I see a smile on Reema's face when I walk into the kitchen the next morning. She must be pleased seeing me like this. She probably feels like she's won. This confirms her superior place in her precious son's life.

Mina walks to the freezer and hands me a bag of ice. "Ouch. I should've warned you about his temper. Delete your messages next time. Rookie mistake, girl."

Before she leaves, she stops to look at me, and I see a sliver of sympathy in her eyes. I suppose she has a heart after all. Her bitch of a mother, however, simply huffs as she walks past me. Her expression says it all. She thinks I've learned my place the hard way. Little does she know I don't want a place anywhere in this world anymore. I will be but a vague memory to her in a short while, and everyone else too.

I find the house phone and call Rajin. "Can you come pick me up in about an hour? It's important."

"Of course. I'll be there soon," he says instantly.

I hang up and set out to find my mother, who's still camping out in the guest room. I wonder why she doesn't just stay at her own relatives' house like a normal person. Why's she staying here when she's clearly unwanted?

She rushes over when she sees the state I'm in.

"Oh Tara, what happened? Who did this to you?"

"Who do you think? Deepa lost his temper again," I say, avoiding eye contact with her.

"Well did you provoke him? What made him so angry?"

"Are you seriously going to blame me for this? My face is bashed in, and you're going to find a way for it to be *my* fault?"

"Stop twisting my words, Tara. Sit down. You look like a mess. Let me take a look at that bruise."

If I'm not mistaken, she's actually tearing up. She sits beside me, her hand resting on top of mine.

Surprisingly, her presence is actually a source of comfort.

We sit in complete silence for a while, until a maid comes up to us to announce that Rajin is here.

"I've got to go. I'll see you later."

"Are you sure it's a good idea to go out? People will ask questions." She gestures to my bashed in face.

"Let them ask. It won't matter soon."

She furrows her brow with confusion and opens her mouth to say something, but I walk out anyway. I have a lump in my throat thinking about how I'm never going to see her again. No matter the hard times we've had, she's still my mother. She's the one who brought me in to this world. Now, I'll be keeping her image in my mind on my way out of it.

I found some rope in the shed behind the house last night. That'll be my final resting place. I'm going to end my misery once and for all after the asshole is asleep tonight.

Rajin sees my face and jumps out the car, "Tara what happened? Did he do this to you? Where the hell's that bastard?"

"Relax Rajin. There's nothing you can do now. Let's just go somewhere. Get me out of here."

"Where do you want to go?"

"Anywhere but here."

"We should get you to a hospital. I was supposed to meet Sunny's brother today, but forget it. You're done, Tara. You're not going back to that place."

"It looks worse than it is. I'm fine. Let's just go wherever you were headed. I'll wait in the car."

"Are you sure? I really think you need to have a doctor take a look at that bruise."

He looks sorrowfully guilty, as if he's the reason I look like a battered wife. Though I suppose that really *is* what I am.

"I'm totally fine Rajin, just drive," I respond robotically. My mind is occupied with thoughts of the thick rope clasped tightly around my neck.

CHAPTER FOURTEEN

I crane my neck to peer into the café Rajin and Dave are meeting in, but I don't see either of them. If last night hadn't happened, I'd be dying to see Dave right now. The marks on my face and my broken resolve serve as painful reminders. I just want to get home so I can write my farewell letters to my loved ones.

Rajin gets back in to the car and says, "I know I shouldn't have...but I told him what happened to you. He demanded I take him to the Gill house right now. I didn't tell him you were with me because I didn't want to blindside you. He wants to meet you, though. Tonight. I told him I'd get you a phone so he can text you when and where."

"Wait, what? Why does he want to meet me? There's no need...I mean, I can't go sneaking off in the middle of the night. What do you think would happen if the in-laws from hell caught whiff of that?"

"He's not taking no for an answer. He would've come out here now if I'd told him you were here. I figured I should at least run it by you first."

"All right, fine." I clench my jaw and try to convince myself I don't feel a twinge of excitement at the thought of seeing Dave again.

We pick up an old school Motorola phone on the way back; I turn it to silent and hide it in the inner pocket of my purse. What I'm doing makes no sense, but for some reason, I can't stop myself.

Luckily, no one's home when I get in. I feel the buzz in my purse of a new text. I feel an urge to read it right away. Once again, thinking of Dave is the only time I'm not consumed by feelings of doom.

I go into my room to check my phone.

DAVE: tara, meet me tonight. I can come to where you are. Just tell me the time and place.

I respond right away.

TARA: i don't know if that's a good idea. if someone sees, i don't even want to think about what could happen.

DAVE: I won't let anything happen to you again. I need to see you. Please.

I can just about hear the urgency in his tone, and it makes me smile.

TARA: okay, there's a small gazebo by the pond behind the house. Rajin will let you know how to get here. i'll meet you out back at midnight tonight. if i don't show up that means i couldn't get out but i'll try my best.

DAVE: If you don't come out, I'm coming in. You can't stay there anymore. See you tonight.

I manage to get through an evening of serving dinner. I have to wait until everyone's finished before I'm allowed to leave the table. I skip out on eating; the food smells horrendous and doesn't look much better either. Not that I have much of an appetite anyway.

I drown out the dull conversations occurring around the room. Everyone sips their masala chai ever so obnoxiously. Deepa never came home tonight; he's probably off somewhere getting high. His family acts like they don't notice anything different about my appearance. I drift off and lose myself in thoughts of meeting up with Dave later.

Regardless of how crazy it's going to make me seem, I'm going to tell him about my decision. I must stay strong and not allow myself to be talked out of anything. I just have this undeniable desire to know what he's all about. Then I'll say goodbye to this stranger who was meant to cross my path for but a brief moment.

The closer it gets to midnight the bigger the knot in my stomach becomes. I'm so distracted by my nerves that I forget about the physical pain of my injuries for a while. Insignificant small talk carries through the rest of the evening. Eventually, everyone returns to his or her respective corners of this dungeon of doom.

I'm pretty much in the clear. I tip toe around the house to check if all the lights are off. As I'm creeping past the parents' bedroom, I overhear Mina letting them know Deepa's staying over at a friend's tonight. This is obviously a load of shit, but who the fuck cares.

Five minutes to midnight, I begin my mission to escape. I try my best to be light on my feet, opening and closing all of the doors as silently as I can. Outside, the dark is spooky and silent. But I suppose if I can sleep in the same house as a man who's attacked me twice, I can handle being in the dark by myself.

"Tara, I'm over here. Follow the light." I hear Dave's voice from a few steps ahead.

I feel like a teen sneaking out in the middle of the night.

He shines a beam of light from where he's standing. I step carefully over a few jagged rocks and push a couple overgrown bushes out of my way, but they still manage to scratch me up. I'm instantly taken back to memories of Whistler, when I was with my friends making my way up to that crazy outdoor rave. How so very different everything has become since then.

"This is a bit odd, isn't it?" I ask. Despite the dark, I'm self-conscious of my bruised face and extremely nervous about being caught.

He grabs my hand and guides me to sit down on a big flat rock. He tries to shine his flashlight toward me, but I turn it off. I don't want him to see me like this.

He squeezes my hand, as if he understands my insecurity, and says, "It doesn't matter that we've only *just* met. I feel like I've known you from some other time. You need to let me help you, Tara, I can't just let you go. I can't leave you there, like that, with *him*."

"I have a way out. I'm working on it."

"What do you mean?" He takes my hand and interlaces his fingers through mine. It should feel odd to be so intimately physical with someone I barely know. But, in this moment, it just feels right.

"Dave, my entire life I've been fighting against the inevitable fact that I'm not meant to be here. I'm a huge waste of space. I only attract negativity and hardship to all those around me..."

He tucks my hair behind my ear and encourages me to carry on.

"…so I've decided to take my own life. It's my only way out."

He jumps up, nearly knocking me to the ground. "Are you crazy? Maybe I got the wrong impression of you after all. I saw you as this brave, courageous, and selfless woman. Ready to put everything on the line to help someone she loves. Now you're just going to take the easy way out and commit the biggest act of cowardice there is?"

"The *easy* way?" I smile wryly. "If you think it's easy to end your own life, you've obviously never felt the way I do right now."

He's sits back down next to me. "That's not what I meant Tara…"

I interject before he can go on.

"My father was *not* a coward. He was the bravest man I know. He fought for so long before he realized he couldn't take anymore. That's exactly where I'm at now. I've crumbled. Actually no, I've been chipped away at, and I'm broken. Physically and mentally beyond repair this time. I just came to see you one more time. You were so kind to me the other day. You've been a brief sliver of normalcy in my outrageous life. But now I'm done with this world. I just can't take anymore."

I stand up, and he gets up right after me. He takes a step in towards me and gently grabs me by the waist, drawing me in so there's no space between us. I begin to melt at the feeling of being so close to him.

He hugs me tightly and begins to whisper in my ear.

"Just let me help you. I know I can bring you out of this. You might not believe it, but I've been where you are. When I heard about my brother I felt like doing the very same thing. I wanted to end it all so I could be wherever he is. I felt like it should've been me who was killed. I was the one who walked out on my family and look what happened. I was meant to protect him, and now he's gone. What kind of older brother am I?"

His voice catches, and it seems like he's trying to hold back tears. I'm taken aback by how vulnerable such a strong guy can be. But like he says, there's this strange familiarity between us.

He faces me head on and even though we can barely see one another I know he's staring at me with that same intensity from the other day. "Look Tara. I believe in fate. I believe you were meant to be there that day walking past the very spot I was standing in support of my brother. Maybe he's even the one who brought us together. Don't you think it's too much of a coincidence that Rajin and Sunny were connected? And the day before I'm due to go back to England – I meet you. You're this stunningly beautiful girl who has this crazy upside down life. Tara, I just know there's something here. Don't you want to find out what it is?" He cups my cheek gently.

"You stayed here for me?" I whisper.

"I stayed here for you and I'm not going back without you," he says. He tips my chin up and wipes away the tears I thought he couldn't see.

At least he hasn't seen my bruises. He seems like the type of guy that would march right into the house and raise hell.

I let my arms fall to my side and move away from his embrace, even though it feels so good to feel safe and protected for once.

"Look Dave. I'm not looking for any romantic adventures right now. I was just nearly beaten to death by my fake husband. My mother has loathed my existence as long as I can remember. It's time I do everyone a favour and just disappear."

"So disappear then. But not in the way you want to. Run away to England with me."

I laugh and exclaim, "I don't even know you!"

"Let's get to know each other then. Tell me every little detail about you. You and I both know you don't belong here. So why are you giving up just because you're in a place you're not meant to be?"

I burst out laughing, "I don't belong anywhere, my friend. I'm an imposter everywhere I go. I wasn't good enough for my old life, and now this one's not good enough for me. I'm constantly grasping at threads of hope, which either snap along the way or lead me nowhere. So you tell me, if I don't belong here, where do I belong?

The clouds part, casting a weak, cold light over his face, and I'm struck again by how handsome he is.

"Well, that's simple." He grins. "With me. You belong with me."

I try not to, but all I want to do is kiss him right now.

"That's awfully bold of you, isn't it? You just met me, and you're ready to be my knight in shining armour. Sorry, but it just makes no sense to me."

"Maybe you think too much," he says. In one swift move, he grabs me and pulls me in close.

He gazes deeply into my eyes and gently rubs the small of my back. Carefully, he traces the bruise from the corner of my eye to the side of my lip.

His facial expression hardens, and I know he's seen the extent of my injuries. "I swear I could kill that guy." He says with shaking anger.

Then we stand in each other's arms for a while before he breaks the silence.

"I know it's crazy Tara. But I just feel so drawn to you. It's like your face is the one I've been trying to picture for years. I can't shake the feeling that I'm meant to know you."

I gasp, but for once it's in a good way. My heart beats so hard, it feels like it's going to burst right out of my chest. Being close to him makes me feel so peacefully complete. I don't want to move an inch.

"But I'm damaged goods," I whisper.

"I don't care about your past. All I care is to be part of your future. I know you're not the kind of girl who needs saving. I just want to be there to see the rest of your story unfold. Because trust me sweetheart, this isn't it for you."

He doesn't look away from me, and I feel myself getting lost in his eyes. I've never felt so vulnerably consumed before. All I want to do is be closer to him.

"You're a game-changer, Tara. You're the type of girl who's going places. I can tell. There's so much more for you out there."

He leans in to kiss me, but we hear a branch break as if under the weight of a footstep. We both crouch down, holding our breath. He tries to calm my trembling body by holding me tight. We know exactly what would happen if we were caught. We wait it out in silence, and luckily no one comes.

"Must have been an animal or something."

"Yeah, but I should really get back," I say, looking around nervously.

"Call me in the morning, okay? I'm getting you out of there. That's final. And no more of this giving up nonsense. Just trust me. Can you do that?"

I want to believe fate brought us together. I want to have hope. The only problem is I just can't shake the feeling that this is crazy because I literally *just* met this guy.

But, no matter what my brain's telling me, my lips can only say what my heart wants. "Okay, Dave. I'll call you tomorrow."

When I get back in, I stay up all night replaying every moment of our meeting. Dave has this irresistible positive force around him that just draws me in. All I want to do is be with him again. I want to tell him more about my life and hear everything about his.

Am I being a typical girl crushing on some hot guy I just met?

Totally.

Am I going to stop?

Probably not.

The next day I step out of my room to a silent house and let out a sigh of relief. After much internal debate, I've decided Dave is right. I can't let this family from hell determine my fate. I'm the one in control of how I allow them to make me feel. I won't succumb to their abuse. I will not give up. I have to carry on fighting to survive. Not just because of what Dave said, and not just for Rajin. But because I *am* my father's daughter, and I know he wouldn't want this to be the end for me.

I just need to refine my focus on what this is all about. Now, it's not only about Rajin. It's also about bringing peace to Dave's brother's memory. Most of all, I must bring an end to all the secrecy that shrouds my life.

I'm so lost in thought that I don't even hear my mother come up behind me.

"Oh, I thought no one was here."

"I just got in." Her voice seems off, and I turn to face her. She looks like she's been crying.

"Everything okay?"

"Yes. But, I think I'll leave sooner than I planned," she says with a tight lip, holding her composure.

"Why's that?"

"I ran into some people I didn't want to see."

"Like who?"

"Your aunt and uncle."

"Well Mom, they do live in the same city. It was bound to happen sooner or later. Why's that such a bad thing anyway? What the heck happened between you all to make you hate them so much?"

"It's nothing of your concern, Tara."

"You snap at me every time I bring this up. Look what happened with dad because of all of the secrets. Maybe I could've helped if you had just let me in. Just tell me, Mom." I plead with her even though it's always been pointless.

"It looks like someone else is interested in airing my dirty laundry. You'll probably find out from her."

She offers more than she usually does, which is typically different ways of saying, *shut the hell up about this.*

"Who?" I press on hoping this is the time she'll finally crack.

"I received a phone call from one of your father's old friends. She seems to think you have a right to know about our family's past. I think she's just sticking her nose where it doesn't belong and stirring up trouble.

She's got to be talking about Ms. Patel. I wonder why she called her. There's no point in asking, though, I know what's coming next.

"Anyway, I need to make arrangements to get home."

There it is. The change of subject and the brush-off.

"After seeing everything I'm going through here, don't you want to take me back with you?"

"You don't belong with me anymore. This is your home now. Make it work," she says with a slight quiver in her voice. Her words sting like a dagger nonetheless.

The first thing I do once my mother leaves is call Ms. Patel. She answers right away.

"Oh hello dear! I was waiting for your call. Do you have time to meet today?" She says over the sound of a blowdryer. She's probably perched up in some beauty salon.

"Yeah sure. Could you pick me up from my in-laws house? I don't really have a way to get anywhere."

"Of course, dear. I can come there now if that works for you."

"Sure, I'll be waiting outside."

She shows up literally five minutes later. She's wearing a long cotton suit with the dupatta knotted around her neck like a scarf. Her outfit's a little too tight around her bulgy bits. It doesn't look all that bad, though. Her over-the-top personality matches her oversized appearance. Her rose-coloured sunglasses balance atop her head. They look like they're going to slide off any moment with her animated way of speaking. Instead, they bobble about on her frizzy hair like they've been there for days and she doesn't even remember. She's chipper and excited to see me. So odd for a woman I barely know.

She gives me a giant hug as I get into her tiny car. "You look *so* much like your father you know! It's so nice to meet you. He used to tell me about you."

"Oh, you guys kept in touch?"

She hesitantly responds, "Yes, he called from time to time just to catch up."

The wistful tone of her voice makes me think they might've been a little more than *just friends* when they were younger.

"So where are we headed?"

"Oh, there's this darling little coffee shop in town."

When we pull up, I realize it's the same one Rajin and Dave met up at, and I get a rush at the thought Dave might be inside. Maybe it's his hang out spot. Jeez, I'm acting like such a dweeb.

We get in and shake ourselves off from the unexpected downpour on the way in. The place is empty.

"Have a seat. I'll go order us something. What would you like?"

I don't usually drink caffeine, but I have a feeling it might be a good idea to pep up for whatever bomb she's about to drop on me.

"A regular *chai* is fine. Thank you."

"No problem at all, love," she says with a warm smile.

She rushes off, and I look down at my phone and see there's an unread message from Dave.

DAVE: hey beautiful, hope no silly ideas today. stay strong, okay? i promise things are going to turn around for you real soon. i have a plan.

I smile at this guy's total disregard for regular social norms. Forget not coming on too strong. To be honest, he's the exact kind of guy I used to imagine myself being with. Well, the kind of guy I yearned for Roger to magically transform into. He's a dreamer and a doer all in one. Trust me to meet the perfect guy in the most imperfect of situations. How so very typical of my life.

"Here you are, dear." Mrs. Patel hands me my tea, and I take a sip right away even though it's steaming hot. I breathe the soothing aroma; it's exactly what I needed on this cold, wet morning.

"So, what do you need to talk to me about?"

"Oh, um, I don't know exactly how to go about this..." She seems to shed her larger than life confidence and become edgy and nervous.

"Just start at what you know about my mother. What's this big secret surrounding her life? And how do you fit into it all?"

"Your mother is not who you think she is," she blurts out bluntly.

"Well, you may be surprised by what I think of her," I say with a laugh.

"Oh? What do you mean?"

"I mean she and I don't get along. Actually, that's an understatement. We despise each other most of the time. We share the same blood, and that's about it."

She cocks one tattooed-in eyebrow at me and says, "Oh, I didn't know that. But, before I dive into what I want to tell you, I just want you to know that I cared for your father very deeply. He was an extremely important person to me…"

"Were you two…together?" I blurt out what had been floating around in my mind since that airy look appeared on her face when she first spoke of my father.

She looks at me with slight surprise, takes a deep breath in and says, "Yes. A long, long time ago."

"When?"

"Before your mother came along," she says bitterly.

It's so strange to see my father as anyone's young lover; all I can picture him to be is that big ol' sad drunk guy.

"Ah, I see. So that's what you have on my mom. She stole your man."

"Not just that. It's not that simple. Your mother only operates on the basis of what she can gain. She's a materialistically driven woman. There are no boundaries when it comes to what she wouldn't do to get what she wants."

"Well, I don't know about *that*," I say, my voice trailing off.

I begin to feel kind of guilty, sitting here bad mouthing my mother with a complete stranger. This woman seems to really have it in for my mom.

"She's a dirty, mean-spirited woman," Mrs. Patel says through gritted teeth.

"Whoa, whoa...my mom might be a lot of things. She's high strung, impatient, maybe a little rude at times. But bad hearted? Nah, I don't see that. If we're done here, I think I should be getting back now," I say, gathering my stuff and standing up to leave.

I suddenly feel infuriated not only at this random woman for spewing such hatred toward my mother, but also at myself for listening to her. No matter what our relationship is like, she's still my mom.

Just as I bid her an angry farewell, she stands up and begins blurting things out to get me to sit back down.

"She slept with your uncle. That's why she left from here. She was the talk of the town. She married your father only to get to his older brother, the heir to the family riches. She thought she could bump his wife out of the picture by getting with the eldest of the family."

Her words hit me like a ton of bricks, and I slowly sit back down with my mouth hanging open.

"Why should I believe you? You could be lying," I say, even though this revelation explains a lot of the mystery that is my life.

"Haven't you ever wondered what was *so* bad that they all stopped speaking? Everyone knows about it. Just ask your mother-in-law if you don't believe me," she says.

This lady just went from being the Indian Mrs. Clause to an all-knowing gossip magazine informant. I don't care that what she's saying makes sense. I just want to get out of here, as fast as possible. The room begins to spin, and I suddenly feel a complete loss of my bearings. I get up again and begin to walk away.

"Wait! Let me at least drop you off at home," she calls after me.

I stop and turn around, as I'm pulling my cardigan on I ask, "I just want to know one thing. Why did you have to tell me? Why did you need me to know?"

"Because your father wanted you to know. He wanted you to know you'd still have a father, even after he's gone."

"What do you mean?"

"I mean, your uncle, he's not actually your uncle. He's your real father."

CHAPTER FIFTEEN

My breathing feels laboured. It feels like I've had the wind knocked out of me. Cheating. Lies. Deceit. Betrayal. How can that be what my mom's all about? Why wouldn't my father just leave her? None of this makes any sense. Everything that woman told me swarms about in my head, making me feel like I'm going to explode. I left the coffee shop in such a dazed state that I've just been walking around the plaza for ages. I ignore the catcalls and lewd gestures of the mischievous young school boys who are free to roam the streets now as it's the late afternoon.

How could they hide this from me? This woman has no reason to lie. It has to be true. This is the big secret. This is why my mother hates me. I represent her disgusting, failed attempt to steal someone's hus-band - *all for money*. I feel sick to my stomach that I share a bloodline with such a manipulative and calculating woman.

I need to talk to someone about this. More importantly, I need to get out of here. I'm sitting on a cement block outside of some shops. Upon closer inspection, the group of local boys aren't as harmless looking as I thought, and are closing in on me.

I better call Dave to come get me. I'd normally call Rajin, but I don't want to be around him right now. He must know all about this too. Everything's slowly sinking deep into my subconscious. All the puzzle pieces of my life arrange themselves into a horrendous reality – but one that finally makes sense. "Hey Tara. I was just thinking of calling you," Dave says in his deeply assuring voice.

I tell him where I am and that I need him to come right away.

"Stay put. I'll be right there," he says without hesitation.

We park in an empty dirt alley by his house. I explain everything to him, and he just holds my hand, squeez-ing it when my eyes brim over with tears. He mostly just listens to everything I have to say. Each time it gets to be too much and I break down, he pulls me into an embrace that makes all the hurt go away.

"Nothing's changed, Tara. You're still the same person. Your father is still your father. No one can take that away."

"But that's the thing. He *wanted* me to know this. My mother never let him tell me. She's the reason he was humiliated in front of his entire family *and* the whole damn village. She drove him into depression. All these years I wondered what I had to do with it. Now I get it. It all makes sense." I trace the lines on his palm and try to hold in another outburst.

This guy must think I'm so messed up.

"Just keep it together. This woman who told you all of this is just some random lady. You owe it to your mom to hear her side of the story too," he says. He runs his fingers through my hair and rests his hand on my cheek.

His comfort and warmth is starting to make me feel strong and capable again.

I shrug my shoulders and say, "She's gone back to Canada."

"Well then call her as soon as she lands. You need to speak to her about this," Dave says like he knows exactly how to make this all better.

His reassuring tone covers up the enormity of the situation. He makes me feel normal, despite the extremely abnormal circumstances I've found myself in. Before I know it, it's beginning to grow dark outside. I check my watch, which is still set to

Canadian time, and quickly gather my things once I do the mental math and realize it's nearly a quarter to nine. Back home, this is when I'd be heading out for a night on the town; here, it's equivalent to strolling in at 4:00 AM or something.

"I really need to get home. Everyone's going to be in a fit about my whereabouts. I'll call you later, okay?"

I'm about to get out of his car, but he grabs my hand. "Tara, you can't walk home from here. It's not safe. This is India, remember? Not Canada," he says with a serious expression.

I smile and say, "Well, you can't drop me off. They'll see you. I have no choice. It's not that far, I'll be fine."

"No. Not a chance, Tara. Why don't I drop you off at your uncle's house? That way you can pretend you were there the whole time," he says, already pulling back onto the main road.

"Alright, fine. You can drop me off up the road from their house. I can walk that far alone. If it's okay with you of course," I tease him.

"Hmmm…should be fine. But I'll be watching until you get in," he says with a wink.

We take turns choosing music to listen to; we have a lot of similar favourites. I haven't relaxed and enjoyed myself like this for ages. No matter what giant bomb

I just had dropped on me, I actually feel happy just being in Dave's company.

Any time I spent with Roger inevitably lead to sex, and I was always very aware of it. With Dave, I feel completely at ease just hanging out with him. He's the perfect confidant during this Indian *Jerry Springer* period in my life.

"Okay beautiful, as much as I'd love to keep you with me for as long as possible, your stop has arrived," he says as he pulls over.

I can tell he wants to lean in and give me a hug, but we both know it's much too risky for any public displays of affection. I'd get my head chopped off if someone thought I was following in my good ol' mother's footsteps and being unfaithful to my supposedly doting husband.

I step out of the car and freeze dead in my tracks as I realize someone's spotted us. A little bit up the way, there's a woman looking right in our direction. My stomach drops even more when I realize it looks a whole lot like Pyaro Bhua. I pray she never saw me.

When I get to the house, I realize that I actually feel relieved to be back here. I never thought the day would come when this place would feel like home. A strange sensation rolls over me as I realize that, technically, this *is* my home.

I don't even know what I'm going to say to them all. *Oh, guess what? I know your big secret. I'm the daughter of this house. Rajin's my half-brother! My cranky uncle is actually my real dad. Aunty is my stepmother!* I think? I don't even know how it all works.

Pyaro snaps me out of my whirlwind of thoughts by grabbing me by the arm and pulling me into the study.

"Who was that? Are you crazy? Do you know what would happen to you if someone else saw you?" Her eyes are the size of saucers.

Crap. Busted.

"He's just a friend," I lie. Even though I'm fully aware that isn't an acceptable excuse any way.

"You're not meant to have male friends when you're someone's wife, Tara," she snaps.

"Oh yeah, about that! What a lovely marital home you all chose for me. Thank you so very much for that!" I say, trying to brush past her and head upstairs to call Dave.

"What do you mean?" she asks, seemingly ignoring the bruises on my face.

I stop and look right at her. "Oh, nothing. Just that he's a wife-beating drug addict. His mother is a complete bitch. His father thinks he's a mafia leader or something. Last but not least, his sister is a nasty, conniving little wench."

"Sounds like a typical Indian marriage to me," she says without hesitation.

"Oh *come on!*" I can't help but laugh at her lack of reaction to all of this.

In her defense, I suppose it's pretty typical in Indian culture to have such issues with arranged marriages. Well, it's not the life I want, so it's not the life I'm settling for.

"You can't just leave, Tara," she says, as if reading my thoughts.

"Yes I can," I say. I stop to examine myself in a mirror. My hair's a dishevelled mess. No wonder she thinks I've been up to no good. I try to put it into a braid, but I'm not doing such a great job. It was the one thing my mom actually did for me as a child–even if she did rip out several strands of hair during the process.

A chill runs up my spine when I remember how good it felt to have Dave's fingers running through my hair earlier.

"Anyway, forget all that. How's your mother doing? I heard she's been staying with you?" Pyaro says, motioning for me to sit on the ground in front of her so she can braid my hair for me.

"Yeah, about that…I know everything," I say with a hiccup in my throat.

She takes an elastic off her wrist and ties it around the bottom of my braid. Then she hands me a blanket, and comes to sit cross-legged in front of me, pulling a bit of the blanket to cover her own legs too.

It suddenly feels like I'm in a high school sleepover with my friends again.

"What do you mean you know everything? What's there to know?" she asks, seemingly confused.

"Let's just say a little birdie told me. Or rather a big, rambunctious birdie," I say.

It takes me a solid hour to get her up to speed about what my childhood after her "death" was like, what the woman told me, and what fuckery has been going on with me in the Gill residence.

Pyaro is completely shocked by everything. She said she knew there was a serious reason why our family ties had been broken, but she had no idea what the reason actually was.

We both sit in silence processing everything we've just discussed. To say it all out loud solidifies it and makes it an even harder truth to accept. I feel like a stranger to myself now that I know my true lineage.

Everything I've ever known seems to be a lie. Yet every uncertainty now makes perfect sense. It's a clarifying but jagged piece of knowledge to have. If only I knew what to do with it. Maybe I was better off in the dark about all of this.

Sometime between hashing out the details and debating about if I should call my mom out on this or not, Rajin joins us. It seems like he already knew about everything, so he doesn't find it all that scandalous. I suppose the current on-goings in his life are even more dramatic than an old affair.

We head up to the roof to avoid my aunt and uncle. Time flies by as we talk, and it's completely dark before long. We have the *munjay* (outdoor cots) laid out and we snuggle up under wool blankets, trying to shield ourselves from the mosquitoes. My eyes are filled with sleep, but the stars spread out across the sky are too spectacular to leave.

It's nearly midnight when I text Mina to ask if the coast is clear back home. I'd stay over here but my absence would cause World War III at the Gill residence in the morning. Rajin offers me a ride home, and although I'd much rather call Dave, I agree and leave with him.

When I get home, I notice a note tucked into the side of the house. It reads: *My phone isn't working. Meet me at the same place tomorrow night at midnight. – Dave*

When I try calling him, I realize my phone says it has no service. How odd. Oh well, soon I won't need it anymore. Dave and I can be together in person once I'm cut free from this ridiculous place. Together, we'll find a way for Rajin to join us in England.

I thought I'd be leaving here with Roger, after hearing his reaction when I told him what was going on. But as usual, he's a no-show. It's so typical of him to give me false hope coated in fake promises. I'm *so* done with him. Him not being there for me in my greatest time of need is the final straw. It's all about Dave and I now. At least he's a real man.

I jump out of bed, realizing I've slept well past noon, since there was no knock courtesy of Ms. Reema to wake me. I slowly creep out of my room after washing up and am met by an eerily normal Sunday morning sight.

Deepa and his father play cards in the living room. His mother and sister sip tea near by, whispering about something. No one even seems to notice I've entered the room.

"Hello, everyone." I test the waters.

"Good day, Tara. How was your evening yesterday?" Deepa's father asks in an uncharacteristically polite way.

"It was fine," I say and head into the kitchen to pour myself some cereal.

Before I can leave, Reema calls for me to join them. I hesitantly oblige and take a seat on the sofa on the opposite end from them.

"So, anything new?" she asks.

"Not really. Just the same old, same old," I say cautiously. They're all acting very odd.

"Your mother returned home yesterday. You must be missing her. You can spend more time with us now," she says, forcing a smile.

These people are being way too nice. Something's up. I wonder what they have up their sleeve now.

Reema fiddles with the fringe on the gaudy flower-printed sofa. "Tara, we're having a very high profile dinner next week. We wish for you to be present. Deepa's grandfather will be visiting from England, and he's very excited to meet you. It was his dying wish to see his one and only grandson married."

"Oh. It's a shame he couldn't make it to the wedding," I say, pretending like I care. All I want to do is get my phone working so I can text Dave. What do these weirdos want from me?

"He hasn't been keeping well, so he could only come once the doctors gave the go ahead. Which was just yesterday," Mina answers for her mother.

"I can't wait to meet him," I say as I get to my feet. Before I leave, I decide to check if they're acting strange because I was out late last night.

"Well, I'm going to go relax for a bit. I got in pretty late, I was at my aunt and uncle's house catching up with everyone."

"That's nice dear. There's tea and biscuits in the kitchen, help yourself," Reema says with another terrifying forced grin.

Wow, this lady should be the star of her own show. She'd win an award for "leading villain" with her ability to hide her evil nature on demand.

I spend the rest of the day journaling and strategically avoiding contact with everyone until it's finally time to meet with Dave. I press my ear against the wall separating my room from Deepa's, I hear the sound of him snoring away like a forty-year-old man. The only problem is, when I get to the forest, there's no sign of Dave. Only a note with a flashlight pointed towards it.

I KNOW WHAT YOU'VE BEEN UP TO.

I look around frantically, waiting for someone to pop out of the bushes.

"Crap, this was a set up," I say aloud as I hurry back to the house.

I close the door quietly behind me and lean up against it, waiting for someone to emerge from the shadows. But there's no one, just dead silence. Who could've set me up like that? Maybe my phone isn't broken after all. Perhaps it's been disconnected. Somebody must have spotted Dave and I together. Now they're using it to blackmail me – but for what?

It would've been catastrophic if Deepa or someone else had been waiting for me out there. And it definitely would've been the end of Tara Sidhu, that's for sure.

I look for the house phone and look up Dave's number in my cell. I call him, but it goes straight to voicemail. This is getting weird. Something's not right.

I can't sleep at all, I'm filled with way too much worry about Dave. The note, the sideshow act the Gills just put on, and our phones not working – something's definitely up.

Everyone's artificially happy behaviour carries on through the morning. Deepa's father leaves for the eight-hour journey to Delhi to collect his father from the airport. Just about as soon as he's gone, I get another wonderful lecture about proper daughter-in-law etiquette courtesy of Reema.

While the staff bustle about, prepping the house, and everyone else is distracted with some minor detail or the other, I try Dave's number again, but there's still no answer. Every fibre of my being is telling me that something horrible has happened to him, so I call Rajin for help.

"Well, are you sure no one saw you when you met up with him?"

"We heard rustling in the bushes but thought nothing of it. What if they know what I'm up to, and that's why they're acting like a bunch of freaks?"

"Try talking to Deepa. Maybe you'll get some answers out of him. They can't carry this on forever. Eventually, they'll drop the façade, especially when Mr. Grandpops leaves. Then what do you think will happen to you?"

"I don't understand why they even need me around for his visit. If they know I'm seeing someone else, then why don't they just off me now?"

"Just go talk to Deepa. He'll end up snapping and letting the truth out. But get out of there if he comes at you," Rajin says.

"Nah. That barbaric behaviour is saved for when he's high or drunk. He's usually bright eyed and bushy tailed in the mornings. It's as if that other side to him doesn't even exist."

"Don't worry, you'll be out of there soon. I'm working on saving enough cash from my allowance to use as a bribe. There's a kid at school who swears he's got an in with the immigration agency."

Before I can respond to this glimmer of hope and a possible exit strategy for the both of us, I hear footsteps come up behind me.

"Who're you on the phone with?"

I turn around to see Mina with her eyebrow raised. She grabs the phone from my hand to check the last dialed number.

"It was Rajin. Is that okay with you? Or is that forbidden as well?" I say in an irritated tone.

Who does this girl think she is?

"Yeah, whatever. Look, I know you're not stupid. Obviously, you know something's up around here. I can let you know what's going on, under one condition," she says, twirling a piece of her highlighted hair.

"Yeah, what's that?"

"You have to promise to tell my dad you'll only be on your best behaviour for papa's visit if they open up to the idea of meeting my boyfriend," she blurts out all in one breath.

"So I take it you know about Dave and I?" I say in a hushed voice.

A smile crosses her face. "How'd you know I knew about him?"

"Because you seem to know everything."

"Ah yes. Years of eavesdropping have benefits sometimes. However, other times I hear things I'd really rather not..." Her voice trails off as her face twists into a disgusted expression.

"Okay. Anyway, do you know where he is? And who left me that note last night?"

She tosses her apple up in the air, catches it, and takes a bite. "The servant saw you two the other night. He reported back to my father. Also, your little buddy's being held at an undisclosed location to figure out what's going on between you two."

"*What*? What do you mean *undisclosed location*? I shake her shoulders. "Where is he? Is he hurt? I swear if anything happens to him because of me I won't be able to live with myself."

She throws my hands off of her and rolls her eyes at me. "Oh chill out, nothing major's going to happen to your lover boy."

"Please tell me where he is," I plead, hoping this is the moment she'll show me a morsel of any humanity she might have in her.

"First promise you'll help me," she says and holds out her little finger for a pinky promise.

I twist my finger around hers and shout, "I promise okay! Just please help me save him. I don't want anything to happen to him."

"All right, fine. Dad's got him locked up in our old house. It's where we lived before he convinced grandpapa to throw us a couple *crore* to build this one."

"I thought your dad's loaded. Why'd he need an allowance?" I ask as I throw my jacket on. I toss Mina her keys; she's going to need to drive me to their place there's no way I could find it alone.

"That's where you come in. Papa will only sign the land over if Deepa is 'cured' of his addiction by being married to a beautiful foreign-born girl. Papa seems to think that's all it'll take to make a man out of him. Some astrologer filled his head with this shit. A wife and some kids are meant to sober him up. What a joke, eh?" She snorts.

I stop for a moment as it all clicks into place. "So I'm just the means to an end. That's just sick. What are they planning to do with me after he leaves?"

"Well, I think you can figure that out for yourself, can't you?" she says, her eyes narrowing.

I swallow hard, realizing I need to get out of here sooner rather than later. "Where's your old house?" I ask.

"Just about ten minutes up the way from here. I can take you there later. If you promise to speak to my father as soon as he's back."

"Can't we just go there now?" I plead. "What if he's' hurt, or worse..." My voice catches when I picture Dave helpless and alone in some abandoned home.

She chucks the keys back into the kitchen drawer under the marble countertop and says, "We can't go now, genius. They'll know something's up if you and I are suddenly buddy-buddy and decide to go somewhere together. Meet me when they're all asleep at the front of the house. I'll roll my car to the road in neutral and then we'll leave, no one will hear anything."

From the confidence in her voice, it seems like she knows what she's doing. I suppose I have no choice but to wait.

"Alright, thank you, Mina," I say, and I sincerely mean it.

Mina might be a cow, but at least she had the decency to let me know what's going on, even if it's only for personal gain. But then again, with a family as messed up as hers, she could've turned out a lot worse.

Everything Mina told me has left me feeling dizzy. But most of all I'm just worried about Dave right now. I bet he's desperately wishing that he never met me at all.

I get into the room, and there's a box sitting on my bed with a note on top.

> *Dear Tara,*
>
> *I brought you your old journals so you always have a piece of home with you. I'm sorry for the way things are between us. One day, you'll understand why. Keep writing. You have a way to make even the worst situations seem beautiful with your words. It might be the only way for you to escape all of this.*
>
> *Love,*
> *Your mother.*

Oh wow. She actually did something kind for once. I bet she must've found out that I know the truth now. Perhaps that's why she felt the need to make amends. So I don't write her out of the family too.

I can't say I'm not happy to have my journals with me. I've truly missed writing. It's helped me make sense of things ever since I was a kid. My teachers always encouraged me to become a journalist or an author. That would be my ultimate dream job. I grab the box and hide it in the closet. Mina's probably been reading my current journal, which's filled with a play-by-play chronicle of my lovely escapades in India thus far. That must be how she seems to know every stinkin' detail of my life. Whatever, I can't be bothered with any of that right now.

What I really need to do is devise a plan to get Dave out of that place. I really hope Mina comes through for me or else I'm going to have to confess the truth to Deepa and hope for the best.

CHAPTER SIXTEEN

Time seems to stretch on forever, until it's finally time to leave. I head out to meet Mina and thank my lucky stars when I see her waiting for me in her car. She looks like she's about to pull off a major heist the way she has a scarf wrapped around her head and the headlights off. I get in the passenger seat and wait for her to start moving.

"What do you think you're doing? The car isn't going to push itself. Get out and help us get up the road so no one hears the engine start," Mina says in the bitchiest voice possible.

I snap because I'm seriously sick of her attitude. "Are you kidding me? I'm doing as much of a favour for you as you are for me. So there's no need to boss me around. Push your own damn car. I'll steer."

I try to shove her over, but she's strong for such a scrawny little pipsqueak.

She leans over to open the passenger door and push me out. "Either you get out and do it, or the deal's off."

Just then, we see Deepa's parents' bedroom light switch on.

"Oh shit! Mom and Dad are awake. We need to get out of here fast," she says frantically.

I hop out and push the car while she pops it in neutral. It rolls down the dirt hill, and she steers it onto the main road.

I can't stand the smug look on her face, so I throw out the ultimate insult to a rebellious young girl. "You're just like your mother, you know."

"I am not!" she cries, just like an angry teenager. In the dark she doesn't see the pothole in the road, so she hits it at full speed, and we both are lifted a foot out of our seats.

"Oh yes, you are. You don't even care that the person I'm worried about could be seriously hurt right now. You're probably getting a kick out of all of this."

"I'm not as heartless as you think I am. I was like you once. I cared about people. Then I quickly realized that doesn't get you anywhere. Being nice only gets you stepped on. If you want something in this world – you have to take it. Nothing comes easy," she says and turns onto a winding uphill road.

"I suppose that's true," I say quietly.

We travel the rest of the way in silence, and before I know it, we're outside a shack of a house with a rugged-looking Rottweiler tied up front.

"He doesn't look too friendly," I say, feeling scared to leave the car.

"Oh, Tommy? Don't worry about him. He's my big cuddly bear. I begged dad to bring him with us to the new house. But of course, he couldn't indulge a tiny bit of happiness, even when I was a little girl," she says with a pout.

The dog growls at first, baring its giant pointy teeth, but as soon as he sniffs Mina, he starts to wag his tail happily.

"I don't think he's going to give me the same warm welcome," I say, still hesitant to cross his path.

"Well if you want to rescue your prince, you have to pass the scary dragon." Mina says, once again enjoying my plight.

She holds him back as I pass by and walk inside. It smells horrid in this condemned-looking house. I scream as something small and furry scurries past my feet and runs up the crumbling wall.

"I wish I was wearing my boots," I say in a shaky voice.

Mina doesn't respond, and I realize she didn't follow me in.

"Mina? Aren't you coming?" I call out to her.

I hear the door shut behind me. Of course she's not going to come in, she seems like a bigger pansy than me. Despite my absolute terror, I carry into the darkness. The floor has giant rotting cracks in it, and humungous spider webs hang down from the ceiling. It's dusty and just plain creepy in here, but I've got to find Dave and get him out of here.

I begin to shout out into the wide-open space. "Dave? Are you in here? It's Tara. Make some noise if you can hear me!"

I hear nothing but the creak of the floorboard under my feet. I try to manoeuvre my way through the place as carefully as possible. I use the light on my phone to see a little better, but it doesn't help much. It's disgusting in here. I don't realize where I'm stepping, and I step right into a giant hole in the floor.

I scream as I fall through and land with a thud on the ground. I stand up and rub my eyes, trying to get a better look at what I'm seeing.

Dave's unconscious and tied to a chair in the middle of the room I've landed in. I run over to him despite my throbbing head and arm. "Dave! Are you okay? Wake up!" I cry out, shaking him.

There's a jug sitting on the filthy plastic table next to him. I take some water from it and splash it onto his face, hoping to conjure him back to awareness. I shine my light around the room once more and see a bottle labelled chloroform on the floor next to him. Thankfully whoever's meant to be guarding him isn't here right now. I keep shaking him, but he isn't waking. I call out for Mina.

"Mina! Help! I found him, but he's knocked out. I can't carry him by myself. Find a way down here!"

No one responds. She must still be outside. I try shining the light in Dave's eyes, and he finally moves a little.

I hold his face in my hands and try to get him to look at me. "Dave. It's Tara. You're okay now. I'm going to get you out of here. Wake up, Dave."

He struggles to peel his eyes open just a little bit more then closes them shut again.

I pour some of the water directly on top of his head, it jolts him awake.

"Tara?" he says groggily. He struggles to keep his eyes open.

I shine the light over him to see if he's badly hurt. His wrists are bleeding from the rope, but other than that he seems okay. His clothes are covered in mud as if he were dragged into this place. I untie his hands and try my best to keep him awake. "Yes, it's me. You need to get up, Dave. I can't carry you out of here."

He grumbles some disjointed response and drops to the floor on his first attempt to stand. I try my best to move him, but it's no use. He's too big for me to move on my own.

I hear footsteps coming down the staircase in the corner of the room. My heart sinks; I'm so afraid that I feel like I could vomit.

"Hello? Who's there?" I call out shakily.

The footsteps get closer, and I try to shine my light, but it's too weak for me to make out the figure approaching us.

Just when I feel like I'm going to pass out from dread, I hear a familiar voice say, "It's just me, Tara."

He comes closer, and I see who it is.

"Rajin? What are you doing here?"

"Mina called me. The door blew shut and she couldn't get it open again. She panicked because she thought you were going to be locked in here forever. I suppose she realized she couldn't cash in any favours with you if you're dead."

His attention switches to Dave passed out on the floor. "Is that Dave? Is he okay?"

"He seems okay...I think he's been drugged, though. Can you help me move him?"

"Yeah, you grab one arm, and I'll grab the other. It's not too far, we can do it."

With much dragging, grunting, and a whole lot of garbled rambling from Dave, we manage to get outside.

"I can't believe all of this is because of my stupidity. I should've never met up with him right outside their fucking house. What was I thinking?"

"You were thinking that you like me–a lot." Dave mumbles with a smile on his face.

"You're slipping in and out of consciousness, and you're making jokes! No more talking, okay? You need your strength to walk. We're almost out of here. I'm so sorry for all of this," I say, trying my best to hold him up.

Even in this bizarrely terrible situation, Rajin cracks a smile at the sight of me tearing up for Dave.

"There you are! I thought I was going to have to call the police. You took ages!" Mina shouts, looking a little more frazzled than I expected her to.

"I thought you ditched me," I say bitterly.

"No! Of course not. I went to grab Tommy a fresh bowl of water and some snacks from the car. Then the door jammed when it slammed shut–I wouldn't abandon you like that."

"Well, we're out now. Thanks for bringing me here. I don't know what they would've done to him if he was in there any longer."

"I think all three of you need to make a run for it, to be honest. My dad's not a very forgiving man. Once he finds out you rescued him from here, it's going to confirm his suspicion that something inappropriate is going on," Mina says.

"I think that ship sailed when he was informed we were meeting up in the dark outside his house. I have to face up to everything now. Don't worry, I'll still help you with your boyfriend," I say. I offer Dave a sip of water from the jug I grabbed from inside. At least they were keeping him hydrated in there. I suppose that means they wanted him to remain alive. This was probably all just to send me a message. I bet this was all so I can't screw up the act they want me to put on for the person bankrolling their lives – Deepa's grandfather.

"Thanks, Tara," Mina says.

We get Dave into the car, and I sit in the back with him; he falls into a deep sleep on my shoulder. I keep rubbing his arm to wake him a little to make sure he's okay. It feels so good to have him safe and close by. But I can't help but think about how everyone I care about seems to end up getting hurt.

We pull up to Rajin's place, and all three of us try to get Dave inside as quietly as possible. Once we get him into bed, Mina and I head home to sneak into our rooms as if nothing ever happened.

I comb out my hair and put it into a messy bun. I look myself in the mirror, I'm grateful my face is starting to look semi-normal again. My eyes aren't as sunken in, and the bruise on my cheek is starting to fade. I really examine myself for the first time since I arrived in this country. I'm not the same girl as when I first got here. I look and feel different, like all the struggles I've faced have hardened my heart and soul.

It's been a few days since we freed Dave. So far, no Gill family fury has rained down upon me. But today's the day everything comes out into the open. Deepa's father and grandfather had to stay a while in Delhi to tend to some business, so they'll be officially arriving today.

The real games will begin when I give Grandpa Big Bucks one heck of a first impression. I've devised a plan to put these twisted assholes in their place.

There's an all too-familiar rap on my bedroom door, Reema begins to speak through it in her fake singsong voice, "Tara dear, are you ready? Dad Ji is going to be here any moment."

I think that's the first time I've ever heard her refer to anyone using the formal address 'Ji'. She's excited, which is evident by the fact that she's nearly breaking the door down. She's probably expecting me to open it dressed in my best good girl outfit with my head covered.

I answer the door wearing my pajamas and a thin t-shirt.

Reema looks me up and down, grits her teeth and says, "Oh. You're not ready yet. Could you get dressed as soon as possible? He's going to be here any moment, and I don't want to give him the wrong impression."

"I'm too tired to get ready. In fact, I feel like meeting him just like this. I was up all night thinking about how I had to free a friend from captivity. He was being held somewhere by this crazy, money-hungry family. The mental and physical exhaustion of dealing with something like that is enough to keep me from getting out of bed at all today," I say, staring her dead in the face.

"Look, you little wench. If you think for a second that I'm going to sit idly by as you screw up everything I've worked so hard for, you have another thing coming. I don't care about your little affair. Deepa's father is the one who didn't want to risk you running off with him. We need you here to convince his wretched old father that you're the daughter-in-law of our dreams. Now get ready yourself or I'll have the staff make you get ready," she snarls, shooting me a deadly glare.

I take a big taunting step towards her. "I have nothing to lose. You have nothing to use against me. My *boyfriend* Dave is free. My mother has returned home. What are you going to do, old lady?"

"Don't test me," she says, narrowing her eyes to terrifying little slits.

From the look on her face I can tell she's *really* not going to take what I've planned very well. But I suppose that's the whole point.

I can't be bothered with this conversation anymore so I smile at her, and slam the door in her face. Ten minutes later, I hear some commotion, and

I assume the old man must be here now. It's show time.

I call Rajin to make sure Dave's doing all right. Rajin says he's fine, and he's going to drop him off at his place soon. Who knows what they did to the poor guy. Dave and I spoke briefly the other day, he repeated about a thousand times that he still wants to be with me – despite my protests. He has no clue who took him or even how long he was there for, but he said that it just makes him want to get me out of this hellhole even more.

I tell Rajin I have to go, and he asks me if I'm sure I don't want him waiting outside for me when shit hits the fan.

"Oh no, I got this," I say confidently.

CHAPTER SEVENTEEN

I can hear everyone chatting away downstairs. I prance down the steps in the teeny tiny jean shorts and a skimpy t-shirt I dug out of the back of Mina's closet. Everyone's jaw drops when I get to the front entrance where they're all gathered.

"Oh hey, *Gramps*! So nice to meet you!" I say, giving him a big ol' hug.

He looks like he's about in his mid-seventies. His distinguished white beard is combed to a perfect V. The folds of his navy blue turban are perfectly pleated and wound tightly on top of his head. He's wearing a brocade paisley patterned *kurta pajama*, accessorized with a diamond-topped golden cane. I guess they weren't exaggerating about his riches.

He pulls back and stares at me with his mouth hanging open. He looks as though he's about to faint. He turns to his son and says, "*This* is your daughter-in-law?"

"...Yes, this is Tara. Tara, take blessings from your grandfather," Deepa's father says through gritted teeth.

I dramatically bow to his feet and touch them with both hands. He reluctantly touches the top of my head.

I smile innocently, then pat the top of his turban, and say, "Why thank you for the blessing. Maybe my shitty ass life won't suck so bad now!"

Mina almost chokes on her water and bursts out laughing. Everyone else looks as pale as a ghost.

"Tara. Go get tea started," My mother-in-law says through tight lips. She looks as though she wants to yank me by the hair and have me thrown out right now.

Everyone gathers in the family room, and I hand each of them a half filled cup of tea with four times too much sugar in it. The old man can't stop staring in disgust at my bare legs. After a few brutally awkward moments of silence, he regains enough composure to start up a conversation with Deepa.

"How's business? Are you taking care of things around here now or still hiding in the shadows of your equally incompetent father?"

"Business is great Papaji. Everything is great!" Deepa says with the utmost feigned enthusiasm.

Damn, these people sure are desperate for that inheritance.

I interject before anyone else can speak, "Actually, you know what's really great, the fact that I didn't even know I was going to be married when I first got to India. Let alone that I was going to be married into a family like *this* one." Everyone stares at me with shocked expressions in response. "Isn't that just so funny grand-pops?" I add with a cackle.

His expression becomes even more grim. He looks at Deepa's parents suspiciously then asks me, "Didn't your mother tell you your marriage was arranged before you came here?"

"No. No one found it necessary to tell me I was going to be the beloved daughter-in-law of this home. It just kind of happened. And boy has it been interesting." I say, pursing my lips and glancing at Deepa's mother.

She looks like she wants to tear me from limb to limb with her bare hands.

"Why don't you let him at least get settled before you start all your nonsense?" Deepa's father snarls at me.

"Oh yes. Where are my manners? I'm so sorry Papaji! Have a seat right here." I pat the grand wooden dining room chair the servants set up for him. I lower my voice but still speak loud enough for everyone to hear, "I don't think this seat's taken. No hostages here today!"

He gives his son a stern look, and I can tell he's starting to figure out that things aren't as they seemed before.

During the next hour, I tell him about my friends back home and the escapades we used to get up to. The remaining colour left in his face faded just about as soon as I mentioned Dave. I swear I heard a collective gasp at the mention of his name.

"It's inappropriate for a married woman to have a male companion," Deepa's grandfather says, looking dismally disappointed.

He looks up at Reema who has sunk so low into her seat she looks like she's become a part of the furniture.

"Why haven't you taught her anything, Reema? What kind of household are you running? How is she meant to keep Deepa on track if she's a wreck herself?" He shakes his head and adds, "This is the bride you chose for my grandson?"

Reema just looks at the ground, but I can tell she's absolutely fuming. She knows I've spoiled her plans of being an insta-millionaire once the poor old fella croaks. Now he knows this is all a sham, and that I have no intention of fixing up their problem child.

"Well, I think I've heard quite enough for one day. I'm exhausted from my travels, I'll retire to my room now. It was…very interesting to meet you, Tara." He shakes my hand and walks out.

"What a prim and proper man he is," I say casually to the remaining Gills.

No one speaks. They must be reeling from the performance I just put on. I carry on chattering any way.

"His English is amazing. It must be all those years abroad. He has less of an accent than all of you!"

Deepa's father lunges at me but I dodge him, and he falls into a pillar. Deepa rushes to help him up, and once again Mina stifles her laughter. At least I managed to make one Gill happy today.

I walk into my room and start throwing all of my belongings into my suitcase as quickly as possible. Once their grandfather lets them know the jig is up, I'm sure they'll come after me. I need to get out of here quick. I use Deepa's phone and text Rajin to come wait for me up the street. It's time to get the hell out of here. I'll find some other way to get Rajin to Canada.

As I'm zipping up my last suitcase, Deepa walks in and slams the door shut behind him. "What's all this? You think you can just fuck everything up and bolt? Like we're all just going to bid you farewell?" he screams, while blocking the doorway.

"Well yes, I have no purpose to you now," I say, trying not to tremble.

"Do you even know who you're dealing with?" he says and reaches out to shake me vigorously.

"Deepa, you need help. Look at you! You clearly have some sort of mommy or daddy issues. You need to face your addiction head on. Money isn't going to make your problems go away," I say as I try to push past him.

He looks enraged, but surprisingly he doesn't come at me. He just looks me up and down, breathing heavily. There's a moment where he just stands there frozen, with a vein pulsing in his forehead. I'm sure he's going to snap and lose it on me, but then he just turns and walks out of the room without a word.

I need to get out of this place pronto. My legs shake, and I nearly collapse to the floor. Despite my firm voice, my insides quiver with dread. There's no telling what these people could do to me right now. I take a deep breath in, gather all the courage I have, and begin to wheel my suitcases towards the front door.

And then I hear it: two thunderous shots. They narrowly miss my head and hit the window behind me, shattering the glass into a million pieces. I turn to face Deepa who holds a shaking gun pointed right at my face.

"Deepa, calm down. You don't want to do this. You'll ruin your whole life. You'll have to go to jail." I try to reason with him as I scan the room, looking for a way out.

"You think you can just walk out on me?" he screams. His eyes are bloodshot and beads of sweat run down his face.

He waves his gun around in the air, laughing hysterically with his eyes closed. I walk slowly backward toward to the door, feeling for the handle.

"What's going on here?" Deepa's father demands. He stands at the top of the stairs, looking oddly vulnerable without his turban on.

Deepa's mother appears. "She's not worth it, son. Let the bitch go. We'll get her another way. Not like this," she says and tries to take the gun from him.

The guest room door opens, and Grandfather Gill comes out in his boxers and undershirt. "So this is what has become of all of you," he says. "Shame on you. Let the poor girl go. It's clear she's no wife or daughter to anyone in this place. You're keeping her here against her will." He looks completely disturbed at the state of his family.

Mina steps forward and shoves me toward the door as Deepa breaks down crying into his mother's arms.

"Now's your chance!" Mina whispers. "Get out of here, go!"

I ditch my bags and make a run for it, sprinting out the door. I keep running until I see Rajin's car. I hurl myself into it and shout, "Let's go! Drive!" He floors it, and just like that, I'm free.

CHAPTER EIGHTEEN

TWO YEARS LATER

"Hurry up! We're going to miss the train."

"But Tara, I don't want to go!"

"Zora, we've been over this. You have to go. It's your sister's dance recital. Don't you want to go show your support?"

"No. She doesn't care about anything I do, so why should I?"

"Oh come on! Dave's going to be waiting for us there. He promised to buy us ice cream! If we're there on time, I'll make sure you get two scoops."

"Okay! Race you to the door."

"Okay, buddy. Ready. Set. Let's go!"

It was my idea for Dave to join the *Big Brother Association*. I feel like it's made a huge difference in helping him cope with the loss of his brother.

I grab hold of Zora's hand as we hop on the underground train. As the rush of recycled air hits my face for the zillionth time, I think back to the first time I ever got on the British tube. I found it rather amusing how it was packed with people, but no one ever made eye contact or small talk with one another. It's such a contrast to Punjab or Vancouver.

"Hi love, thanks for grabbing Zora." Dave hugs me hello and hoists Zora onto his hip. We hold hands as we head inside the theatre.

"So, did you find out what time your friends are getting here?"

"Yes. They're arriving at 8:00 PM tonight. I just can't wait to see them! It feels like it's been a decade," I say, taking off my beige trench coat and closing my umbrella.

"Well, quite a bit has happened since then. Do you think they'll even recognize you with that hair?" he asks me, folding away a piece of newspaper into his briefcase.

"You know, I always joked around with them that I was going to go blonde. But I don't think they thought I'd actually do it, and especially not in order to remain incognito," I say as we take our seats in the back row of the theatre.

"You gotta do what you gotta do," Dave responds, and he tousles Zora's coiled head of hair.

My phone buzzes in my bag. I fish it out and look at the screen. It's a blocked number again. It's the fifth call this week. Every time I answer, no one responds. I wonder who keeps prank calling me.

"Who's that?" Dave peeks over my shoulder and sneakily kisses my ear.

"Oh just my editor, I'll call him back later" I lie and chuck my phone back into my oversized bag.

No need to worry him that the Gill's or their minions are after me. It's been two years since I escaped them. It's not like they're going to suddenly think I came back from the dead and know my whereabouts. I still can't believe how that all went down. I thought I was scot-free and that it was all over. But that evil family just couldn't let it go. They couldn't let *me* go.

A week went by with no word of them after I escaped that dreaded place. I was hiding out at my aunt and uncle's house. At first, they were infuriated that I'd ditch the marriage they'd arranged. But after letting them know I knew who my real father was, my uncle decided to let me stay. I told him how they treated me, and how Deepa tried to kill me. Thank my lucky stars, they actually cared.

Then came the men in hooded shawls into my room at night. They tried to drag me out and take me to God knows where. Luckily, my uncle foresaw something like that happening and hired around the clock security to stay just outside our home. They saved me and brought me back.

But incidents like that kept occurring. They kept coming for me, and I kept narrowly escaping. They told me if I didn't surrender, they'd come for everyone else too. No one would be safe for the embarrassment and everything else I'd cost them. They even threatened to have goons go after my mother in Canada.

So then, at last, I agreed to what Dave had planned for me all along. They wanted me gone. So, he made them think that's exactly what I was–dead and gone.

We faked it all pretty darn thoroughly. Right down to a staged fiery crash. All the gory details were published in the local Punjab newspaper with my name and picture splashed across the front page.

To our ultimate surprise, the women of the Gill household and their extended relatives all showed up at our house in mourning. They expressed their deepest condolences (to keep up appearances of course). Nobody else had caught whiff of Deepa's and my "separation" yet, so they all assumed I was visiting my uncle's home when *the accident* occurred. The house was flooded with people from near and far all mourning the loss of a foreign beauty who was but a young bride.

The Gill's told my uncle they appreciated him *"taking care"* of me in such a manner. They thought he had it all arranged. They were smugly pleased that it was done, and no blood was on their hands. They felt they'd received closure for the way I had played and betrayed them. Little did they know I was running off with the guy who pulled me out of the depressed slump they had thrown me in.

The clapping around me snaps me back to the present. The show is over, but I didn't even see the poor kid's performance. I was too busy lost in my thoughts about everything I've endured over the last few years.

As we walk back to the station, I think of how lucky I was to have met Dave when I did. Living with him in his two-bedroom apartment, overlooking London is a tweaked childhood dream come true. I've been holding up my end of the expenses with freelance writing jobs here and there.

He takes care of the majority of stuff for me, though. He says as long as I'm happy, he's happy. We've talked about getting married, but it just doesn't feel right yet. I always end up making some excuse to stall the process. As perfect as our fairytale life has been—evading the evil villains and all—I can't yet vow to commit to a life with him. I usually tell him it's because he needs to make amends with his family first. But he's so hesitant to do so. He says he's not ready to let them back into his life, let alone into *our* picture perfect world.

Things *have* been pretty perfect. A little *too* perfect and *too* easy if you ask me. Things with Dave have become extremely comfortable. I can't help but feel like I still have so much more of my life to live before I settle down. Every now and then memories of my past gnaw at me too. I miss my house, my friends, and even my mom. We speak every few weeks, but I've never had the nerve to bring up what I discovered about her in those last few weeks in India.

For safety reasons, I don't call my relatives in India much. They understand. They send me e-mails every now and then, and I send them picture and video updates of my life here. There's just one enormous distressing problem. I left all my things—including my journals—back in India. I often feel the urge to contact Mina via Facebook (while pretending to be my mother) and have her ship them to me, but I know that would be much too risky.

I snuggle into Dave on the tube ride back to our area. I gaze out the window and let out a dreamy sigh. What I've fallen most in love with in my new life is this country itself. I love the old buildings with so much history engrained into each brick. I love the carefree social culture of after work drinks. I love how there's no need for casual banter. Everyone here is direct and serious. Until it's time to let loose and have fun–then this is the best place to be.

Although our living space (like everything else in England) is extremely constricted, I wouldn't trade it for the world. I feel safe and secure in my little bubble with Dave. He makes me feel like the luckiest girl in the world.

As if he can read my thoughts, he pulls me in by the waist as we drop Zora and his sister off at home after our weekly outing.

"What are you thinking about beautiful?" he asks with a smile that makes his eyes crinkle–just the way Roger's used to.

Whenever he's an inch away from kissing me, my mind flashes to the only other person I've ever been this close to. Roger's the one person I completely lost contact with. After his false promises of being my knight in shining armour, I couldn't be bothered with him anymore. I realized that he's always let me down when the going gets tough.

I haven't even asked Serena whether he's with someone or not. He may even be with her. There's no need to reopen old wounds, though. I've been through far worse, which overshadows all of that any way.

After too much time had passed without hearing from me, Roop and Serena began harassing my mom day in and day out, asking when I was coming back. She filled them in on everything when they just wouldn't let up. I would've paid to see the looks on their faces.

We've kept up via e-mail and the occasional phone call, and I truly can't wait to be with them soon. They're the missing keys to my life having some sort of normalcy again. I'm hoping once they're here I'll be able to stop looking over my shoulder every second, wondering when the boogieman's coming for me next. They'll reassure me that all that is behind me now. Maybe then I'll be able to move on to the next chapter of my life–with Dave.

"So when should we head out to grab them?" Dave says, holding our front door open for me.

This is what I learned I love most about him–his ongoing quest to be respectful and chivalrous. It's almost like he's too perfect of a boyfriend.

"Well if you're tired from work, you can just hang out here while I go. I'll grab food on the way back," I offer.

"Oh, no need. You know that Chinese place you love near the firm, I got some take-out from there before the play. It's probably still warm, I left it in the oven," he says with a smile.

"This is why I love you. You're always thinking ahead. Especially about what matters most to me – food!" I say jokingly. I kiss him on the cheek and set the table.

It's our nightly ritual to get our meal ready first, then go out for a walk and have dinner later. We're not exactly party animals, so it helps make us feel like we actually leave this tiny place every so often.

If you really think about it, we're more like an old married couple. Our routine's pretty consistent, and we don't have much of a social life due to Dave's crazy busy work schedule. His first year as a lawyer has been very taxing on him, and a lot of the time he has to work late or leave super early, so I end up staying in and doing some reading and writing to pass the time.

"Okay, I'll wait for you guys, and we can all eat together once you're back. I can't wait to meet them. I'm actually a bit nervous too," Dave says as he uncorks a bottle of red wine.

"Oh, they're going to love you. Don't worry!" I say, grabbing two crystal wine glasses from the cabinet and handing them to him on autopilot.

We're so engrossed in our regular chatter about his work that I don't realize I'm late to pick them up. I grab the keys to his BMW and head downstairs to the garage. I don't typically drive his car alone since I'm still getting used to the whole opposite side of the road thing, but I know I'm going to enjoy going on the motorway today. I've been stuffed up at home for most of the day, with nothing but my thoughts to entertain me. It can get a bit suffocating and lonely at times. So a good long drive is exactly what I need. England's speed limits are the exact opposite of limiting; they're actually rather exhilarating.

I pull up to the arrivals section of the airport with a huge fleet of butterflies at war in my stomach. I'm so nervous and excited to see them that I think I might be sick. I spot them from a mile away. They run towards me while trying to keep their trolley under control. They're already attracting stares from the uptight Brits around them.

A group of businessmen in flashy, perfectly tailored suits pause their conversation to watch our reunion with stifled amusement.

My friends jump on me and give me a huge hug.

"Oh my goodness! Look at you, you European bombshell. Your hair looks amazing! And you're even skinnier than before, if that's even possible. You look *so* good," Roop says.

They both grab me again in a three-way bear hug. "We missed you *sooo* much, Tara. You have no idea what it was like without you," Serena says with a shaky voice.

We stand there hugging, and I can't hold back the tears. Seeing them makes me unravel. They both look so very different, with mature haircuts and perfectly applied makeup, yet they have the same youthful energy as before. I suppose I lost my light once I left home. I wonder if the feeling of being a carefree young adult will ever return.

"I can't believe you guys are really here," I say through tears.

"Here to stay toots – at least for a week, anyway. That's about as much time off work we could get. Now where's this British hottie of yours?" Roop says, looking past me.

"He's waiting for you guys at home with some takeout. I think he figured you'd enjoy some flavourful comfort food after all that bland airplane stuff," I say.

"Oh yes! Bring on the greasy food, and the tea and crumpets too! It's London baby!" Serena jumps up and down with excitement.

Oh man, I missed these guys. This is going to be a fun couple of days.

By the time we get in, Dave's fast asleep on the couch. He's surrounded by dozens of work documents scattered across the living room. The poor guy's been working so hard, all while keeping our relationship afloat. When we first got back, he was absolutely fixated on avenging his brother's death. Eventually, the guilt got the best of me, and I told him everything. It took a whole lot of persuasion to stop him from getting on the first flight back to India to go after my uncle and Deepa. But he eventually let it go, since that would jeopardize my safety. I suppose that's an easier pill to swallow rather than accepting that what's done is done, and there's nothing he can do about it.

"Holy shit! He's so freakin' hot!" Roop whispers to me as we tip toe past him.

"I know right? He's pretty darn gorgeous. Hey Serena, don't get any ideas," I say, nudging her playfully. An awkward silence fills the air, and neither of them says a word in response.

Once we get into the guestroom, I figure I may as well address our unresolved issues. "Hey, about everything that happened between you and Roger, I just want to say I'm over it. It was such a long time ago, it's water under the bridge now," I say and smile reassuringly at Serena.

Her eyes brim with tears, and she says, "I never brought it up because I didn't have the right words to apologize. I guess there are no words that can make up for what I did."

"No. There aren't. But that's why it's better to just leave it behind us and never speak of it again," I say.

"I agree," she says and pulls me in for a hug.

"So, how is Roger anyway?" I ask trying not to sound too interested.

Serena rummages through the front pocket of her Louis Vuitton suitcase and pulls out an envelope with my name on it. I recognize Roger's handwriting straight away.

"Here you go. This will tell you how he is."

"A letter? What could he possibly have to say to me now? He left me high and dry after I told him what I was going through in India," I say and shudder at the memory.

"Just read it, Tara. There's a lot you two need to discuss…when you're ready of course," Roop says.

I take the envelope from Serena and trace my fingers over the writing. I feel strangely nervous to know what's inside. I'm itching to ask Serena if they're together. Maybe they're engaged, or even married. But I don't, because I probably won't be able to handle it if they are.

"All right guys, I'll let you get some rest now. We've got a jam-packed day of sightseeing tomorrow! Roop, I'm sure you've done some research about every place you want to visit. Am I right?" I say while refolding the towels I'd set out for them on the dresser.

"You know me so well, Tara." Roop grins at me.

"Of course. You two are like my sisters. Goodnight guys." I walk out of the room and hide the letter in my sweatshirt. Even feeling excited about reading it makes me feel like I'm doing wrong by Dave. He knows all about my history with Roger, and despite the fact he's the complete opposite of the jealous and possessive type, I don't think he'd be too pleased about him reaching out to me like this.

Each time I go to open the letter, I just can't. I get a flashback to the last conversation we had. He pretended to be so worried about me and then that was it. I never heard from him again. I think back even further and remember the sting of learning the truth about him and Serena. I don't want to go back to that place again. So, I leave the letter sealed shut. It's best I don't go there yet. I just don't feel ready.

CHAPTER NINETEEN

We're all chatting away as we begin our full day of fun we have planned in downtown London. Per Roop's itinerary, we're going to the London Eye first. It's essentially a huge Ferris wheel with cubicles from which you can see the entire dazzling city.

"Whoa. Watch it, buddy!" Serena snaps at a guy who bumped into her as we're stepping on to the tube.

"Oh no. I should've warned you about pickpockets. You've got to watch your stuff here, girls," Dave warns. Serena frantically confirms that all of the contents of her purse are still there.

"I don't think he got anything that quick, Serena," Roop reassures her.

"I thought he was just trying to cop a feel," Serena says.

"Well, yes…that may have been it too." Dave stifles his laughter.

He's not used to Serena's upfront, open character yet.

"Okay guys, it's a long walk from here. You sure you don't want to catch a cab?" I ask them. They're both a little wobbly in their brand new matching heels.

"Yes! We're here to see the sights, aren't we? May as well soak in as much as we can on the way there," Roop says, bouncing up and down.

Today seems like an extra special day here in London. There's an exhilarating buzz in the air. There are countless rows of street performers, ranging from men performing cheap magic tricks to acrobats doing dangerous fire throwing stunts. Hundreds of foreigners and locals wander the alley-ways. The smell of fresh pizza from a parlour around the corner, mixed with the scent of the crisp air and lightly drizzling rain draws me in and makes me feel right at home.

I've lived here for two years, but I haven't truly experienced this place yet. It has its own subdued yet deeply historical vibe. An exciting maturity exists in this monochrome but lively place.

I reach into my bag and feel for Roger's letter. I still haven't opened it. I didn't want to risk leaving it lying around, so I kept it on me. It's strangely reassuring to hold something that he recently touched.

When we finally arrive at the entrance to the London Eye, we all stop and admire it with awe.

"Wow. It's *huge*," Roop says, staring up at it with wide eyes and her hands on her hips.

"I didn't expect for it to go so high. I thought you said it's like a Ferris wheel Roop. I ain't getting on that thing," Serena says, taking a step back.

Dave links arms with the two of them and says, "Ladies, there's no backing out now. You've come all this way for a royal London experience. Now that's what you'll get."

He winks at me, and I can't help but grin as I look at the three of them. What a great catch Dave is. I'm *so* lucky to have him. And I'm so very stupid for allowing Roger to mess with my head just because he sent me some stupid letter. I'm going to throw it out when I get home. Nothing he says can make up for him not being there for me when I needed him most.

"Tara love, hurry! The queue is getting super long. Let's squeeze in quick," Dave calls after me.

"Coming!" I shout back as I jog to catch up with them.

I decide that I'm going to enjoy today and stop thinking so damn much. Today's about being with my friends, and feeling like myself again with no drama – I just have to get Roger and his letter out of my head.

We spend the rest of the day popping into random bars, watching Serena work her charm on the locals. They love her accent, and she loves theirs. She's decided that she's going to move here just for the edgy British guys. I guess that confirms that she and Roger are no longer an item.

Damn it, there I go again letting him dominate my thoughts.

The drizzle turns into a classic London torrential downpour, and we all run to huddle under the nearest canopy. It hangs over a cobblestone door, which leads to a nearly hidden restaurant. We're all shivering, and I button my coat up and draw my hood over my head; I've caught one too many colds courtesy of the ever-lovely British weather since I've moved here.

"Sorry girls, it's really starting to come down now. I should've known better than to bring you guys out for a day in London with no umbrellas," Dave says apologetically, wrapping his jacket around my shoulders.

"You know what Dave…you've been a wonderful tour guide. I would've never thought this city would have so much life and excitement packed into it!" Roop says.

Judging by her ear-to-ear grin and the way her curls are bouncing all over the place, it's clear she's buzzing from her last few shots at the bar.

"Should we head back now?" I ask while trying to shield my face from the wind.

"Hey, why don't we check this place out? It looks kind of cool." Serena points to the medieval looking place we're huddled in front of.

My feet ache and I'm soaked to the bone but I begrudgingly agree, and we head in. The restaurant's entryway looks more like the opening to a dark and dreary cave. Flickering candles line the wall of the entire pathway, which opens to a narrow stairwell that must lead to an underground restaurant.

"Welcome, ladies, and gentleman." A stunningly beautiful waitress with a blonde slicked back pixie cut and a septum piercing greets us. She's eyeing Dave up and down so I step up and grab his hand. It's odd that she wouldn't assume he's *with* one of us. Or perhaps she doesn't care because she knows she's prettier than all three of us combined. Not to mention the crucially sexy edge her British accent gives her.

She bats her eyelashes at him and says, "Table for four?"

He smiles politely and puts his arm around my waist and says, "Yes please...my girl and her friends wanted to pop in for a drink."

"How lovely," she says. She continues to smile at him and snub the rest of us.

He clears his throat and shifts his weight. He's probably noticed that this exchange is a little inappropriate. I realized some time ago that girls here have no problem very obviously checking out another girl's man.

I always feel a little self-conscious while out and about with Dave. My last brutal encounter with my psychopath husband from hell left me with a faint scar on the right side of my face. I'm sure people are wondering what a perfect guy like Dave is doing with a damaged-looking girl like me.

As if he can read my thoughts he whispers how beautiful I look and places his hand on the small of my back, guiding me through the dimly lit hallway. There was a time when his subtle touches would send a shiver up my spine, but lately, I've just been feeling extra coddled by him in public. It's like he's always got his guard up, like memories of the past haunt him just as much as they haunt me.

"This place is like out of a movie! Or an old time story book. It's strangely eerie but cool," Roop exclaims.

"Well I don't know about you three, but I'm going to get very wine drunk off far too many bottles from this fancy list," Serena says giddily as she glances over the menu.

"You know, I think I've heard about this place," Dave says. "I'm pretty sure it used to be a torture chamber way back when. They left most of the building structure as is, to create this ancient wine-bar feel. It's spooky to think about all the screams embedded into each stone of this place, huh girls?"

Roop and Serena's mouths hang open and their mood goes from peppy and cheerful to somber and serious as they soak in the atmosphere of this intensely creepy but alluring place.

"Hey guys, where's the bathroom?" I ask, realizing I haven't checked my reflection for a couple of hours.

The results could be catastrophic as the London air usually turns my overly fried and dyed hair into a complete frizz ball in about twenty minutes.

"I think it's in the basement. I saw a sign pointed that way," Roop says. "You want me to come?"

"Nah. I'm good. I'll be back in a sec."

I slide out of the booth, grab my bag, and head down the tiny stone steps.

"This place really does look like a dungeon," I say to myself as I shudder and brush away a few cobwebs in my way. It seems like it's getting even darker as I travel further below ground. I notice the cracks on the wall, and I'm instantly hit with a flashback to when I rescued Dave from captivity back in India. I suddenly feel like I don't need to go to the bathroom quite *that* badly anymore.

I try telling myself to get a grip and keep walk-ing, but there's no sign of the bathroom, so I turn back around. On my way up I notice a corridor, which seems to lead to a wine cellar. I poke my head in there then jump when my phone begins to buzz.

I shake my head at myself for being such a scaredy-cat and then pull my phone out to check my messages.

PRIVATE NUMBER: *we're always watching. we know you're not dead, but you will be soon.*

What the fuck?

I run back up the stairs, and a door slams shut behind me. I miss a step and trip, falling to the ground and cracking my phone screen.

I text them back, despite my desire to simply throw my phone down the stairs and leave it in this cavern forever.

TARA: *WHO THE HELL IS THIS? HOW DID YOU GET MY NUMBER?*

I begin to quickly walk back to the table.

"We need to leave *right now*," I say in a panic. I use the napkin to wipe away my tears and swat the dust off of me.

"What's wrong? What happened?" Dave stands up and grabs my hand.

"Come on, guys. I'll explain everything once we get home," I say as I put my jacket on.

Dave throws some money down on the table, and Roop and Serena rush out after us.

"Can you please slow down and tell us what happened?" Roop says.

"Yeah, you're acting like you saw a ghost or something, Tara," Serena says as she struggles to keep up with our fast paced jog back to the tube.

I look at Dave and shakily say, "They're here... they know I'm alive, and they're here."

CHAPTER TWENTY

"I suppose that's the end of our sightseeing." I overhear Serena saying to Roop in their bedroom the next morning.

My eyes are bloodshot, and I feel absolutely exhausted. I spent the entire night trying to get a hold of Rajin. Each time I called, the number didn't go through.

Dave was up all night with me too. He kept reassuring me that he wouldn't let anything bad happen. But if they were able to get my number, and they know I'm alive, then clearly they have a way to get to me.

The phone finally connects when I try an old number of my uncle's that my mom begrudgingly gave me. I called her last night, frantically asking for any sort of contact information she might have. Not only was she annoyed that I'd even ask, but she also sounded very unwell.

"Rajin? It's Tara. I've been trying to reach you for ages," I say, breathing heavily with anticipation into the phone.

"...Oh hey, Tara. How are you?" he asks in a completely offbeat way.

"Why do you sound so weird?"

"What do you mean? It's not safe for you to be calling me. I'm just surprised to hear from you."

"Rajin, they know I'm alive. Do you know how? Have they said anything to you guys? Did you tell them anything?"

"Just get out of England Tara. You need to get out of that place as soon as possible," he says with a quivering voice.

"What?! How did they find out?" I shout.

"We don't know. But you need to go. Okay? Do you understand? We're claiming we didn't know you were alive. That's why it's better if we just don't speak, okay?" he says.

"Rajin I risked *everything* for you. I'm in this situation because I was trying to save *you*...and you couldn't even warn me?" I ask him. I'm shocked by his sudden change in demeanour.

"I'm leaving for Canada in a few weeks. They offered me a visa if I told them what really happened to you. But I'm not the one who blew your cover. They must have found out it was all a lie somehow," he says sounding a little more apologetic.

"So you're free, and now I have to look over my shoulder for the rest of my life? You sold me out Rajin," I say. Tears well up in my eyes.

"I did what I needed to do. They kept coming at us Tara. It all got too much. You left and went on to live your life freely. But we were stuck here to deal with the aftermath. I'm warning you now. Just leave as soon as you can. Forget Dave and your whole life there. You must go before they turn your fake demise into reality."

I hang up the phone and chuck it across the room. There's no point listening to any more of his crap. I just can't believe him! I guess that's what having an easy exit strategy does to people. He saw his chance and took it.

I walk out of my bedroom and just watch Dave for a while. He's silently staring out our living room window with a furrowed brow. He looks downright exhausted and stressed out. I'm only weighing him down with all this shit; I have been since the moment we met. I don't want to be a burden anymore. It's time for me to finally go home.

Roop pokes her head in through the door and asks, "Hey Tara? Can we talk to you for a second?"

"Yeah, sure. What's going on?" I say, trying to mask the mixture of fury and fear in my voice.

"Could you come over here? We need to tell you something," Serena calls from the other room.

I walk into the spare bedroom, and they both gather nervously in front of me.

"What's up?"

"Your mom told us not to tell you. But she really hasn't been doing well. We want you to come back with us and be with her. She's been in and out of the hospital because of terrible dizzy spells and major anxiety. She's not even working right now," Roop says.

"Why didn't you guys tell me before?" I say, beginning to feel shaky from all the crap going on.

"You just seemed so happy here. We didn't want to ruin that for you. But now I don't think it'd be such a bad thing for you to get out of here for a bit," Serena says.

"When will this ever end?" I whisper.

Roop hugs me tightly. "It'll be okay Tara. Just come home. We'll make sure you're okay there."

My head reels from everything going on. I walk out of the room to go check flight times and let Dave know about my decision. I shut the door and pause, leaning against it and trying to catch my breath. There's that feeling of having the wind kicked out of me again. I knew my life couldn't remain simple for long.

When I sit down in front of Dave and take his hands in mine, I realize that there's a possibility of him getting roped into all of this again. What if they come after him to get to me? The thought of something happening to him again, all because of me, sends a shiver up my spine. I guess we have no other choice, though. I must get out of here as soon as possible. The more distance between us, the safer he'll be.

We're all gathered in the living room with the television on. None of us are even watching the cheesy British comedy Dave switched on in an attempt to cheer us up.

"How long could they really stay in England for? Who knows if they're actually here anyway?" Serena asks, breaking the gloomy silence in the room.

"Yeah, Tara. Just come visit home for a couple weeks. Wait it out. Then come back and carry on with your life here as normal!" Roop says, trying to put a positive spin on all of this.

"Are we just supposed to stay holed up here until we leave?" I say, letting out a sigh.

Dave sits between us on the couch. He puts his arms around our shoulders and says, "You girls don't need to be afraid. We're going to stick to Roop's itinerary and explore every crevice of London. Do you guys really think I'd let anything happen to any of you?" Dave says with a reassuring smile.

He doesn't get a response from us, so he jumps up and throws some of his lame jazz music on.

"Get ready girls, we're going out! Enough is enough. I bet you they're just empty threats coming from thousands of miles away. We can't let them scare us. Dinner and drinks are on me, get your arses up!"

Dave always becomes a bit more British whenever he's trying to be authoritative. I can't help but smile at his attempt to salvage whatever's left of Roop and Serena's butchered trip.

I know he doesn't truly believe that I'm not in danger. But he probably feels confident in his ability to keep us safe until we leave. Although, I highly doubt he'd be saying this if he knew that Rajin confirmed that the Gills *are* indeed coming after me.

We shuffle into our rooms to change our clothes and make ourselves look presentable, despite our sour moods. Serena and I take ages straightening our waist-length hair, while Roop leaves her shoulder length curls bouncy and free as ever.

The three of us look like doe-eyed dolls after Serena's done with our makeup. She always had a way of accentuating our features and making us look like the Instagram models we used to obsess over when we were younger. We pause to examine ourselves in my bedroom mirror before heading out.

Dave whistles and asks if he needs to put out the fire from the "smoke show." I roll my eyes and laugh at him, but secretly I'm happy that he's being so positive. It can't be easy since he's probably anxious about what's going to happen to "us" once I leave.

"We may as well look like we're ready for a fun night even if we don't feel like it," Roop says and links arms with Serena and me.

Before we leave, Dave takes a picture of the three of us. We all force smiles on his command. I think back to the last time the three of us were dressed to the nines and ready for a night out. Circumstances certainly have changed since our carefree road trip to good ol' Whistler.

"Alright loves, let's have a great night and forget all this bollocks. What do you say?" He says and hands me my beige trench coat, the one reserved for rare but special nights out.

The three of us exchange an amused look amongst ourselves at his cute attempt to cheer us up.

"Thanks, honey. We needed this." I kiss him on the cheek, and we walk out, locking up behind us.

There's a club on the floor below us blaring UK's top underground hits, but we've been quite content drinking ourselves silly here. The weather's been good to us so far. The air is surprisingly warm, or maybe it's just the alcohol in our system keeping us from shivering our butts off. The place is packed with a variety of people ranging from freshly legal teenagers to sophisticated looking business people. But there's one thing everyone has in common: we're all here for a good time.

After ordering one too many fruity shots at the most popular rooftop bar in downtown London, we find ourselves reminiscing and letting Dave in on the escapades of our younger years. He's our "DD" of the night, and protector from any psycho stalkers who might be lurking around the corner. I sit back for a moment in our cozy booth and simply enjoy my surroundings without allowing any fears or worries seep into my mind. It's so wonderful to see my three closest friends from two completely different times in my life come together and enjoy themselves.

Dave pulls me on to the dance floor even though it's empty. He draws me in close, tucks my hair behind my ears and kisses me on the tip of my nose. I smile at him and feel a huge wave of gratitude for a man who truly saved me from a doomed fate. Regardless of the fact that our future together is so up in the air right now, I'll never forget just how much he's done for me.

"What're you thinking about, babe?" He whispers into my ear and twirls me around, making my navy blue cocktail dress flare out as I spin.

"Oh, nothing. Just about how great you've been to me."

We stop moving, and he stares deeply into my eyes and says, "I'll always be here for you Tara. No matter what comes our way, I'll always be here to take care of you."

I smile, but for once, the feeling of being someone who needs taking care of doesn't sit well with me. I don't know how to express to him that I feel like I'd do just fine on my own.

Before I can say anything, he points at our table with the most bewildered expression on his face. I look up to see Serena table dancing dangerously close to the edge of the patio. The staff try to coax her to get down, but she just keeps screaming, "It's London, baby!"

Roop looks like she's going to crawl under the table any second, so we head over, laughing hysterically.

"Sorry about our friend here. She's just hoping her carefree nature could rub off on some of us." Dave offers an apology to an extremely annoyed security guard. He looks just about ready to give Serena a shove over the edge himself.

I grab her hand and yank her down; she comes tumbling down on to the floor and nearly snaps her heel in half. She gets up and tries to casually slide back into the booth, but it's clear she's hurt her knee.

"Oh man! Remember that time Tara nearly fell out of the window of our high school when we were trying to spray paint it for our senior prank? Luckily Roger saved her ass," Serena exclaims. She slaps her injured knee, then howls with pain.

Surprisingly, I think I notice a faint hint of jealousy on Dave's face at the mention of Roger's name.

"He was so scared to get caught! But he'd do anything for Miss Tara here," Roop says with a smile.

"Yeah, tell me about it. Like, travel to the other side of the world only to go right back the next day." Serena carries on while scooping the ice out of her drink and rubbing it over her knee.

Roop gives her a huge kick under the table.

"Ow! What was that for?" she says, rubbing her other knee now.

"What did you just say? When did he travel across the world for me? What are you talking about?" I ask, suddenly feeling rather sober.

Dave excuses himself, chucks his napkin on the table, and heads to the bar.

"Oops," Serena says, looking down at her plate of fancy cheese and crackers.

"Great job, Serena. You weren't supposed to bring that up. The *one thing* I told you not to tell her and you let it slip the moment you get a few drinks in you," Roop says glaring at her.

"Tell me what you guys are talking about right now. Did Roger come to India?" I say, feeling a rush of emotions that throw me into a whirlwind of anxiety.

"Yeah, he did. He went there as soon as you called him and let him know what happened. Then he saw you in the car with Dave by some coffee shop and assumed that you were okay. He thought you were just saying all that other stuff to piss him off and get back at him for the Serena thing. He saw how happy you were and didn't want to bother you. So he left the very next day."

"He came for me," I say with complete shock and an extreme sense of nostalgia.

Dave slides back in to our booth, tight-lipped and visibly annoyed, so we all shut up.

He clears his throat and says, "So girls, another round?"

"Oh yeah, that's a great idea!" Serena says nearly knocking over her glass of water.

"I think you've had quite enough Serena," Roop says.

"Yeah, perhaps it's time to call it a night," I say. I suddenly wish I hadn't thrown that letter away.

After a busy couple of days of endless wandering, shopping, and even more bar-hopping; today's the day of our flight back home to Canada. I can hear Roop shuffling around in the kitchen at the crack of dawn. She's probably trying to whip up some fancy breakfast for us to enjoy before we head out. I lift Dave's heavy arm from around my waist as gently as I can without waking him.

Just as I'm about to get out of bed, he mumbles, "I can't believe I'll be waking up without you tomorrow." Then he pulls me back down and tugs the covers back over us.

"We still have time before your flight, let's just forget you're leaving and enjoy ourselves," he says, pushing himself right up behind me and kissing my neck.

I know where he's going with this, but I don't feel right getting close to him when my mind's filled with thoughts of Roger. I reach out and touch his face, studying every inch of it. He has this natural manliness to him and a charm that never comes across as forced or insincere. He owns his wit and good looks without being cocky about it. That's rare for a guy who seemingly has it all.

When we first arrived in London, we couldn't keep our hands off each other. Every moment we spent together felt like a romantic movie scene. He had successfully rescued me from the "bad guys," and we were shacked up in his cozy apartment overlooking the city. But after a while, when there's no fights to make up from, or fear of losing one another, or *any* sort of passion – things become complacently dull, just plain *boring*.

Being with Dave is comfortable and safe. It feels too simple. About a year into our time here I began to yearn for adventure. I needed a crushing and all-consuming love. I wanted to remember and feel the intensity that comes from being with someone who pulls the best out in you. Not just someone who covers up the bad and makes everything just... okay.

I take his arm off from around me, sit up and say, "It's just for a little while, then I'll be back. At least this way you won't get sick of me." I hop out of bed and wrap my robe tightly around my silk nightie.

"I could never get sick of you. I feel homesick thinking about you being gone," he says, yawning and stretching his perfectly toned body.

"You can't be homesick for people, silly! I'm the one leaving, not you." I'm beginning to feel a little suffocated by his clinginess.

"You can when somebody is your home. I'd follow you anywhere, you know that?"

"Then follow me to Canada," I say even though I don't mean it.

"I think I might have to if Roger's waiting around for you there."

"Oh come on. Don't start with that. I haven't even talked to the guy for two years. There's nothing for you to worry about," I say, grabbing a fresh towel from the closet.

"When I know how amazing my girl is, I've got to worry. He's going to realize what he threw away like a dumb little kid, and he's going to want you back. You know it too."

"Well, it doesn't matter. I'm committed to you, even if I am half way across the world," I reassure him.

I say exactly what I know Dave wants to hear, but deep down I'm not sure if it's true. After learning the truth about how things really went down with Roger, I have all these strange conflicting thoughts in my head. I thought he had left me stranded. Now, all I see is this image of him standing there, completely gutted watching me flirt my ass off with this new dude I'd just met. Laughing and talking away, without a care in the world, as if everything I'd told him on the phone was a complete lie.

There's a knock on the door, and I already know it's Roop becoming nervous about being late – five hours before departure.

"Yes, Roop! I'm about to jump in the shower. Don't worry, we won't be late."

"Okay. Just making sure! Give me your passport and tickets I'll keep all three sets together in my bag." she says through the door.

"Are you kidding me?! I'm not a child, Roop. I can take care of my own stuff! Jeez, relax woman," I say with a laugh.

I hear her walk off, and I know it's going to eat away at her that she can't have things perfectly organized and ready to go in her own way. She'd probably charge in here herself and get me dressed and out the door if she could.

"Just stay. No one's going to get to you while you're with me. And once I get some time off I'll take you to see your mom myself," Dave says as he pulls on a clean pair of his tight boxer shorts over his huge muscular thighs.

"It's your first year as a lawyer at one of the top firms in London. You're not getting time off anytime soon, hon," I say, tousling his hair like he usually does to Zora.

Before I close the bathroom door, I see him glance at me with a quizzical and then sad expression.

"The sooner you let me go, the sooner I'll be back," I call out to him while stepping into the shower.

He comes into the bathroom and sits at the edge of our tub but doesn't say a word.

"What is it?"

"I should've made you my wife the moment we landed here. I want this to be our forever. Just me and you...alone in our own little world."

The *old* Tara would've jumped for joy upon hearing something like that. Now the thought of being eternally hitched to Dave makes my stomach feel like it has a huge tangle of weeds in it.

After some chaotic packing, a couple of cold showers (courtesy of Serena using up all the hot water), and a rushed breakfast, we all gather by the front door to head to the airport.

A picture of Dave and I smiling happily catches my eye. I think back to that time and how exciting it was to begin our lives together. We didn't have anything or anyone else to worry about. It was nice living in a secluded, carefree existence for a while, but reality always comes back with a vengeance.

"I knew you were going to make us late Serena! How did you manage to have so much more stuff to take back than you came here with?" Roop's high-pitched panicky voice snaps me out of my thoughts.

"It's called shopping, Roop! The fashion here is like ten years ahead of ours. Don't you know anything?" Serena says as she struggles to drag her suitcases out the door.

"I'll get you there on time, Roop. Don't worry love," Dave says with a wink.

With a lump in my throat and a small voice hinting that this might be the last I'll see of this place, I glance around my tiny sanctuary for the past two years one more time. Then I shut the door on this chapter of my life and lock it forever.

Dave buzzes up the motorway at the customary British lightning speed of travel, and we're outside the airport within literally half an hour – an extremely impressive amount of time to get anywhere in England.

Quite pleased with the half hour to spare Serena says, "See Roop, there was no need to get your granny panties in a twist. We've even got a few minutes to spare to check out the duty free!"

Roop shoves Serena playfully and rolls her eyes. I stretch out in the front seat trying to feel for my passport and tickets in my jacket pocket. There's just one problem – they're not there.

"Uh guys, we have a slight problem here," I say nervously.

"What is it, babe?" Dave asks while paying for parking.

"I may have left my passport and tickets in a very secure location…back at the apartment."

"Are you kidding me?" Roop shouts at me with her eyes bulging out of her head.

"Don't worry Tara, we have some time to spare. We'll just pop back home and grab it," Dave says reassuringly.

"Well, I don't know my way around this giant airport, we're going to get lost just looking for our terminal!" Roop says.

"How about this, you take them to the gate and wait for me. I'll take your car and quickly go grab my stuff. I'll be right back," I say, already grabbing the keys from his hands.

"You sure? I can get you there quicker," he calls after me, but I'm already halfway to the exit.

Roop calls after me, "Don't speed Tara!"

"I'll be right back! Don't worry," I call back over my shoulder, rushing back to the car park as fast as I can.

I pick up my pace a little, realizing I'm going to be cutting it super close with this. I hop into the car and drive just about as fast as I can. It's taking some extra concentration to remember to stay on the correct side of the road as I'm in such a panic.

Gosh, I'm such an idiot! I should've just given Roop my things, I think to myself as I take the exit back to Dave's place.

I pull up to the building and I'm in and out within minutes. I check my watch and realize I'm still pretty okay for time. I can still make my flight if there's no traffic on the way back.

Just as I reach for the car door, I feel a hard thud on the back of my head. I fall face first onto the hard concrete road, and everything fades to black.

"Got you, you lying little bitch."

CHAPTER TWENTY-ONE

I turn onto my back, feeling unbelievably hazy and I try to reach for my phone. I look up and then I see who's hovering over me. Deepa and his equally smug looking mother watch me struggle to get up.

"You were right after all; the little bitch is alive." His mother looks down on me with disgust and kicks my phone out of reach.

Before I can consciously process what's going on, I intuitively reach back to feel the throbbing bump on my head. Then I feel a trickle of blood going down my neck.

I begin to hyperventilate and look for any way out of this situation, but they have me cornered.

"Yes, she's alive. But not for long," Deepa snarls down at me.

"Get up," he demands, delivering a swift blow to my side with his pointed leather shoe.

My body shakes like a withered old leaf. I can't believe this is really happening. It's a nightmare come to life. I blurt out whatever I can in hopes of receiving some mercy.

"I don't know what you want to do with me, but just know that this isn't going to solve anything. You're not going to get your money from your grandfather this way. You're not going to feel better about yourself this way either. What I did was wrong. I know that. But you left me no choice," I say, rising shakily to my feet and frantically looking for a way to get the fuck away from these people.

"Just shut up and get in the damn car," Reema barks at me, gesturing to a black sedan parked behind me.

"We can still make that return flight, mom. We'll just book her an extra ticket. Oh how convenient, she's got her passport on her," Deepa says as he shakes out the contents of my purse onto the front seat of the car.

"We have to take the subway. We can't take the car, it was due back at the rental place an hour ago," Reema says.

I try to collect my thoughts and think rationally. Okay, they're dumb enough to take me to a public place. I'll get away from them at the tube. I'll cause a scene and break free.

"Why don't you just kill me here? Why do you need to take me all the way back to India?" I ask with feigned bravado.

"So your uncle can see what our family is capable of. They betrayed the wrong people. Plus, what happens in India stays in India. We don't want to bother with what'll happen when the British authorities discover your body," Deepa says without a morsel of empathy in his voice.

I swallow hard, and suddenly I feel extremely faint from hearing the way he so casually describes their plot to kill me. No matter how terrified I am I have to get away from them. I absolutely *cannot* get on a plane with these people, or that'll be it for me. I must distract them. I must show them I'm not afraid.

They push me into the back of the car and tie some rope around my hands so I don't try to jump out.

They seem to be driving to the tube station, but I can't be sure, as my eyes aren't focusing quite right after that hit to my head.

"How did you find me?" I say looking directly at Deepa. He's been avoiding making eye contact with me.

"It wasn't hard. You signed off on all your little newspaper articles with your real name. Somebody posted one of your pieces titled, '*The Holy Un-sanctity of an Indian Marriage*' online. Mother caught Mina reading it. She tried to deny it was you, but we knew she was trying to cover for you."

My heart feels like it's going to burst through my chest as the car slows; for all I know they might be taking me to where I'll be sent to meet my maker. Maybe they're just pretending they're taking me back to India, so I don't start freaking out beyond belief.

"I'll drop you two at the side of the station. Wait for me there while I go drop this shitmobile off," Deepa says.

"Okay. What about the ties around her hands? You have to take them off, or it'll attract too much attention," Reema says, as if this is perfectly casual banter to be having with your son on a Tuesday afternoon.

He grabs a pocketknife and crawls into the back seat from the front. He presses the blade of the knife against my cheek, and I begin to sob profusely.

He pushes his disgustingly chapped lips right against my ear and whispers, "I should've fucked you in that field when I had the chance." I begin to cry out for help and kick my legs against the back of the front seat. He holds my legs down as he cuts the ties off from around my wrists. Then he squeezes his hands around my throat and says, "Don't fuck around. Or I *will* kill you."

I tremble uncontrollably. I can't believe this is happening. I was almost away from all of this and on my way home. Now I'm going to die just because I forgot my things.

"Get out the damn car, you stupid girl!" Reema pulls me out roughly by my arm.

We draw some attention from passersby, but no one stops to ask if I'm okay. *Why can't someone just stop and ask if I'm okay?*

Reema digs her claws into my arm and makes me walk toward the stairwell leading to the trains. She hands me a tissue and tells me to get a hold of myself.

"There's no need for the theatrics. Nothing's happening to you right now, now is it?" She asks in the most detached manner a woman could muster.

"You're taking me somewhere to have me killed. How do you expect me to react?" I say while trying to catch someone's attention enough to let them know I need help.

Dave and the girls must be thinking something terrible has happened to me. This is even worse than crashing on the motorway. I would've rather actually died in a fiery crash, than be in this situation with these twisted fucks.

Just as I lose all hope and contemplate throwing myself in front of the next moving train, I spot him. At first, I think I'm hallucinating. I blink real hard and realize that it really is him.

Roger stands on the other side of the platform, waiting for the train going the opposite direction.

Please just look up. Look up Roger. I'm right here. I don't know why you're here, but I need you to see me right now.

He doesn't look up. A train is about to pull up and block my view of him. I have to do this. It's now or never. No matter what happens to me because of it.

I call out to him as loudly as I can over the sound of the incoming train. "Roger! It's Tara! I need your help...they're after me again!" Just as I'm shouting, the train breezes by us and comes to an abrupt stop.

Reema begins shouting, "You dumb slut! How many men are you with? We watched and waited for that big fool of yours to leave the apartment for days, and now you're trying to get someone else to come save you!" She yanks me back towards the stairwell. I dig my nails into her arm and desperately try to break free from her grip.

Deepa charges down the steps. "What's going on here? Didn't you understand us? The more you fight this, the sooner you die. You get it, Tara?"

"I don't care! Kill me right now! Throw me in front of the train! I'm not going anywhere with you sick people," I scream, frantically trying to loosen their grip on me.

I finally break away and Deepa chases after me. He tries to grab me, but I trip going up the stairs and smack my head against the railing.

"Get the fuck away from her. Take one more step, and I swear I'll kill you with my bare hands."

I look up to see Roger standing there, holding Deepa's wrist. He looks absolutely furious.

Deepa backs off and says, "Of course. The whore has two men watching after her."

Roger stands an inch away from his face, "What did you just call her? So it *was* all true. Are you the one who hurt her? You must be the asshole who tried to ruin her life!"

Roger shoves Deepa back toward the flyer-covered tile walls, and people begin to gather around us to see what all the commotion is about.

I catch Roger's gaze; his eyes are filled with a rage I didn't even know he was capable of. I begin to weep uncontrollably and fall back down to the steps, clasping my head in my hands. He notices my fragile, terrified state, and his eyes instantly soften. He rushes to my side, grabs both of my hands, and quietly asks me if these were the people who were torturing me in India.

My throat feels so very dry, and I just don't feel like I can handle anymore of this; I can't even respond.

"Tara, are they here to take you away?" He rubs my back, trying to reassure me that everything's okay now.

I look up and see Reema's sinister face; instinctively, I stand to get away. I stumble and lose my balance, but Roger catches me by the waist before I hit the ground again. He follows my gaze and glares at Deepa and his mother. Now they look like *they're* the ones who want to disappear.

I respond before anyone else can speak and turn this into another argument. "Yes. I was on my way to the airport to go back home, and they caught me outside of my apartment."

"You people are something else." He takes a step toward Deepa, looks him up and down and says, "She left you, buddy. Take a fucking hint. She doesn't want to be with you."

"They don't want me to be their daughter-in-law or wife any more. They were taking me back to kill me," I say, leaning into his shoulder and feeling faint from one too many blows to my head.

His jaw clenches and his facial expression becomes even more terrifying than before. He very slowly says to Deepa, "I'm going to give you five seconds to get the fuck out of here. Take your mother and get on the first flight back to India."

Deepa's mother starts pulling her son away, realizing that there's no way they are going to be able to take me away now. We stand there, and Roger doesn't seem to blink as we watch them get on the next train headed God knows where.

"Roger, I don't feel so good," I say just before I collapse to the ground.

"Tara, are you okay? Please open your eyes." I wake up in Roger's lap on the steps outside the train station.

"Roger? What happened?" I ask, feeling the nauseous and uneasy.

He pulls me upright and hands me a bottle of water.

"You fainted. They were trying to take you away," he says, holding my face in his hands and checking if my head's okay.

"Are they gone? We need to get out of here. They're going to come back. They're probably watching us," I say frantically.

I try to stand up, but my knees give out. Roger breaks my fall and catches me. He helps me slowly sit back down and says, "No one's coming to get you now. I took care of them. They're gone, okay. It's over." He pulls me into a tight embrace, and suddenly I wonder how he's here right now.

"What are you doing here Roger?" I ask, looking right into his eyes.

"Your mom finally told me everything. I knew she was keeping me in the dark about something, but I just didn't know what it was all about. So I came to see you to clear everything up. I realized that you probably never even knew I came to India for you. I saw you there with that guy, so happy, looking like you were dealing with nothing at all like you described on the phone. I thought that goof you were with was taking care of you. I didn't know there were people after you and everything you said was true," he says with a furrow in his brow.

I examine his face and realize how different he looks. He looks *so* much older. It's unbelievable how terrifyingly angry he was. He never would've become that worked up before.

"Dave's not a goof."

Suddenly, I feel rather uncomfortable practically being in another guy's lap right now. Specifically, my ex's lap.

"Oh yeah? Where is he then? Why wasn't he here to protect you?" He says, seeming quite annoyed.

"Well, he's not sleeping with my best friend, that's for sure."

He ignores my jab and says, "Let's just get you out of here and cleaned up. That fucker hit you again, didn't he?" He holds up a napkin to the back of my head.

"Yes, or his psychotic freak of a mother. I'm not sure which one it was this time," I say, limping towards the nearest cabstand.

We hop into the next one that pulls up, and argue back and forth about whether I need to be medically examined or not. He finally gives in, and we head to the airport so I can find Dave and let him know what happened. In all the commotion my phone got left behind, so I can't even call him.

Roger reaches for my hand but stops himself from grabbing it when I flinch. After being physically, mentally, and emotionally attacked, I'm a little on edge. Not to mention that it's inappropriate for him to think we can just pick up where we left off just because he's here now.

"We can't do that, Roger. I'm with Dave, you know that."

"I don't care who you're *with* right now. You *belong* with me. You always have, and you always will." He stares right into my eyes with an agonizing look of complete adoration and love that I would've died to see a few years ago.

I clear my throat trying to break the awkward heat between us and say, "I hope Roop and Serena got on their flight."

"I'm sure they did. You know Roop can't willingly miss a deadline," he says with his same old half smirk.

I take a deep breath in and out when I see Dave standing where I left the three of them. He's on his phone looking frazzled as hell. The poor guy's probably called and received my voicemail about a trillion times now.

"I wish we'd thought to get my damn phone back from them. Now they're going to have an inside look at my entire life and plot their next attack," I say sadly as I step out of the car. I'm not sure how to explain to Dave why Roger of all people is bringing me back to him right now.

"There won't be another attack. It's over now. I saw the look on the dude's face. He knows I'll come after him for his life if they ever come at you again," Roger says. He swallows hard and narrows his eyes at Dave; he probably recognizes him from India.

When we get out the car, Dave sees us. A look of confusion and relief crosses his face at the very same time.

"What happened? What took you so long? Are you alright?" he asks taking in my blood-stained clothes and dishevelled appearance.

Before I can respond Roger steps forward, "You must be Dave. I'm Roger. I'm sure you've heard a lot about me."

Dave's jaw drops and he looks absolutely bewildered. "What the heck, Tara?"

I step forward to grab his hand, but he pulls it away.

"Dave, I'll explain everything. Just take a seat," I say, feeling desperately guilty for the way this all looks.

"No Tara. Tell me *now*. How did you end up with him? And why do you look like that?" He takes a huge step back, and his eyes dart back and forth between the two of us.

"Oh come on, buddy! I thought you were a lawyer. Put two and two together. They came after her, and you weren't there. So I had to save her," Roger says. He takes a rather unfriendly step toward Dave, as if challenging him to a duel for my love right in the middle of the airport.

"Roger. That's enough," I say moving between them. "Stop with the pissing match. I can't deal with this petty bullshit right now."

My head still throbs, and I feel sick to my stomach. Yet these two feel the need to brawl it out over who's the bigger hero the moment they meet.

"They found you? How?" Dave asks, turning toward me.

Roger interjects before I can even open my mouth and snickers, "I'm sure it wasn't hard. Man, you sure are a genius! They had probably been watching you two for weeks."

"Look, bloke. I appreciate you being there and saving *my* girl. But I've got it sorted now. Thanks," he says and grabs my hand, which is still sore from the grip Deepa had on it.

"*Your* girl? You didn't even get her out of that house when you knew what the fuck was going on there. Her mom told me everything. She freed and saved herself, how exactly is she *your* girl?" Roger says, raising his voice.

I try to release my grip from Dave's hand, but he unknowingly squeezes tighter. I scream from the pain, and because I just want them to stop.

"What happened?" They both ask in unison.

"I am no one's *girl*. You two aren't any better than Deepa. He and his family treated me like I was a piece of property they owned, and now that's how you're both making me feel. For fuck sakes, I was just nearly abducted. Yet all you two care about is laying your claim on me like I'm some piece of meat. You know what? I think I'm going to choose to be *neither* of yours. Maybe it's time for me to simply be alone, and away from the *both* of you. I don't need saving anymore. I'm out of here," I say and walk away in a huff.

I head in to book myself a new flight to Vancouver. These two can stay here and fight over a girl that's quite frankly over this whole 'damsel in distress thing.' They call after me, but I just keep walking.

Dave jogs to catch up to me and asks if I'm sure I want to go back after everything that just happened. "You should wait a few days? You need a shower and a change of clothes, don't you?" he says, gesturing to my disastrous appearance.

I point to the suitcase that he's still lugging around and say, "I've got plenty to choose from right here."

I motion for Roger to come join us so I can break this to the both of them.

"Look, guys, I need to leave. I don't even know if they're really going to leave me alone or not. I also don't feel like being battled over like this is high school or something. You two can stay here and duke it out."

"Actually, if you're leaving the country I have no need to be here either. I'm coming with you," Roger says.

"Like hell you are!" Dave shouts.

"Oh come *on* Roger, no you're not! You're free to go wherever you want, but there's no need to escort me home. It's an airport, I'm safe here," I say, feeling even more exhausted from these two than everything that just happened with the Gills.

I look at Dave who really hasn't done anything to deserve me being this way to him, but I can't help but just want to be free of both of them, and everything else too.

I take his hand in mine and say, "Dave. I'll call you when I land. Okay?"

He brushes me off and says, "Yeah, okay. Whatever you say."

Then he leaves my suitcase right in front of me, and in that moment, I can sense a feeling of finality between us. Like this just summarized what had been brewing between us for months. That I was mentally checked out of something he was much too invested in.

I stand there in silence, watching him walk out of the airport and out of my life, most likely for good. Even though it wasn't his fault, I know he's going to take it to heart that he wasn't there to protect me when the "bad guys" came to get me.

Roger clears his throat and says, "Well this is a lot less awkward now that *he's* gone!"

I roll my eyes at him and sigh. "Roger, go to your hotel. Stay the rest of your trip. Enjoy England. Come home when you're ready. We'll talk when you're back."

I give him a kiss on the cheek and sincerely thank him for being there for me. Then I head in to security, to make my way to my departure gate, and finally return home.

CHAPTER TWENTY-TWO

S IX MONTHS LATER
"*Grande?* Why can't they just say medium? What's this nonsense?" Rajin says, struggling to make sense of the Starbucks menu.

"He'll have a Grande White Chocolate Mocha," I order for him before the barista turns from red to purple because of the growing line behind us.

"I think I see Serena pulling in. Roop said she's running late. She had showings all day." I pay for our drinks and step aside, pulling Rajin out of the way of the next customer.

"Her real estate stuff is doing really well, huh? Good for her!" Rajin says. He finally notices the guy on his laptop who's been checking him out since we walked in, and his eyes go wide.

"Go talk to him," I whisper.

"Nah, I'm not ready for anything like that yet. Let me get fully settled in first."

Rajin just arrived to Canada a couple of weeks ago, but from the looks of it, you'd think he was born and raised here. He's really come into his own since being here. He's always dressed to the nines and perfectly groomed, all prim and proper. In fact, we often joke he's the guy version of Serena.

Speak of the Prada-wearing devil: "Hey guys!" Serena walks up to us as if she's on a runway, and she absolutely must flash that big ol' rock of hers around.

She only met her *gora* boyfriend a few months ago, but they're already engaged. Even though her ring's about two sizes too big, she hasn't taken it off since.

We slide in to a table by the fireplace, and I spot Roop coming in. With her kitten heels, fancy jet black blazer, and perfectly sleeked back high ponytail waving behind her, she looks the picture of elegant professionalism.

"Whoa. Hottie alert!" Serena says as Roop takes a seat next to me.

"Oh come on. Tara's still the knockout of the group," she says, nudging me.

I know she's just making me feel better about myself, because lately all I've been sporting to our weekly meet-ups is sweats and bags under my eyes the size of my Hermes.

My all-nighter writing sessions have been taking quite the toll on me. It's seriously crunch time now. My publishers have already mentioned the possibility of an international book tour, and I still haven't sorted out the ending of my book yet.

"So, are you ready to be headed to the big N-Y-C?" Rajin asks me excitedly.

That's the first leg of my tour before heading even further east. It still feels like a dream, but my friends keep reminding me that this is all well deserved.

About two weeks after I arrived home from England, a parcel arrived for me. It had all of my journals in it. I couldn't believe it. I thought they were gone forever, but Mina had the decency to give them to Rajin once she discovered them. He had them couriered to me when we reconnected.

My book project started as a therapeutic way for me to process everything that had happened over the past few years. Then, after pulling bits and pieces of my most personal entries, and a few nosy instances of Serena reading over my shoulder, it became something more real. I decided to publicize these real life glimpses of what it meant to live through a severely twisted reality created by my own family.

I forgave everyone, including my mother and Rajin, for all the lies and apparent betrayal. After some solitude and reflection, I realized they were both backed into a corner. Plus, I *did* leave Rajin high and dry with that crazy family after him. I tried to make things better for him, but instead, I left him worse off than before.

Once I made the decision that I wouldn't be returning to London, or my life with Dave, I let him officially know it was over between the two of us. He still holds a major place in my heart, but after everything that had happened, there was just no way to force the promise of a future between the two of us any longer.

Things have been so crazy since I arrived back home; it's been hard to keep up with everything. As Roop, Serena, and Rajin chat happily amongst themselves, I think back to my first week back.

Once I felt my mom was well enough for us to have that necessary talk, I finally put it all out there. I told her what I'd heard about her, and she sat there completely baffled in response. In that moment, I knew from the look on her face that I'd been fed lies.

The entire truth of what really occurred is something I'm still having trouble accepting. My mother was never the one in the wrong. As hard as it was for her to tell me, she finally cleared up so many things that just didn't make sense. She didn't seem like the type to sleep with someone for personal gain.

So, when she told me that my uncle was the one who forced himself on her, I believed her right away. There was so much anguish and horror in her eyes at revisiting that memory, which she'd tucked away in the deepest corner of her subconscious. Telling me about it was a haunting truth that she'd finally let free.

My uncle (and biological father) had raped her. That was the root of her pure hatred for my father's family. That was the way in which I was conceived. Hence her long displaced negativity towards me. She associated me with everything that had happened to her. She lashed out at my father too; she never had the heart to tell him about all of this, but she suspected he knew what truly happened all those years ago.

She also told me the reason she and my father faked Pyaro's death was because my mom demanded all ties to his family be severed, and that Pyaro be sent back to India. Mom threatened to leave the both of us and expose my father's family for what they truly are. My father obliged, and my young heart grieved a death that never happened.

My dad was most caught up on the betrayal of being duped out of his share to the family land. To him, his brother was a crook who had taken away what was rightfully his. He consciously focused on this, because the subconscious truth of what his brother had done to his wife was much too deep a wound to bear.

My mom finally allowed me access to the mysterious wooden chest in our basement, and in it, I found the rest of the missing pieces of my childhood. It held my birth certificate, pictures from when I was born, and other tokens from when I was little.

"Hello? Earth to Tara! You look like you're a million miles away," Serena says, snapping her fingers in front of me.

"Sorry, I was just lost in my thoughts."

"Serena, you're so rude! You know how much she's been through. She probably has scary flashbacks sometimes," Roop says, reaching out to squeeze my hand.

"Yeah, but those flashbacks are her ticket to famous author-ville," Rajin says teasingly.

"No, no. I wasn't thinking about all that," I lie. "It's all behind me now. Writing it all out actually helped close that chapter of my life – no pun intended."

"So, have you spoken to *him* yet?" Roop asks me.

"No. I haven't. Not yet. It's too soon," I say, and quickly change the subject.

We share the amusing bits of our week, and laugh until our sides ache. When our drinks have been standing empty for a while, we head back to our brand new grown-up lives.

When I get back to my apartment, the place I bought with the small fund my father left for me, I see a bouquet of flowers with a note on it. It read: *I'LL NEVER STOP TRYING.*

How funny. I think to myself. A couple of months ago, an ominous message like that would've sent a chill up my spine. Now I can't figure out which one of my exes it could be from.

At first, I felt like things with the Gills couldn't possibly be over. I'd obsess over every sound that went bump in the night. I felt like they were going to appear from no where and take me away. Then my agent took it upon himself to send them all the wonderful bits of my novel which featured their role in my plight in India. He let it be known that should they ever act upon their desire to have me killed again, we'd print and publish their names, leaving them susceptible to arrest by the Canadian authorities.

After that, I felt much more comfortable being on my own. But I wasn't alone for long. Roger followed me home the very next week after I arrived to Canada. Things were so confusing between us. Despite my desire not to do so, we once again fell into the on-again-off-again spiral of intermixed love and lust. He won me over by telling me everything the wounded Tara needed to hear. I still remember what it felt like to hear him say that he couldn't allow himself to believe I was truly gone from his life and that he was never going to let that happen again. He explained the general gist of his letter as well. He wanted me to know he never stopped loving me.

But things just didn't feel right for me. I needed to do some soul-searching. I had to gather all the jumbled up pieces of me left over from the turmoil and drama that was my life. In order to be whole again, I had to had to tear myself to shreds. Now I'm stronger and more focused than ever before.

It certainly wasn't easy letting him know things weren't going to work out between us. I've since cut all communication with him, but he won't stop trying. Just like the note says, it seems like he'll *never* stop trying to be what I needed.

But that's just it. As a timid, afraid little girl I did need him. But he's not what I need *now*, as a grown woman. I finally realized that when the time is right, what I need is someone I can't live without. Not just someone who I'm with for comfort. With both Dave and Roger, that's all it was. Safety, ease, and most of all, protection. At first, it was protection from unknown demons, and then some very real ones. They were the warm, strong arms I turned to whenever I was scared. I didn't think myself capable of being on my own and fighting whatever battles needed to be won.

Well, now I'm ready. I'm ready to leave the past behind me, and to simply focus on myself. To jump in with both feet and see what I can become *all on my own.*

I look out at my view of the city through the floor to ceiling glass windows of *my* apartment. It's my very own place of solitude. I uncork a bottle of wine and pour myself a glass. I bring it out to the balcony and snuggle up on my favourite chair. With my feet up and my shawl wrapped around me, I feel like I've done pretty damn well. Despite all of the loss, drama, and misery–I survived it all. Now here I am, living my dream to be independent, and to simply be okay.

Sometimes that's all you can be. Just okay. Living life how it's meant to be lived. Without any fear, and knowing you have what it takes within yourself to take on *anything.*

Maybe fate will bring on even more woes and heartache. Or maybe it'll take me to bigger and better places than I ever could've imagined. I know one thing for sure though; I can handle anything that comes my way. Because I'm Tara Kaur Sidhu – a shooting star headed straight toward whatever the universe has destined.

THE END

ACKNOWLEDGEMENTS

First and foremost, I'd like to thank my husband for bearing with me through this journey.

From taking care of our son while I edited, to helping develop the storyline when I first began – this project wouldn't have been possible without him.

I'd also like to thank my family for being so open-minded and understanding about putting this story out there to the world.

A lot of people may become focused on *who* this story and the events in it are about, truth be told it's the story of every single Indian girl who must struggle to find her way.

Although this is a work of fiction, the cultural tenets laced throughout the story are very real for so many individuals all over the world. This story is for them, and anyone else who has ever been minimalized by the constraints of society.